A Postcard from Italy

Alex Brown was born in Brighton, Sussex and ran away to London when she left school at sixteen, where she found the streets she lived on for a while weren't paved with gold. After twenty years working in a variety of jobs as a live-in nanny, cinema usher, T-shirt printer, telephone operator, bank cashier and sat-nav voice recorder, Alex started writing and found she couldn't stop.

In 2006 she won a competition to write the weekly City Girl column for the *London Paper* and her first novel, *Cupcakes At Carrington's*, was published in 2013.

Now living on the Kent coast, with her husband, daughter, and two very glossy black Labradors, Alex is working on her eleventh book. When she isn't writing, Alex enjoys knitting, watching Disney films with her daughter and going to Northern Soul nights, and is passionate about supporting charities working with care leavers, adoption and vulnerable young people.

Alex loves hearing from her readers, so please visit her website – www.alexbrownauthor.com or join her for chats on Facebook at www.facebook.com/alexandrabrownauthor, Twitter and Instagram @alexbrownbooks.

Also by Alex Brown

The Carrington's series
Cupcakes at Carrington's
Christmas at Carrington's
Ice Creams at Carrington's

The Tindledale series
The Great Christmas Knit Off
The Great Village Show
The Secret of Orchard Cottage
The Wish

Short Stories
Me and Mr Carrington: A Short Story
Not Just for Christmas: A Short Story

A Postcard from ITALY

ALEX BROWN

HarperCollins*Publishers*

HarperCollins*Publishers* Ltd
The News Building
1 London Bridge Street
London SE1 9GF

www.harpercollins.co.uk

A Paperback Original 2019
2

A catalogue record for this book is available from the British Library

ISBN: 978-0-00-820666-6

Set in Birka by Palimpsest Book Production Limited,
Falkirk, Stirlingshire

Printed and bound by
CPI Group (UK) Ltd, Croydon CR0 4YY

For all the people who care for other people

'The best thing to hold onto in life is each other.'
Audrey Hepburn

PROLOGUE

Tindledale, in rural England, 1939

The flip of a coin is all it had taken to seal seventeen-year-old Constance Levine's fate.

'Heads, she goes to Aunt Rachael in Manhattan,' her mother had declared, barely able to even look at her 'wanton' daughter, the word she had used on first discovering Connie's condition.

Manhattan. In America. That might not be so bad . . . Connie remembered thinking as she had dared to lift her downcast eyes to look at her father's hands, one stacked on top of the other, primed to reveal her destiny, the scent of his sandalwood cologne permeating the air between them. But then it had all gone wrong. The coin hadn't displayed the King's head. And that was that. So there would be no sailing to New York and visiting exciting American landmarks, like the Statue of Liberty, which Connie had seen pictures of in her *Britannia and Eve* magazines. Or maybe a show on Broadway where she could watch professional dancers move with the grace and elegance that she always aspired to in her weekly dance classes. But none of it was meant to be. Not now the course of her destiny had changed for ever.

Instead, she had been dispatched on the next train from her home in Blackheath, London, to the countryside where nobody would know her. To stay with her grandfather's sister, Aunt Maud, in the sleepy little village of Tindledale, surrounded by undulating fields full of lumbering cows and oast houses flanked with rows of hop vines reaching almost up to the sky. Aunt Maud was a dour woman who Connie had never met until the day she arrived here. But that was the point. Banished before her parent's influential and, more importantly, highly respectable friends found out what she had done and shame was brought upon the whole family.

'No, the matter must be dealt with swiftly and discreetly,' is what her father had instructed when she'd tried to venture an alternative solution. That she marry her sweetheart and they live happily ever after. But Jimmy wasn't Jewish and so her parents had forbidden any such union, plus he swept floors at the packing factory in Deptford, and that would never do.

Connie had met Jimmy at the funfair one Saturday evening on the heath when she'd gone with her best friend, Kitty. Jimmy and his best friend, Stanley, had been seated on the painted carousel horses behind them. It had been a gloriously balmy evening as they rode round and round and up and down with the sound of melodic organ music floating in the breeze, making Connie feel carefree and happy. Later, after winning a coconut and a fluffy pink teddy bear for her on the rifle range, Jimmy had walked Connie home, making her laugh with his range of silly accents and slapstick humour. His sweep of hair, as black as treacle, bobbing into his impish green eyes, had her swooning when he'd winked and tilted his head after saying goodnight at the gate like a proper gentleman.

They had arranged to meet by the duck pond the following afternoon and, just before she had to leave to be home in time for tea, he had swept her up in his arms and kissed her with such passion that she knew he was going to be the one for her. Love had blossomed for them in the weeks that followed; meeting in secret, of course, as her parents had taken an instant dislike to Jimmy. They hadn't even given him a chance to show his worth when he called at the house one time with a beautiful bunch of wild flowers that he'd picked himself from the hilly field section in Greenwich Park. He'd even bought a jolly yellow satin ribbon from the haberdashery shop near the station to tie around the bouquet, but Mother had refused to even let him into the house before sending him away with a flea in his ear. And then later, right after Mr Chamberlain's wireless broadcast declaring war on 3 September, Jimmy had signed up to do his duty for King and country, and it was as if the light had gone out in her life.

Connie had promised to wait for him to return, and had prayed every morning and evening that her darling Jimmy would stay safe and come back home from wherever it was they had sent him. She couldn't bear to even consider the possibility of a different outcome for her truelove, and believed in doing so was only to tempt fate. Although Jimmy hadn't replied to any of her letters since he went away, or even sent one of those miniature, colourful post-cards like her best friend, Kitty, had received from her own sweetheart, Stanley. Kitty kept it tucked inside a compartment in her handbag so as to feel close to him, and Connie so wished she had a post-card too. A few words from him to hold on to. To keep Jimmy close to her always. All she had was the pink teddy bear. If she had heard from Jimmy, then perhaps she would have found the courage to tell him about their unborn child before now, instead of waiting until he came back to her. Or maybe it was better this way. She would be eighteen soon and knew that Jimmy would marry her right away when he heard about the baby . . . and they wouldn't need her parents' permission after all.

Pressing the palm of her right hand into the small of her back, Connie carefully lowered herself into the high-backed chair next to her bed in the spartan bedroom. Aunt Maud was a frugal woman who saw no virtue in home comforts or niceties, preferring to live a martyred existence that Connie was also expected to endure for the duration of her incumbency. Her punishment, it seemed, for falling in love and then allowing Jimmy to be intimate with her that one time. If only she had known their moment of passion would make a baby, then she would have held out until their wedding night.

So now the joy of being with Jimmy, the music and gaiety, cushions and comfort and glorious indoor bathroom that Connie had grown up with at home in London's exclusive Blackheath, were all mere memories. There was no softness or joy in

Aunt Maud's world. With an outside privy at the end of the long garden, which even in the summer months was grim and cold, making the chilblains on Connie's toes itch and throb with pain. The inside of the cottage was no better either, with its hard stone floor and damp walls, and so it was as if all the colour had drained from Connie's life. When she had first arrived in Tindledale, Aunt Maud had let Connie take a walk out into the village where she had met a couple of farm girls sitting on a bench in the village square sharing a bag of chips. Sisters Winnie and Edie were around the same age as Connie, and so she had enjoyed chitchatting with them and pretending, if only for a short while, that everything in her life was still the same. Happy and gay. But Aunt Maud had stopped the trips to the village as soon as Connie's fecund belly had started to round, and so she hadn't had the pleasure of Winnie and Edie's company since. Aunt Maud had even instructed Connie to remove her jaunty but 'sordid' magazine cuttings from the bedroom wall, so they were now confined to an envelope inside her diary that she kept hidden in the groove behind the headboard of the bed.

At least it will all be over soon.

I'm going to be a respectable married lady.

Mr and Mrs J. Blake.
And a mother, to boot!

Connie held on to these thoughts as she felt around the headboard. Then, after slipping the diary from its hiding place, she propped it up on the mound of her swollen belly and took the fountain pen from its holder. She checked the date before drawing a line through another day. Only a few more weeks to go. She couldn't be sure though. Her mother had said it would take nine months, or thereabouts, for the baby to be grown enough and ready to be born, but Connie didn't know when to count from. Was it afterwards when she had lain in Jimmy's arms feeling all dreamy and on top of the world, with her body still tingling from his touch? Or the first time her monthly didn't appear? And she hadn't dared to ask.

But Jimmy would be home soon, bringing with him an end to her feelings of fear and shame. She had to believe this. It was all she could do, because Connie had never felt so alone as she did right now . . .

London, England, present day

Grace Quinn loved her job at Cohen's Convenient Storage Company. In fact, it was the only thing that gave her real pleasure these days. Alongside her knitting and a large mug of hot chocolate with a dash of cherry brandy dropped in of an evening as she escaped into one of her favourite old films. She loved the classics. The feeling of being swept away into a world of nostalgia and glamour, where nothing bad ever happened, or so it seemed. Musicals especially, with plenty of dancing. Fred and Ginger. Doris Day. Whipcrackaway! She was a big Doris Day fan and had learnt so much about timing and precision from watching Doris, which in turn had helped Grace hone her own dance skills. Gene Kelly too. *Singin' in the Rain*. She'd never grow tired of watching that masterpiece. Although her absolute all-time favourite was – of course – the legendary Audrey Hepburn in *Funny Face*. It really was *'S Wonderful, 'S Marvellous*, as Audrey and Fred sang in the Technicolor scene where they floated down the river in the grounds of that idyllic chateau in Paris. But the magic could never happen for Grace until her bedbound mother, Cora, had eventually fallen asleep, which recently had been getting later and later.

So, slipping her shoes on as she brushed her hair, and then wound her rumpus of copper curls up into a more manageable bun, Grace kept one ear out for Cora upstairs in her bedroom, silently praying that she'd make it out the door to work without her mother bellowing again for more breakfast cereal and toast. Grace had already taken her a large bowl of cornflakes and two rounds of butter and jam, but the shop had run out of the extra-thick crusty bread, 'so it takes more to fill me up, Grace' is what Cora had said on calling out for yet more toast. And recently, Cora had been yelling too for the lamp right beside her on the cabinet to be switched on because her own hand, mere millimetres away, was 'playing up' again. That had happened four times last night.

But it wasn't to be.

'Grace. Grace. *Grace. For the love of God where are you?*' Cora thundered in her dense Irish accent, thumping the floor with her walking stick and making the plastic lightshade, hanging from the ceiling in the lounge, sway precariously above Grace's head.

She put down the brush. Gripping the edge of the mantelpiece with both hands, she closed her eyes, dipped her head momentarily and inhaled deeply before letting out a long breath, searching every fibre of her being just to find another iota of resilience somewhere within her. She was tired. *So tired.* After opening her eyes, Grace inspected her face in the mirror and saw bloodshot flecks around her green irises from lack of sleep and her fair, freckly skin seemed even paler, if that was even possible. Cora had had a bad night and Grace had been up until almost 3 a.m. This would be the third day in a row now that she would be late for work; even though her boss, Larry, was very under-standing, he was also getting on. And after his knee surgery last year it wasn't so easy for him to do the rounds, walking the length of the warehouse corridors, checking the temperature controls and pushing the heavy metal trolleys back to their place in the bays beside the lift. Yes, he had been good to her, so the least she could do was to turn up on time. Grace really didn't feel it was fair to leave it all to him.

But then nothing much was fair these days as far as she could see. Not for Larry. And not for her. How could it be fair when none of her siblings helped out? Cora had four grown-up children, yet it had been left to Grace, the youngest, to care for their extremely demanding mother, single-handedly. Apart from the occasional visits from her best friend, Jamie. He lived in the terraced house next door and they had grown up together here in Woolwich. He worked as a midwife now at the Queen Elizabeth Hospital and popped in whenever he could to help turn Cora and pick up a pound to buy her a scratch-card. Cora loved a scratchcard and was convinced that her 'big win' was just around the corner. And when that day came she was going to 'employ an expert carer and book into a suite at the Savoy Hotel in London where they know how to do things properly'.

Grace had heard it all before a million times over and, if the truth be told, she really hoped that 'big win' would hurry up and happen soon for both of their sakes. Cora flatly refused to consider a council-run care home, claiming only a high-end one, akin to a five-star hotel, would do for her, and she wouldn't let 'riffraff', aka strangers, in the house to help out either, so it really had all been left to Grace to deal with. And Grace knew that she was crumbling under the strain of caring for her mother and trying to hold down a full-time job, but couldn't see another way. Especially since Cora had flatly refused to be assessed for any sort of carers' allowance, so Grace's income was all they had to get by on. Grace had tried getting her siblings involved, but they had moved away or had important jobs in banking in the City of London . . . well, more important than her job at the storage company on an industrial estate in Greenwich and only ten minutes to get to on the bus, is what they really meant. So Grace ploughed on . . . because she couldn't just abandon her mother, turn her back on her when she was unable to leave her own bed unaided due to her health problems exacerbated by her bulk.

No, Cora needed her.

'What is it, Mum?' Grace asked, on entering Cora's bedroom, near choking on the foggy air, thick with the fragrance of lily-of-the-valley talcum powder.

'What did you get this one for?' Cora complained, her doughy face wobbling into a frown.

'What do you mean, Mum?' Grace scanned the room.

'Look!' And Cora lifted up the corner of the duvet. Her fleshy bare legs and arms and nightie-covered body were coated in white talcum powder. Grace's heart sank. It was twenty-five past eight, according to the gold carriage clock on the chest of drawers, and she was supposed to be at work by nine. There was no way she could sort this out in time – strip the bed, being careful to turn her mother as she did so – just as the care assistant from social services had shown her, and then replace the talcum-powdered sheet with a clean one. Before finally washing the powder from Cora's body and finding a fresh nightie for her to wear. Grace had taken the last nightie from the drawer earlier this morning before putting a load of washing in the machine, ready to peg out on the line to dry when she rushed back home in her lunch break. But she couldn't leave her mother like this for a whole morning. Cora was already wheezing from inhaling the powder and her skin would sweat and then get sore which would involve more creams and extra-frequent turning to avoid painful bedsores.

So, resigned to letting Larry down again with another late start, Grace pulled her mobile from her jeans pocket and swiftly tapped out a text message to him before galvanising herself into action. If she moved fast and Cora complied with her instructions to hold the handle of the hoist when she rolled her onto her side, then she might be in with a chance of making it to work before ten o'clock.

'So how did this happen?' Grace asked tentatively, because her mother was prone to rages and that was the last thing she needed right now. Cora would never help her then and the whole routine would take twice as long.

'You bought the wrong one!' Cora accused. 'I said to get the nice Marks and Sparks one, not the cheap Pound Shop one. So the lid fell off when I shook it.'

'But why were you putting talcum powder on, Mum? I did all that for you after your bed bath this morning,' Grace reminded her as she made a start on pulling the corners of the sheet away from the mattress.

'No you didn't.'

'I'm sure I did,' Grace responded softly, knowing that she definitely had.

'Well, you must have forgotten. You always were a forgetful girl. Now, your older sister, Bernadette . . . she *never* forgets. Every birthday, Christmas and Mother's Day, a lovely card arrives. And flowers. Will you look at them over there on the side. Beautiful they are. And fresh. The smell of them is just terrific,'

Cora rhapsodised. Grace glanced at the big bunch of pink lilies that had arrived earlier that week with a card of apology from Bernie for not coming to see Cora on her birthday, on account of her husband, Liam, taking her and her children out to lunch. The same thing had happened last year. And the year before. 'You could learn a thing or two from our Bernadette now, sure you could.'

'Shame she didn't visit, though. It would have been nice to see her, don't you think?' Grace mused as she heaved her mother on to her side, unable to remember the last time her sister had been here to their family home. But then instantly regretted the words as soon as they left her lips.

'Well, she could hardly do that now, sure she couldn't! She has a busy life herself. It's important for a mother to spend time with her children,' Cora lectured. 'And Bernadette works so hard on the reception desk of that private bank – you know the customers have to press a special bell *just* to be allowed inside the building. That's how important it is – so why would you begrudge her one day off?' she puffed on, and then, '*Ouch!*' Cora slapped the back of her daughter's hand as a strand of her silvery-grey hair got accidentally caught around a button on Grace's shirt.

'Sorry, Mum,' Grace flinched, pulling her stinging hand away as she gently untangled her mother's hair.

'Well, be careful. No wonder that boyfriend of yours has gone off the boil . . . if this is how you are with him. Poor man is probably scared you'll hurt him too with your rough-handedness. And you're not getting any younger, Grace, sure you aren't.' Cora paused to shake her head in dismay, or was it disgust at her daughter's perceived inadequacy? 'You can't keep on letting what happened with that wonderful Matthew ruin the rest of your life. No, you need to buck up and make an effort with this new one or he will also end up dumping you for someone much younger and prettier.'

Grace inwardly groaned and glanced at the ceiling, having heard this tirade a trillion times at least, or so it seemed, over the last few years. She thought of her ex-fiancé, Matthew. The love of her life. But he was married to someone else now.

Grace and Matthew had met at dance school and fallen in love as they worked together on the cruise ships after graduating. Then, later, they had both landed parts in musicals back home in London. Everything had been carefree and fun, until Cora had become increasingly more demanding of Grace's time, often persistently phoning late at night and waking her and Matthew up when they were exhausted after having danced two shows that day. Not to mention the impact on the following day's performances where they would dance and end up making silly mistakes through sheer fatigue, until Matthew sustained an injury to his ankle which cost him a part in *The Lion King*, in the West End, his dream opportunity. With hindsight, Grace could see that was when the tension between them intensified, with her feeling compelled to help her mother, and Matthew constantly biting his tongue whenever Cora found ways to erode their relationship.

And now Matthew was blissfully happy with his super-fit and bouncy-haired, perky yoga-teacher wife and cherub-cheeked toddler twins, living in a proper chocolate-box cottage in the Cotswolds with an actual stream along the end of his back garden (that was really a meadow) full of wild flowers. And if that wasn't enough bliss for one person . . . he'd recently got a chocolate Labrador *puppy*. And Grace knew all this from his Facebook posts, which she still looked at from time to time. Usually in the evening after she'd had too many cherry-brandy hot chocolates and her self-esteem was somewhere on the floor. Because the image from that day – when she had found him in their bed with the Perky Yoga One – would be forever indelibly inked inside her head.

Two years ago it had happened, and Grace's heart had shattered into an infinite number of unrecoverable pieces as the Perky Yoga One had nonchalantly untwined herself from straddling Matthew's naked hips and sauntered off to the en suite. Stopping only to do a bend and snap to retrieve her postage-stamp-sized thong from the floor. Later on, Matthew's reasoning for being naked in their bed with another woman was that he thought Grace would be 'out for the whole day looking after your mother again like you always are'. He got lonely, apparently.

Struggling to function for weeks after he moved out, Grace had slumped into a depression brought on by sleepless nights full of flashbacks of Matthew being caressed by a tight-bottomed, naked woman in the very bed that she was trying to sleep in. And unable to pay all of the rent on her own, she had lost the flat they had shared. It was then that she'd moved back into her childhood home here with Cora.

Her mother hadn't been bedbound back then, but had still needed help with day-to-day tasks. So with

Grace in a dark pit of grief for the relationship and future life she had thought she was going to have with Matthew, and her passion for the performing arts having dissipated, she had left her job dancing in the chorus line of a West End show and dwindled into becoming her mother's carer instead. A solitary role, which had suited her just fine at the time, as it meant Grace was able to retreat even further into herself, away from the outside word and all the dangers it held . . . like predatory, perky yoga-teacher types! Being reclusive felt like a protection of sorts, where Grace could keep herself safe from potential heartbreak. Because on that horrible day her world really had fallen apart. She had trusted Matthew with her life, and it was as if he'd sucked the air right out of it and she had been over and over this a million times inside her head. Constantly replaying that moment when Matthew had opened his half-closed ecstasy eyes and spotted her in the bedroom doorway where she had stood. Frozen. Watching the scene as if by satellite on a time delay. The two beautiful bodies moving as one in perfect symphony and slow motion, immersed in their sensual delight of each other.

The weeks of staying indoors had turned into months until, a year later, knowing she couldn't carry on that way any more, Grace had managed to summon up the courage to seek help from her GP. Agoraphobia, brought on by depression, was what the doctor had diagnosed, before referring her to a counsellor who set her a programme of tasks aimed at building her confidence and self-esteem back up. And it had worked, to a point. It was soon after that she had started working for Larry at the storage company; she had been there for a year now as their Girl Friday – the counsellor had a friend who knew somebody who knew his wife, Betty, and that she was looking to bring in some help; with her and Larry not getting any younger these days, and their grown-up children living and working abroad, they were finding it hard to manage the business between just the two of them.

So with Larry's kind patience and the counsellor's encouragement, Grace could now venture out to familiar places, if she took a familiar route. Like going to work or to the library or to the end of the road to the convenience store on the corner. Nice and simple. Safe. She knew where she was at then, even if it did mean counting the steps to the bus stop to help calm her breathing. That's how she had met 'this new one', Phil. He had seen her muttering to herself, counting the steps as she reached the bus stop one morning on the way to work, and had struck up a conversation. He had been there again on her way home from work and had offered to walk with her to the front door. Things between them had sort of trundled on from there.

'And you'll be thirty-five soon so you need to think about that before you scare any more men away. If you don't get a move on and find one to marry you then you'll never be a mother.' Cora cut in to Grace's thoughts. 'And I shan't be around for ever, you know, and then you'll be all on your own!'

Grace pulled her bottom lip in and bit down hard as she vowed to talk to her brother and sisters again. Something had to change. She worked hard too. And what she wouldn't give for even one day off from her mother's foul temper and cruel words . . . let alone a leisurely family lunch! And Phil was always complaining about Grace never having any time for him these days. Cora was ruining his life, apparently. And even though Grace wrestled with her emotions for having such guilt-ridden thoughts about her own mother, she had to admit that she was rapidly feeling the same way too.

2

'There you are, my love.' Larry's homely wife, Betty, bustled out of the little kitchenette area and placed a mug of steaming tea down on Grace's desk before popping a plate, with an enormous slice of still warm, traditional Jewish babka on, beside it. 'I've put a smidge of sugar in your tea too . . . to keep your energy levels up. You look done in, dear, if you don't mind me saying.'

'Oh thank you, Betty.' Grace put down her knitting; she was making a cable-stitch scarf for Jamie, and grinned up at the older woman, admiring the new lemon hand-crocheted waistcoat over her usual navy serge shift dress. Her black wig was coiffured into a wavy halo around her face.

'Another late night?' Betty asked, getting cosy in a brown leather bucket chair in the customer waiting area. Grace nodded hungrily through a mouthful of the chocolatey and cinnamon swirled bread that

Betty frequently made from scratch and which she absolutely loved. She hadn't had time to eat at lunchtime as the washing had taken longer to peg out than she had anticipated, and then Cora hadn't liked the lasagne that Grace had cooked last night in an attempt to make life easier today. Instead, she had insisted on a time-consuming freshly made chicken salad with an oven-warmed baguette. And then the bus back to work had been stuck in traffic for what felt like ages.

'Yes,' Grace nodded, 'and I'm sorry for being late again this morning . . .' She turned away; there were only so many times one could apologise before it just felt embarrassingly superficial.

'You do your best, my dear. That's all any of us can do,' Betty said kindly, rummaging in her crochet bag before pulling out a glorious candy-pink-coloured yarn. 'It's going to be a dolly blanket for our little Hannah in America,' she chuckled, looping a length of the wool around her fingers as she worked the hook.

'I think she's going to treasure it,' Grace smiled, remembering fondly when Betty and Larry's granddaughter and her husband had visited from America to introduce their first great-grandchild, beautiful baby Hannah.

'I hope so. It's important to keep our family members happy. And how is your mother, dear?'

'The same as always, Betty. Still refusing any outside help . . . but thank you for asking.' Grace felt her cheeks flush on criticising Cora. Not being accustomed to doing so to anyone outside the family, it felt disloyal, and she had been brought up never to air her dirty laundry in public. Her mother had been fastidious about it, forever wagging a finger and shushing them as children in case the neighbours overheard their business as they walked to church on Sunday for Mass in their best coats and shoes. Appearances were everything, and nobody needed to know that the electric meter had run out again or the TV had been returned to the rental shop because Dad had lost his job at the printing factory and so hadn't been paid in weeks.

'Oh dear. Well, if there's anything I can do to help . . . I'd be happy to call in some time with a pile of magazines or one of those Sudoku books. If only to give you a bit of a break. You do look a little peaky, my love, if you don't mind me saying so,' Betty smiled kindly, 'although still beautiful with your gorgeous red curls and English rose complexion.'

Betty's words hung in the air as Grace stirred her tea, knowing that she would never take Betty up on her kindness. She had been making the offer for nearly a year now, but Grace knew that her mother would never forgive her if she brought a stranger into the house, even if it was only to keep her company over a cup of tea. It was a shame, though, as it couldn't be much fun lying in bed all day long watching the same daytime TV shows over and over, with only a word-search puzzle book to break the monotony. No wonder her mother was foul-tempered and ungrateful. Grace had tried getting Cora interested in reading, even borrowing a selection of books that she thought she'd like from the library, only to see them thrown aside with complaints that they were boring. The same had happened with Netflix. Cora had hated that too, berating Grace for 'interfering with my telly' and 'wasting money on silly subscription services for rubbish box sets set in foreign places like Sweden or America'.

'Thanks, Betty. I'd love to take you up on your offer, but . . .' Grace let her voice fade away.

'I know, my love.' A short silence followed, broken only by the sound of Betty's crochet hook as she looped the yarn around it and got to work on Hannah's dolly blanket. 'Now, Larry has something special for you to do this afternoon.'

'Ooh, sounds intriguing.' Grace finished the last of her tea and stood up as Larry walked through the door. A clipboard and a bunch of keys were pressed against his uniform of a black suit, including waistcoat and tie with a freshly laundered striped shirt. With his swept-back silver hair, he had been making an effort to look dapper since he was first introduced to Betty at a tea dance back in the day. They had both been nineteen and it had been a mutual love at first sight. Grace loved hearing all about it from Betty. It gave her hope, that there really was such a thing as 'happy ever after', where two kind souls could love and cherish and, most importantly, respect each other as they shared a life together.

'That's right, Grace. Your favourite job. Unit 28 needs opening and cataloguing for sale or disposal.' Larry removed his bifocals and slipped them into his breast pocket before handing the clipboard to her, then started sorting out the key to the padlock on the door of number 28.

'Thank you!' Grace particularly loved this part of her job. Not that she was nosey – well, maybe a bit; her mother always said she was as a child – 'with your constant questioning'. 'Inquisitive' was how Grace liked think of it, as she did get a thrill of anticipation when the door to an abandoned unit was first opened and she got to peep inside and then sort through the contents. Somebody else's cast-off stuff was always another person's treasure.

Mostly, it was the usual items of furniture stored after a house move, or sometimes catering equipment, packs of party blowers and joke hats belonging to event planners whose businesses had gone bust, that kind of thing. But every now and again there would be a veritable treasure trove of intrigue. She once found a pair of stuffed parrots. Another time a collection of fossils – she'd contacted the Natural History Museum in London on that occasion and they had sent a curator to collect them when numerous attempts to make contact with the owners had proven fruitless. And then there was the World War II medal collection a little while ago. Grace, Larry and Betty had all agreed that it just wouldn't have been right to sell the medals to recover the rental arrears when they hadn't been able to contact the owner. It had then turned out that the owner had died six months earlier. Luckily, Larry had managed to find a relative . . . the son of the deceased soldier, who had stored his medals at Cohen's for over fifty years in one of the small safety deposit boxes, and that had been a happy day. The grateful son had travelled all the way from Scotland to collect the medals in person and to shake Larry's hand. A reporter from the local newspaper had even come along too, and then written a lovely piece featuring a black-and-white photo of the man in his soldier's uniform during the Second World War.

'I can do that for you,' Grace offered, indicating the bunch of keys that Larry was fiddling with. 'They can be very tricky sometimes,' she added tactfully, knowing how Larry struggled with arthritis in his age-gnarled fingers.

'Thank you, Grace. You are kind.' He smiled gratefully, handing the clipboard and the bunch of keys over.

Having found the right key, Grace had pushed an empty trolley along the length of the corridor on the ground floor and was now standing outside the door to unit 28. It was one of the oldest large walk-in units, occupying a corner space, and Grace wondered when it had last been opened as the key was stiff in the padlock, which had rust all around the edges. So after walking back along the corridor and locating a can of WD40 in the cleaning cupboard, she had returned and managed to spruce up the padlock and get the key to turn.

Gingerly, she pulled the metal door, which scraped

across the floor as if it hadn't been opened in years, and felt around for the light switch. Larry had first set up the storage company in the Fifties, and the older units didn't have automatic motion-sensor lighting installed. She felt a whoosh of anticipation in the middle of her stomach as the old-fashioned strip light flickered into action before eventually settling to bathe the contents of the unit in a bright, wondrous light.

Grace stood in silence for a moment.

Blinked a few times.

Then gasped on registering the sight set out before her.

She took a few steps forward until she was standing in the centre of the storage unit.

It was incredible.

And breathtaking.

And on first glance it appeared to be the best unit she had ever had the pleasure of opening.

Right in front of her was a beautiful Aladdin's cave full of ornate vintage items with a sumptuously soft, deep-piled dusty pink rug beneath her shoes. But the contents weren't stacked higgledy-piggledy on top of each other to make best use of the space as was often the case. Not at all. Someone had taken a great deal of care to present everything in the best possible way. Someone with an eye for design and sumptuous living, because the unit was organised like a glamorous 1950s boudoir. It was just like stepping onto a Hollywood film set – Elizabeth Taylor's bedroom would have looked like this for sure, Grace thought, as she folded her hands, one over the over, and tucked them up underneath her chin in glee.

Then, double-checking the paperwork on the clip-board, Grace saw that the unit belonged to a Mrs Constance di Donato and the last payment had been made by cheque over two years ago. The final cheque had been for a whole year's rental payments, making Mrs di Donato now one year in arrears, which was far longer than they usually waited before opening an abandoned unit. Grace made a mental note to mention it to Larry, as she wondered if there was a special reason for letting the payments lapse for so long. She flicked on through the rest of the paperwork. There were copies of the three letters that Larry had sent to the address they had for Mrs Donato in London; all of them had been returned, unopened, with 'Not known at this address' hand-written on the envelopes in large, flamboyant letters. Grace had to be sure they could show they had tried to contact Mrs Donato several times before she touched anything and started sorting through the items.

She didn't know anything about antiques, but even she could see that the ornate French Louis XV style dressing table with its carved cabriole legs and marble top was of significant value. Not to mention the large leather jewellery case on top of it. Moving further into the unit, Grace gasped again as she lifted a dust sheet to reveal an exquisite silk chaise longue with a petrol blue peacock-patterned fabric that had been placed at a jaunty angle over in a corner. A clothes rail ran the length of one wall with at least twenty, maybe thirty, sparkly evening gowns hanging neatly on satin padded hangers. Each gown was carefully tucked inside its own transparent plastic protective cover. A mink coat was draped around a mannequin, presumably to help keep the coat's shape, Grace figured, remembering how the costume staff in the theatres where she had danced had used this trick too. Stacked in one of the other corners were four old-fashioned brown utility suitcases, and next to them were three expensive-looking leather handbags – Italian design by the looks of them, as one had the famous gold Gucci badge on the front. A selection of paintings had been carefully placed behind the chaise longue, with a large oval-shaped rose-print hatbox beside them on the carpet.

Grace lifted the lid of the hatbox and drew in the nostalgic aroma of musty paper as she peeped inside to see a collection of old magazines. *Variety. Britannia and Eve.* Dated 1938 and through to 1941, 1942, and so on, she noticed, carefully sorting through the pile. In jaunty, faded primary colours there were pictures of women wearing headscarves and dungarees like the Land Girls did during the Second World War. Another cover, dated 1950, was much more glamorous, with a woman wearing a ball gown and holding a champagne glass. A faded brown envelope was tucked down the side and contained a handful of dried pink rose petals. Grace turned the envelope over and saw *Glorious day, Portofino – 1955* handwritten on the back.

Grace could feel her spirits rising, and couldn't wait to get started on cataloguing the contents of storage unit number 28. But where to start? She felt like a child in a sweet shop, elated and overwhelmed by the mesmerising selection of goodies on display. Smiling to herself, she stepped towards the suitcases, figuring this would be the best place to begin as there might be some paperwork in one of them with an address of a relative or a friend they could contact

– there was no way Larry could just dispose of these items without them trying hard to find Mrs Donato. But as Grace reached out her hands to release the two brass clasps of the suitcase that was sitting on top of the pile, her mobile rang in the back pocket of her jeans.

'Where are you?' her sister, Bernie, demanded on opening the conversation, and making Grace bristle.

'At work,' she stated, in an equally cursory tone.

'Well, you need to get home right away. I've just had Mum on the phone. She was put through via the switchboard, so I had to come out early from eating my lunch in the staff restaurant especially to deal with her . . .' Grace was sure she heard Bernie tut with frustration, which made her bristling intensify. She crossed her free arm across her body as if to soothe herself. 'And she was crying—'

'*Crying?*' Grace interjected, panic starting to trickle through her, as it was unlike Cora to cry. In fact, Grace wasn't sure she had ever seen her mother cry. Not even when their gentle, kind dad, had died. Cora had said, 'It was your father's time to pass.' And that was that. No more emotion required.

'Yes. That's right,' Bernie kept on. 'Crying. Sobbing she was, so hard she could barely get her words out. Took me ages to calm her down. Apparently, you rushed off so quickly after your own lunch break that she didn't even get a chance to use the commode. So now she's had an accident and feels really dreadful about it.'

'But—'

'No buts, Grace. You can't just leave her like that. She'll get sore and then likely get an infection or whatever, and you'll never forgive yourself if that happens.' Grace swallowed hard as she tried to formulate a response. 'Are you still there?' Bernie barked a few seconds later, and Grace could hear office noise now in the background.

'Yes,' she managed in a dejected voice, her earlier elation on seeing Mrs Donato's belongings having suddenly vanished, not to mention her feelings of guilt and confusion. She hadn't rushed off, and she was sure she had asked Cora if she needed to use the commode, but had been told off for fussing . . .

'Look, I have to go. But sort Mum out and let me know later, OK? Oh, hold on.' The instruction was so swift and fleeting that Grace automatically acquiesced. 'If you take a seat over there, someone will be with you shortly,' she heard Bernie say in a far nicer voice, and then, 'I really do need to go, Grace. I'm just so busy. I've a queue of people who all need my help and . . .' Grace wasn't listening any more;

all she could think about was something she had read online last night at around midnight as she stood waiting for the microwave to ping time on Cora's request for a mug of warm milk with a sprinkle of nutmeg on top. The article was about people being busy being busy and so somehow managing to fill their time, regardless of their actual workload, and thereby convincing themselves they were busier than everyone else . . . she figured that Bernie must be one of those 'busy' people.

'I'm busy too,' Grace uttered, but wasn't heard as the line went dead. Seems Bernie had gone back to being too busy to be bothered by troublesome phone calls from their bedbound mother.

Grace turned and left Mrs Donato's glorious unit 28 behind for another day. Monday to be exact, seeing as today was Friday! The disappointment of having to wait three days to go through the contents was crushing, but at least she had something nice to look forward to now . . . *or maybe I could come into work tomorrow? Just to take a peek inside one of those suitcases? Or I could take the one on the top of the pile home to make a start?* But Grace knew this could never happen as there was no way Larry would allow her to remove one of Mrs Donato's suitcases from the storage company's premises – he was very fastidious about things like that and rightly took pride in looking after his customer's belongings as if they were his own. Plus Grace knew that her mother would never agree to her leaving her home alone over the weekend. And Bernie was right . . . she couldn't leave Cora lying in a wet bed, so there was nothing for it, Grace would have to go home now. And strip and then remake her mother's bed, for a second time today.

So after closing the door behind her and securing the padlock back in place, Grace put the clipboard on to the trolley and braced herself to face Larry and Betty to explain that, not only had she turned up late this morning . . . but that she was now going to have to let them down again and go home early.

3

'Babe, why do you even bother working at that storage place?' Phil moaned, pushing his bushy beard towards Grace's left cheek. They were sitting side by side on the Dralon sofa in the lounge below Cora's bedroom having a film night. *Breakfast At Tiffany's*. Grace had seen it a million times before but when Phil had said it was her turn to choose, she hadn't hesitated, keen to rekindle some of the glamorous Hollywood magic she had felt on entering unit 28 on Friday.

It was Sunday evening and she had thought about Mrs Constance di Donato and her beautiful vintage belongings all weekend. Even her name sounded sophisticated and glamorous, and Grace couldn't wait to get to work tomorrow to find out more about the woman she imagined lived the kind of life that she had only seen in films and read about in those lifestyle magazines. It was exciting and intriguing.

Grace had even decided to put Cora's breakfast of toast, cereal, a little jug of milk and some fresh-fruit salad with a flask of hot tea on a tray like they did in hotels. If she left it all ready on the table by her bed, then Cora could have it whenever she liked after her morning routine of bed bath and selecting her TV programmes for the day. This way, Grace could get off to work on time for a change, instead of having to wait around while her mother ate . . . usually very, very, *very* slowly as she complained through every mouthful! A genius plan, and Grace didn't know why she had never thought to do this before now. In fact, she had done a lot of thinking over the weekend, and talking too – she had called Bernie to 'let her know' how their mother was . . . as per the instruction in the telephone conversation on Friday afternoon, and to moot the idea of them setting up a care rota for Cora.

Bernie had actually gasped out loud on realising that Grace was implying the rota would be shared between the four of them! And then said she might be able to manage a contribution to pay for a professional carer to 'give you a break, Grace, if that's what you really need.' Grace had then tried her other sister, Sinead, who – to be fair – had acknowledged that Grace 'pulled the short straw when it comes to looking after Mum, and I wish there was more I could do but it's so difficult with me being so far away these days.' Grace had pointed out that Chelmsford in Essex wasn't really that far away. A weekend, or even just a Saturday here and there was manageable, surely? And it really would make a great deal of difference to Grace to have a few hours to herself. She was in desperate need of a haircut and some new clothes, or even just the chance to visit the library or browse the chunky yarn section of the craft shop a few streets away. Plus she fancied trying a salted caramel smoothie in the pop-up bar that had opened up. It had been months since her counsellor had set these activities for her to accomplish on her own, and she hadn't made any progress whatsoever on them yet.

But the call with Sinead had somehow moved on to her offering to chip in for a private carer too, or 'better still, get on to the council, Grace, and see if they can send someone round for free. My neighbour has a woman who comes in three times a day to help out. And it's all paid for by us taxpayers. Just make the call!'

Grace had tried to point out that it wasn't as simple as all that – there were forms to fill in and assessments to be carried out and Cora would never allow a stranger inside the house for all that in any case. There had been no end of recriminations from Cora for that one time Grace had managed to get the care assistant from social services to come and show her how to lift her mother and see to her basic needs. As soon as she had left, Cora had gone on strike and refused to even hold the handle on the hoist for days after that. But Sinead had breezily suggested if Grace found someone Mum liked then it would be 'absolutely fine', before ending the call because her Waitrose delivery driver was lugging her shopping through to the utility room and it would be rude not to give him a hand.

Lastly, Grace had spoken to her brother, Mikey, the hedge-fund manager, who in his usual fashion had got straight to the point: 'Stick her in a home and be done with it, Grace! I can't be hearing all this crap about her not wanting strangers in the house – did she ever give a toss about what we wanted when we were kids?' Silence. 'No, we did as we were bloody well told or a whack around the head and no dinner was the punishment. That woman is a bully, and believe me I know what I'm talking about: I deal with them all day, every day, and the sooner you wake up and realise that, Grace, the better. Now, if you call my PA, Annabel, on Monday, I'm sure she'll sort you out with a list of half-decent places you can visit. Just pick one. A cheap one. And make them come and collect her if you have to. I'll pay for it all and recoup my losses when we flog her house. Annabel will probably go with you if you're still getting in a state about going out on your own. Or if you just want a second opinion! You know, to make sure the staff aren't slapping the old dears around like you see on those undercover documentary programmes on the telly. Mind you, what goes around comes around, so it would serve Cora right to get a taste of her own medicine!'

Grace had hung up at that point. Frustrated and weary. She could just imagine the look on her mother's face if she selected a care home for her, a *cheap* one at that. Then bundled her off there without so much as a conversation about it, let alone without seeking her consent, which she knew would never be given. Deep down Grace also knew that she was scared of her mother. Scared of her rages and scared of what she would do or say to hurt her if she ever turned on her . . . and that is exactly how Cora would see it if Grace did what Mikey suggested. A betrayal.

But Grace was decided on one thing . . . if her siblings weren't going to help out, then she was going to help herself and implement a few more changes to make her own life a little bit easier . . . like encouraging Cora to manage her bed bath, for starters. Grace knew that her mother was perfectly able to sit up in bed by herself, and she could rub the edge of a coin over a scratchcard too, so surely she could utilise that hand action and replace the coin with a flannel and move it over her own body? This would give Grace a precious extra ten minutes or so to go towards doing all the other things that had to be sorted before she was able to leave for work each morning. It was only a small change, but it was a start at least. A small step towards taking back the life that she used to have and that had got lost along the way. Along with her dancing career . . . her dreams and aspirations of being blissfully happily married to Matthew, with perhaps a cherub-cheeked child of her own – but that had all vanished on that terrible day when she caught Matthew cavorting with the Perky Yoga One.

'I work at the storage company because I enjoy my job and because Larry and Betty are so kind,' Grace answered, bringing her thoughts back to Phil and his beard, which was now burrowing into the side of her neck and making her skin all irritated and itchy.

'But you could do yourself a favour and just pack it in,' he suggested.

'Why would I do that?'

'Well, it's not like you need the money or it's a proper career or anything! Not when you're all set up here.' Phil paused burrowing and glanced around the room. 'If you play your cards right, this house will be yours one day. And you must get a fair whack in benefits and stuff, what with you being your mum's carer. You might even get more if you didn't work and looked after her full time.'

'I don't, actually. And I do need the money. Plus the house will probably be split between all four of us . . .' Grace leant forward to reach another slice of pizza.

'What?' Phil said, aghast. 'But that's not fair. Surely it should be all yours seeing as you are the one doing all the work, and saving the rest of them a fortune on care-home costs? When my nan was old and had to go into a home, my dad sold her house to pay for it so there was no money left for any of us.' Grace could see that Phil had given her mother's care needs a great deal of thought . . .

'Anyway, let's enjoy the film while we can before Mum needs me upstairs,' Grace said, keen to move the conversation on. Phil lifted his arm away from around her shoulders and swivelled his body on the sofa until he was facing her.

'How about I need you upstairs?' he grinned, wiggling his eyebrows suggestively as he picked a stray curl of red hair away from her face. 'Come on, Gracie . . . bet your mum is fast asleep by now. She's probably snoring.' And he pressed pause on the TV remote control to cock an ear up to the ceiling, as if to prove his point. Grace swallowed her mouthful of pizza and looked at Phil. She did fancy him but, to be honest, she really didn't feel like going to bed with him right now. She was exhausted, and with her mother in the bedroom next door of their tiny terrace house where the walls were paper thin . . . well, it just didn't feel right.

'Not tonight, Phil. It's late and I have work in the morning. And I'm tired, I was up again with Mum last night and—'

'You see! There you go again . . .' Phil sat back and folded his arms like a petulant child.

'What do you mean?' Grace asked tentatively. She really wasn't in the mood for this kind of conversation.

'Well, I thought we had sorted all this out and agreed we would put each other first for a change, instead of you always putting your mother first. I even let you pick the film!'

'I'm doing my best, Phil.'

'Are you? You know, I reckon you don't even want to put me first.'

'Of course I do.' Grace heard her voice jump up an octave. 'But I can't just not bother with my mother . . . what would become of her if I just did whatever I liked and wasn't around to care for her?' She cringed as the sense of déjà vu shot through her, for she was certain she had said the exact same words to Matthew shortly before she had found him in bed with another woman. 'My mother can barely even move on her own, so she'd end up dying of hunger,' she added, bleakly, desperate to make some kind of sense of the situation she was in now, and with no way out anytime soon that she could see.

'Doubt it! The size of her,' Phil muttered as he drained the last of a can of beer.

'Pardon?'

'Nothing. Only joking.' He marshalled a swift smile on to his face before carrying on with, 'I know you can't just "not bother" with her and I wasn't suggesting you abandon her or anything. But you could get someone else in to look after her. It doesn't have to be you all the time. Anyone would think you like being the only one she can count on . . .'

Grace sighed and decided to fast-forward the next part of her plan to make her own life easier, and because in all honestly she really didn't have the energy to argue with him or explain the situation any more than she already had done, umpteen times. And she could see the way the relationship was going, only this time it was worse as she was actually living with her mother. Back when Matthew had started complaining about Cora's demands she had mostly been visiting and helping her out of an evening and at weekends. In addition to the late-night phone calls, of course. Sooner or later, Phil would have enough and find someone else too, just like Matthew had, and she really couldn't put herself through all that again.

'Maybe we should have a break!' she blurted out.

Phil's face froze.

There, she had said it, and felt a wave of relief. Better out than in is what her mother would say. Cora was a great believer in speaking your mind and had drummed it into Grace to do so too . . . 'I'm only being honest,' she would say, even if the words were spiteful and hurtful. Grace had been carrying the thought of slowing things down with

Phil around inside her head for a while now. But having told him, she panicked, never having been one for confrontation, so felt the need to add, 'It's not fair on you. My mum needs me, and you are right, I don't put you first . . .'

'What?' Phil spluttered. 'Don't be daft, Gracie. You can't dump me.'

'I'm not dumping you, exactly.'

'Yes you are. Everyone knows "a break",' he paused to do sarcastic quote signs in the air, 'means dumped!'

'But I can't put you first, Phil.'

'That's not what I meant. I didn't say you need to put me first. I said we should put each other first.'

'Did you?' Grace felt confused now, her head crammed full of cotton wool . . . from the exhaustion most likely.

'Of course, babe. Me and you. Always has been. It's about us.' And he stroked a finger over the back of her hand.

'That's just it, Phil. I don't think I can put us first. You want more than I can give you right now . . .' She dipped her head and twiddled with the butterfly pendant that hung on a delicate silver chain around her neck. She had bought it as a gift to herself on the day of her first visit to the GP to ask for help.

A symbol of new beginnings. Only it hadn't really worked out that way as she didn't have a new life. In fact, she now felt even more trapped. Stuck in a rut as her mother's carer, with a mediocre relationship and an old engagement ring that Matthew had refused to take back when she'd offered it on the day he came to collect the last of his belongings from the flat. 'Why don't you sell it and use it to pay the rent, or treat yourself to something nice . . . it's the least you deserve after everything that has happened. I'm so sorry, sweetheart, for the way things have turned out between us. I never meant to hurt you, but . . . I guess we fell out of love with each other,' is what he had said, followed by a hug and one of his wonderful warm smiles that had almost broken Grace in two. Only holding it together until the front door had closed behind him, when she had slumped down on to the hall carpet and sobbed. Because all the time she hated him she could cope, just about, with losing him . . . but he had to go and ruin it all by being nice. And she had never fallen out of love with him. Oh, she had tried to, but somehow couldn't quite make it happen.

She never had sold the engagement ring, which was now relegated to a velvet box kept in the drawer beside her bed. Sometimes, when she was at a low ebb, usually after one of her Facebook stalking sessions, she would get the ring out and allow herself, for the briefest of moments, to pretend it was still real. Her and Matthew. Happy in love with a wedding to plan. That hadn't happened for a while now. But tonight that could all change as she yearned for the simplicity and lightness that had been her life before, with Matthew. Now it just felt heavy, like wading through treacle all the time.

'Babe, come on . . . don't be like this.' Phil moved his finger to her chin and gently lifted her face up to his. 'I know you've got your hands full, but—'

'No buts, Phil,' Grace jumped in, and then cringed on realising that she sounded just like her sister, bossy Bernie. 'I can't be the girlfriend you want me to be.' Grace had known this for a while. After meeting Phil at the bus stop about a year ago, at first it had all been fine. He had been happy to sit in and watch TV with her and said he 'got it' that she struggled to go out. He also seemed to accept that there was no space in her life for dates and trips out to the cinema or to a nice restaurant. Or an art gallery or a sightseeing day like other couples enjoyed. The ones who weren't carers, and who were therefore in charge of their own lives and free to do whatever they liked with it. It bothered her, if the truth be told. Being an onlooker in her own life, letting Phil down, and herself too. Not to mention feeling guilty for resenting her own mother.

'Look, you're just stressed that's all. And you're the only girlfriend I want.' Silence followed. 'Is this because you had to pay for the pizza? Because I'll sort you out for the twenty quid when I find my debit card, promise.'

Grace studied Phil. His forehead creasing. His blond hair swept back from his blue eyes. His easy, sideways smile. But before she could answer, he carried on talking. 'Look, how about I take you away for a weekend. A spa hotel, where you can put your feet up and let the flunkies wait on you for a change. Champagne and massages . . . what do you reckon? And it's your birthday soon too. Let's make it a special one, babe. My treat!' He nodded at her eagerly and she felt touched that he had remembered and wanted to plan something nice for her. 'You need a break. And is it any wonder when you work all the hours you do? At least think about packing in your job too . . . we'd have all the time we wanted then to do stuff together.'

Grace instinctively shook her head, knowing that a weekend away was an impossibility. She couldn't afford it, for one thing, and dreaded to think how many steps it was to the nearest spa. Just the thought of it was already making her feel panicky. Plus how would she organise it all? Cora would never go for it, and even if she could be persuaded, it would take time and energy that Grace just didn't have right now to find a potential weekend carer, interview them and train them to do things the way her mother liked. Cora was so particular. But it was really lovely of him to suggest it and she could feel herself softening towards him.

'Oh Phil, I'm not sure I can . . . you know that,' she told him, gently.

'You could if you really wanted to,' he suggested, kissing her on the lips, then after pulling away, added, 'if you found a private carer . . . listened to your sisters and actually got someone in. They'll pay for it. Hell, I'll even chip in too if it means I get some bedroom time with you. When was the last time we had sex?' Grace turned away to stifle a yawn, the softening towards him now dissipating.

'I don't know.' She could barely keep her eyes open, so love-making was the furthest thing from her mind right now, which instead was crammed with thoughts of *I'd do anything right now for a whole night of blissful, uninterrupted sleep.*

'Exactly. So do it, Gracie. Get the carer in and . . .

let me take "care" of you!' Phil laughed at his own joke as he pushed her back on the sofa and slid a hand up and under her T-shirt in one deft move.

'I'll think about it,' she conceded into the side of his neck, knowing it wouldn't be as easy as all that. But if she was serious about helping herself, and it seemed that was her only option, given that Bernie, Sinead and Mikey's intentions were purely monetary when it came to caring for their mother, then it had to be worth a try. Plus it might be nice to be able to participate in her own life again. Maybe she was ready for that new beginning now. Grace had a feeling that she had allowed her grief over the break-up with Matthew to take over and exonerate her in some way from making an effort until now – it was easy to excuse herself from doing the things that brought back happy but painful memories, of the life she used to have with Matthew – when she had the perfect excuse: that her mother needed her. Maybe Phil had a valid point. And because, at that exact moment, Cora pounded her walking stick on the ceiling above them and bellowed,

'Grace. Grace. *Grace! For the love of God.* Where is my bedtime drink? I'm near dying of thirst up here while you're pawing that poor man of yours.'

4

Monday afternoon at work and Grace was engrossed in another, more fabulous world, where parties on board yachts on the breathtakingly beautiful Italian Riviera drinking limoncello cocktails and pure glamour prevailed. Connie was happy, meeting and mixing with Italian socialites and a new friend . . . a glamorous, vivacious Italian woman they all called Cristal due to her love of champagne.

Grace carefully turned the page of the red leatherbound diary embossed with gold initials, CD, on the cover and eagerly read on, revelling in how very 'Elizabeth Taylor and Richard Burton in their heyday holidaying in Portofino' it all was. Connie seemed to be having the time of her life, as if living inside an incredibly romantic Hollywood film.

Italy in springtime really is exquisite. We drove all the way along the old coastal road today from Santa

Margherita to Portofino with the top down and the glorious sunshine hot on our bare heads. With glistening waves swirling around the rocks on one side and lush green grass dotted with pastel-coloured houses on the other, I couldn't resist untying my headscarf and truly throwing caution to the wind as it ruffled my hair and lifted my spirits.

The boat was waiting for us in the harbour and after climbing aboard I rather enjoyed my first time at sea! The waves propelled us, quick as flash, to our destination, the tiny bay of San Fruttuoso, where we swept ashore to explore the atmospheric old Benedictine monastery. Mind you, I had a terrible fright when a squealing wild boar piglet scampered from the under-growth and almost ran right into my legs on its way off into the pine-clad hillside. Thank heavens I had kept my gloves on as I had to pat its little rump in order to shoo it away as it double-backed and came at me for a second time.

Later, after a scrumptious supper of roasted octopus on a bed of velvety tomatoes and olive tapenade under a honeysuckle-entwined trellis on the beach, we strolled arm in arm across the sand and then ventured up and down the steps around the monastery, picking wild mint on our way, which we later discovered was a rather splendid idea, as we dipped the leaves into our cocktails

*when we got back on board the boat for the moonlit
voyage home to Portofino . . .*

Sighing in contentment and wishing she was there,
hundreds of miles away in the sunshine, eating
roasted octopus and patting wild-boar piglets in the
tiny bay of San Fruttuoso, Grace closed the diary.
And then, on hearing Larry call out her name, she
glanced at the time on her phone and realised that
she had been sitting (very carefully on the dust sheet
near the edge, so as not to mark it) on Mrs Donato's
peacock-patterned chaise longue in the corner of
unit 28 for almost an hour. Larry was probably
wondering what she was doing and, more importantly, why she hadn't come back to the office yet to
make a start on sending out this month's invoice
letters.

'Coming,' she called out in reply, and hurriedly
stood up, but then Larry was in the doorway. 'Sorry.
I was just . . .' She stopped talking and looked at
the floor, mentally kicking herself for losing track
of time.

'It's fine, Grace.' He smiled kindly, gesturing with
his right hand for her to sit back down. But she
remained standing, keen to see what his reaction
would be as he properly saw inside the unit. His

face didn't disappoint. After casting an eye over Mrs Donato's belongings, he let out a long, impressed whistle and raised his wiry eyebrows.

'Wow! This is quite something.'

'It sure is. And it's going to be a proper adventure going through it all.' Grace's face lit up.

'Well, there's no immediate rush. The items aren't going anywhere soon, not after being here for almost thirty years. But before you get stuck in, I wanted to make sure everything was OK? Betty and I were getting worried about you; you've been gone ages. We thought you must have fallen asleep or something.' He smiled gently. 'And who could blame you . . . I just checked my emails and saw one from you earlier this morning . . . sent around 4 a.m. Is everything OK, Grace?'

'Yes, I . . . I'm sorry about that . . .'

'Why would you be sorry? I was fast asleep at that time, but how come you weren't?' Larry chuckled, making his shoulders bob up and down.

'Oh. I . . . um, I couldn't sleep,' she said, not wanting to go into the real reason she had been awake all night. That Cora had insisted Grace sit by the window in her bedroom on lookout duty, convinced she'd heard a noise coming from the garden below, and telling her, 'You'll never live with yourself, Grace. Sure you won't, if someone breaks in and strangles me in the middle of the night while you're fast asleep now without a care in the world.' And Grace had loathed herself for not reasoning with her mother and telling her that it was highly unlikely someone was going to break in and strangle her . . . because it was more likely the person to strangle her would be her own sleep-deprived daughter who was already inside the house! But seriously, Grace knew she should have been stronger and stood up to her mother for the sake of her own nocturnal needs. But it had been late and she had been at a low ebb, knackered and not in the mood for another fight. So instead she had done as her mother had told her to, and sat in the armchair dozing as she tried to stay awake 'just in case' her mother's fears turned into a reality. Because, at the end of the day, Grace knew that what Cora said was true, especially once she had planted the seed of doubt inside her head . . . how *would* she live with herself if something happened to her mother on her watch?

'I'm sorry to hear that, Grace. Especially if it was work that was keeping you awake . . . I'm sure Mrs Donato's whereabouts could have waited until today,' he said, shaking his head as he referred to the email that Grace had sent to him in the early hours.

'Sure, Larry, I know . . . but I didn't want to forget any of my ideas. So that's why I typed them into my phone and emailed them to you.' Grace lowered her eyes, grateful not to have to go into detail about her own ineptitude when it came to standing up to her mother. Plus she didn't want to complain about Cora and then come across as self-pitying. 'I've not been able to stop thinking about Mrs Donato and wanted to give you some suggestions of how we might find her. I guess I got carried away and . . . well, it is pretty exciting seeing all her glamorous belongings in here. And I was also wondering why we had let her account go so far into arrears? It's well over a year,' she added, remembering the dates in the paperwork on the clipboard. 'We usually do something long before now.'

'Hmm, well that's true. We do.' Larry looked momentarily evasive, then a little embarrassed as his cheeks dotted pink. 'Between me and you . . . well, I . . .' He coughed. 'I'm not going to lie . . . I guess I have a bit of a soft spot for Mrs Donato,' he confessed. 'But, please not a word to our Betty, because you know that I adore my dear wife.' He lifted his shoulders to emphasise this fact. 'Plus, she'd have my guts for garters if she ever knew.' Larry pulled a mock-petrified face then, making Grace laugh as she swiftly nodded her agreement, touched by his gentlemanly consideration for his wife that came from a bygone time where honour was everything.

Grace doubted Betty would have his guts for garters though. She would probably chuckle and admonish him to busy himself to keep from distractions! Just like she had when Mrs Bassett, a willowy blonde widow, had swept in to the customer waiting area to retrieve her late husband's stamp collection and had flirted outrageously with Larry in the hope of him waiving the closing bill. He had been just about to as well, when Betty had stepped in and said that payment would be very welcome, thank you very much, as she plucked a credit card from Mrs Bassett's grasp.

'So you've actually met Mrs Donato?' Grace asked excitedly. 'Oh, I can't wait to meet her too – that's if we can track her down. What's she like? I've been reading this.' She lifted the diary into the air to show him, but then fell silent on feeling her cheeks flush pink. 'Sorry. I . . . probably shouldn't have been so nosey.' She waggled the diary around before bringing her hand back down beside her.

'Oh it's fine,' Larry said gently. 'I won't tell if you don't,' and he tapped a finger to the side of his nose. 'Besides, how else are we going to get in touch with her. Which year is it? The diary . . . anything recent to give us some clues as to where she might be now?'

'Sorry, no. And at first glance there doesn't seem to be any kind of order to the diaries and notes written on scraps of paper. Everything is very sporadic and with some of the diaries completely empty, or with just a few lines written in them here and there. Though I did manage to find this one, dated 1955, which is pretty full up – where she's living in Italy and it sounds so idyllic. Listen to this.' Grace quickly reopened the diary and read a section of it aloud. '*The warm, salty sea air is infused with the marvellous scent of citrus from the lemon and orange groves further down on the hillside. The dazzling azure-blue sea laps gently in the distance and I simply can't imagine a more perfect place to be than standing here on the veranda with my truelove watching the plump, pink sun setting on the horizon.*'

'Well I never!' Larry folded his arms and nodded slowly, clearly impressed by Mrs Donato's prose. 'Those are mighty fine words, and with a clue for us right there too.'

'A clue?'

'Yes . . . a truelove! With any luck, he's Mr Donato by now. So we'll find him and he will lead us to Mrs Donato. Yes, that's what we will do.' Larry nodded, clearly resolute about the best way forward for solving this matter.

Grace pulled out her phone and tapped through to her To Do list to make a note to read on through all the paperwork in unit 28 to see if she could find mention of a Mr Donato. Or a wedding. Surely, Connie, being the romantic she appeared to be in the diary, would write about her own wedding.

'It's all there in gorgeous detail. Connie is an incredibly romantic writer,' she told Larry. 'Reading her diary is like reading a beautiful, romantic novel. And she lived in a powder pink villa surrounded by lemon and orange groves on a hilltop in Santa Margherita. I googled it and it's part of the glamorous Italian Riviera and just along the coast near Portofino in Italy, apparently. Imagine living somewhere as wonderful as that? Or she did in the 1950s! But I'm guessing that's not the case any more if her stuff is in our storage unit here in drizzly south London.' Grace patted her curls, which had turned into a giant auburn frizz ball after falling victim to the inclement weather at this time of year in London, when she got caught in a sudden downpour while counting the steps to the bus stop this morning.

'Connie?' Larry asked.

'Yes, Mrs Donato. Connie is short for Constance. That's her first name . . . well, the name her family and friends call her. It's on a number of letters and cards in the first suitcase. From what I can make out, she grew up in London and then moved to Italy later. But I'd have to put it all together into a proper timeline to be sure . . .'

'OK, Grace. But do we have a current address for her? Or a relative? A son or daughter perhaps? A bank statement? Anything to give us a clue as to her current whereabouts and why she hasn't paid us? Or how about a first name for Mr Donato?'

'Not yet. But I'm working on it. Please can I have a bit more time to go through and catalogue everything properly? There's a lot of paperwork. But a week or two should do it.'

'Hmm, I know I said there was no immediate rush, but we can't afford to have units unpaid for, so we need to start getting an income for this space asap. I've already been a sentimental fool for far too long over this one. Perhaps we should make a start on getting it listed at auction and hopefully someone will buy the whole lot swiftly. Then we can recoup our losses and re-let the unit right away.' He shook his head as if deep in thought as he tapped the tip of a biro on the doorframe.

'I understand,' Grace conceded, reluctantly, but then had an idea. 'Some of these items are antiques and must be worth a fortune . . . much more than she owes us in missed storage payments, so we'll easily recover our losses if we can't find her and have to sell them. What do you reckon?' She felt alive at the prospect of piecing together the life story of Connie Donato or, to use her gloriously glamorous full name, Mrs Constance di Donato. 'And you did say that you have a soft spot for her . . .' she added, hoping to appeal to his better nature. 'It doesn't feel fair to not even try to track her down.' Grace inhaled, willing him to agree. 'Surely, her belongings are as important as the old soldier's medals? There's a whole lifetime inside this unit waiting to be discovered . . .'

A short silence followed as Larry creased his fore-head and gazed around the unit, seeming to take it all in. Grace inwardly crossed her fingers, because if he let her have a week or two, she was quite certain she could unearth something in amongst Connie's belongings that would give them a clue. If not to her whereabouts, then a relative, or even a friend who might be able to help. The items in the unit were unique and far too personal to be sold off at auction.

'OK,' he eventually agreed. 'A week or so. Two tops! But only because I feel sorry for her.'

'Thank you,' she breathed out, only realising then that she had been holding her breath for too long making her feel dizzy. 'But why do you feel sorry for her?' she asked, blinking a few times to clear her head.

'Because,' he started and then paused. 'I don't really know, to be honest . . . I mean, it was donkey's years ago, of course, yet feels like only yesterday, that's how distinctive she was. But I still remember when she first came here to sign up for the unit. Mrs Donato stuck in my mind. You see, there was an aura about her.'

'An aura?' Grace felt intrigued and widened her eyes in anticipation of hearing more.

'Yes. Imperious. Regal almost. But kind of sad and lonely too. She was smartly dressed, in a mink coat with leather gloves and a hat . . . it was still OK to wear real fur in those days,' he quickly clarified. 'And she was wearing this expensive scent . . . I don't know what it was – not something our Betty would wear. Anyway, I remember it lingered in the office for ages afterwards. Betty and I joked about it for weeks, saying, "Mrs Donato is still here" every morning when we unlocked the office door and got a great big walloping whiff.'

Grace immediately wondered which perfume it was, and from what she had already deduced about Connie, imagined it to be something romantic yet sophisticated, classic and expensive, like Cartier or Van Cleef and Arpels. Grace had been walking through Selfridges' beauty hall one time on a shopping trip with Matthew, and the sales assistant had spritzed her with both of these fragrances and then given her some small sample sprays. She had treasured those tiny phials, eking them out as a way to hold on to that moment in time with her own true-love, as it was later that very day, over lunch, that Matthew had proposed.

Perfume was such a powerful evocation of memories: one whiff and Grace was back there with Matthew by her side, oohing and aahing over the dazzling display counters in Selfridges. Then, after the shopping trip, they had found an authentic Italian café in a quiet back street with round tables covered in red gingham tablecloths and candles in wine bottles with wax trickling down the sides. They had sipped limoncello cocktails and tucked into big bowls of buttery soft ravioli stuffed with shrimp and drizzled with pesto and pecorino shavings. Creamy raspberry gelato was for pudding, followed by mugs of hot chocolate so deliciously thick they had been able to stand their teaspoons up in it and take bets to see whose spoon would topple over first.

Matthew had joked about the leaning tower of Pisa being right there inside his mug and how they should book a holiday to Tuscany to see the tower and all the other glorious Italian sights for themselves. He had then pushed back his chair and actually performed the whole chivalrous ceremony of asking her to marry him amidst much whooping and cheering from all the other diners. 'Of course I will marry you,' she had laughed, 'but only if you get up off the floor at once.' She had never been one for showy displays of affection. The way everyone had stared and then come over to shake Matthew's hand and tell him how marvellous he was. She remembered his smile, like he was the happiest man alive. And it had felt right. A perfect day.

'But her eyes. I'll never forget her eyes,' Larry continued, bringing Grace back to the moment, so she tucked that particular memory away for now; it was probably for the best as it never did her any good to remember the good times with Matthew . . . it only made her current, lukewarm relationship with Phil feel like a consolation prize. 'You can tell a lot about a person from their eyes.' Larry leant against the doorframe and tilted his head upwards as he ruminated.

'Here, do you want to sit down? Come and rest your knees,' Grace offered, gesturing to the chaise.

'Ah, no thank you, my dear. My orthopaedic consultant said that I have to keep active if I don't want the old joints to cease up. Road to ruin that is . . . not keeping active.' And he did a halfhearted knee bend as if to punctuate the point, making Grace wonder if she should try to encourage Cora to be more mobile. Maybe she could manage some arm stretches at least. It certainly wouldn't hurt for her to try. She could sit up in bed and reach up for the hoist and bash her walking stick hard on the floor, so it was worth a go. Plus she was younger than Larry by over a decade. Grace made a mental note to mention it to her mother when she got home from work.

'If you're sure . . . ' Grace smiled at Larry. 'So, what were they like, Connie's eyes?'

'Deep and pensive. As if she had lived a life of note, but with adversity and sorrow. Haunting, almost. That's why she's stuck in my memory. I've not ever seen eyes like that since . . .'

'Oh, poor Connie,' Grace said, even more determined to find her and discover her story. 'And thank you for giving me time to find out more.'

Larry smiled and moved into the centre of the unit.

'Two weeks tops!' He shook his head and sighed good-heartedly. 'Come on, how about I give you a hand to sort through some of her things . . . let's see what we can find. If we have no luck in finding a lead of any kind, then we can always get Betty to ask her pal, Maggie – the one from the knit-and-natter group, to look on the computer.

'Maggie who works at the coroner's office?' Grace said, optimistically.

'Yes, that's the one. She does family trees for people too and has even managed to trace right back to pirate times for some of her clients.'

'Really? I didn't even know that was possible,' Grace said, fascinated, and wondering if she could be related to a proper pirate. She quite fancied the idea of that. It was quirky and unusual and certainly sounded more interesting than coming from a long line of potato farmers who had lived in stone huts on the desolate, windswept fields of the remotest part of southern Ireland.

'It's all there in the computer these days,' Larry confirmed. 'Maggie was very helpful when we were trying to track down the owner of those medals that time. We would never have known he had died or had a son up in Scotland without her help.'

'True.' But Grace really hoped this wasn't the case for Connie. After retrieving a picture from the carpet that had fallen out of the back of the diary, Grace studied it and found herself looking at a slim, elegant young woman, with a row of yachts and small sailing boats moored behind her in the background. Rows of narrow, tall houses with shops and cafés with the awnings out curved along the water's edge to her right, a church or a lighthouse peeping over the top on the pine-tree-clad cliff. She was wearing a silk scarf knotted at the side of her neck, pedal pushers and a stripy, boat-necked sun top and looked very 1950s chic – just like Audrey Hepburn in *Roman Holiday* – another one of Grace's favourite films. With a handbag in the crook of her elbow, sunglasses and leather gloves in her hands, Connie looked breezy and happy at first glance, but on closer inspection there appeared to be a sadness surrounding her too, with her almond-shaped eyes gazing sideways and ever so slightly downcast. Or maybe she was just shy and didn't like having her picture taken.

It was hard to tell for sure. But Larry was right, Connie did indeed have pensive eyes. And a dazzling smile. And was strikingly beautiful . . . if the faded black-and-white photo was anything to go by. Grace really hoped she hadn't died.

Grace showed the photo to Larry who turned it over and read the old-fashioned cursive words in faint black ink on the back.

'Connie. Portofino harbour. 1952,' he read aloud and then commented, 'very nice indeed.' He passed the picture to Grace who slid it back where it belonged inside the diary.

'But why hasn't anyone been in contact? There must be someone – who took this photo? And who wrote Connie's name on the back? A family member? Mr Donato? Connie's child?' Grace was sure Connie had a daughter as she had seen mention of a baby in one of the letters she'd found in the first suitcase. And then there was the pink fluffy teddy bear. It was tucked inside a bundle of delicately hand-knitted baby clothes – a pretty matinee jacket, a bonnet with satin ribbons and bootees in soft pink and white wool. And all of a sudden a wave of sadness came over her, for she knew that Connie was dead. In her heart she just knew. It was the most likely reason for her storage payments to have stopped, it was usually the way, and she couldn't bear the thought of the unit being sold at auction to whoever was willing to stump up the highest bid, as had happened on rare occasions when all avenues to trace the owner or a relative had been exhausted.

Grace felt it important to make sure it didn't happen this time; that a complete stranger should rummage through Connie's things with scant regard to the life that she had lived. She wasn't really sure why she felt so strongly about it. Maybe it was seeing the photo; it had somehow made Connie real, and now Grace cared about her. Or maybe it was the pair of worn-out pink satin pointe ballet shoes that she had found in a black leather oval-shaped dancing case underneath the chaise longue. Was Connie a dancer too? Was that where the feeling of affinity came from?

Whatever it was, Grace knew that she had to find out more about the elusive Mrs Donato with her sad eyes. And who knew, maybe Grace's intuition was wrong and Connie was still alive: it was possible. Perhaps she had returned to Italy and was living the high life in her powder pink villa on the hillside and just didn't give a damn about a load of old stuff deposited back in London, having long ago forgotten about its existence. Or perhaps she was old and senile and didn't even remember the contents of her storage unit. Maybe someone else was managing her finances and had simply forgotten, or didn't even know they were supposed to send cheques to pay for a storage unit in London.

There were so many possible scenarios and Grace felt determined to find out more. Compelled to, even. And if there was a daughter, then surely she would want to sort through her mother's belongings herself. It was even possible that Mrs Donato's daughter didn't know that her mother had died . . . if they were estranged for some reason. So it was entirely possible she had no idea the items were stored here . . . just like the soldier's son in Scotland, who'd had no idea that his dad's medals were here at Cohen's Convenient Storage Company on an industrial estate in southeast London.

'Who knows, Grace.' Larry shook his head. 'Something I've come to realise in this line of work is that human beings are complex. Families, especially. We've had all kinds of situations over the years with the storage units. Divorce, deaths, affairs, even marriage, and that's supposed to be a happy time for people. But weddings can cause tension too, especially when a newly married couple come to clear out a unit. Do you remember the Marples?'

'Oh yes, how could I forget?' Grace pulled a face on remembering the debacle that had ensued when Mrs Marple discovered that her new husband had stored a load of memorabilia of his time with an ex-girlfriend. Photo albums, clothes, letters, souvenirs from their travels were all dumped in the big rubbish container amidst much shouting and flouncing after Mr Marple had settled the bill.

'So, where shall we start?' Grace said cheerily as she put the diary down on the dressing table and looked at the jewellery box, determined to unravel the mystery of Mrs Connie Donato's life and reach a happy outcome.

'Here is as good a place as any,' Larry nodded, lifting the padded lid of the jewellery box.

A moment of silence followed.

Grace glanced inside, looked at Larry, and then they both gasped in unison.

'These stones can't be real . . . surely?' Grace managed, going to touch the sapphire- and diamond-encrusted bracelet nestling in its own little velvet tray inside the box. She hesitated, unsure if she should let the tip of her finger even dare to make contact with such an exquisite piece of jewellery. What if she damaged it somehow? She would spend a lifetime trying to save enough money to replace the bracelet, if it turned out to be real and therefore worth an absolute fortune.

'I sure hope not.' Larry carefully picked up the bracelet, worry etched on his aged face. 'Because if it is, then Mrs Donato definitely isn't insured for such a valuable item.'

'I wonder why she stored it here then? Surely a bank deposit box would have been more secure?' Grace looked at the other items: a dazzling ruby ring, a silver – or was it platinum? – short chain with a Star of David dangling from the end, a small diamond at each of the star's six points. A tiny silver expanding bangle, the kind that babies are some-times given soon after they are born. Three pairs of sparkly drop earrings – one pair with diamonds, another with the darkest blue sapphire stones and the third with the palest, creamiest pearls haloed with yet more diamonds.

'This is way out of our league,' Larry exclaimed as he swept a hand through his hair. 'We'll need to get these jewels examined to see if they are genuine, but if it turns out they are then . . . well, I can't believe they've just been sitting here for all these years.' And after carefully closing the lid, he lifted the jewellery box up with both hands.

'What shall we do?' Grace asked.

'Let's get the jewellery box into the safe at least, just in case the jewels are the real deal, and then decide where we go from there. We need a contact, a lead, something to get us started on our quest to find Mrs Donato.'

'So we're definitely not going to list the unit for auction?' Grace checked optimistically, feeling excited.

'No. But, like I said, let's give it a couple of weeks. You go through all the suitcases, read the letters and see what you can find. I'm sure Betty won't mind holding the fort in reception. And I'll make a start on sending out the invoice letters tomorrow; it'll give me a chance for a nice sit-down . . . now that I've done my exercise for the week by coming over here to the oldest and furthest part of the warehouse to find you,' he laughed.

'Thanks, Larry. I'll get on it right away!' And she turned towards the pile of suitcases, keen to get started. Then an idea came to her. 'How about your nephew? The one in America?' she suggested hurriedly, pivoting to face Larry again. Her mind was working overtime now in figuring out the quickest and best way to find Connie Donato, who was clearly a woman of considerable means . . . if the jewellery was genuine.

'Ellis?'

'Yes, doesn't he work at an auction house?' Grace looked at Larry.

'He does!' Larry jubilantly lifted the jewellery box up, as if in celebration of this fact. Something to set them on the right path in tracking down Mrs Donato.

'Then perhaps he can tell us if the jewellery is real . . . or if it's just paste with pretty coloured plastic bits and nothing to get excited about after all.'

Larry brought the jewellery box back down as he added, 'Ah, but Ellis works in the Fine Art department. He won't know about diamonds and suchlike.' And he turned to leave with a deflated look on his face.

'But . . . hold on.' Grace darted around the back of the chaise longue. 'Maybe he can take a look at these instead.' She gestured to the framed paintings. 'I can take photos of them and you could email them to Ellis.'

'Yes. Good thinking, Grace, you're always full of good ideas.' Larry put the jewellery box back on the dressing table and walked over to where she was standing by the paintings. He lifted one out to take a look. 'Now I'm no art dealer but this looks pretty impressive to me. None of your mass-produced printed stuff here! You know, the kind of thing that you find in IKEA. No . . . this is a proper oil painting. And thankfully we have the correct climate control in all the units, even the older ones such as this, as I wouldn't want to be held responsible for such a wonderful work of art getting ruined with mould or mildew. It'd be a travesty.'

He carefully touched the corner of the canvas with a look of relief on his face. An exquisite scene of Venice's famous Grand Canal was displayed before them, with tall, creamy-caramel-coloured buildings flanking either side of the water's edge. Gondolas on glittering blue water under an atmospheric cloud-streaked sky led up to two marble domes with delicately intricate detailing. 'And a skilled artist by the looks of it . . . see how he or she has captured the detail of the cornicing on the domes right there?' Larry paused to point at a beautifully impressive building in the top right corner of the painting. 'The famous Salute. It's a church. And built as a thank you when the plague ended in 1630, if I'm not mistaken.'

'Gosh, that must have taken the builders years to create. It's incredible.' Grace studied the picture; it reminded her of the 1950s film, *Summertime*, starring Katherine Hepburn. She'd only watched it again a few months back and had been swept away in the gorgeous, romantic scenery of Venice's magnificent waterways.

'It's breathtaking up close,' Larry said, carefully placing the painting on the chaise longue.

'Have you actually seen it in real life then?'

'Oh yes, I took Betty there on a mini-break back in the day. We were young and carefree, and this was long before the nippers came along and you could just up and do all that spur-of-the-moment stuff.' He smiled wistfully, as if remembering the lovely time he'd had with Betty in Venice. 'And we hadn't been married long, so it's a wonder we saw anything much at all outside of our hotel room,' he added, doing an exaggerated wink. Grace put a hand over mouth to stifle a giggle as she really couldn't imagine Larry and Betty cavorting in bed all day and night long. 'Ah, those were the days.' He pondered quietly for a moment before rubbing his palms together. 'Anyway, enough of the melancholy – shall we make a start in snapping some pics then?'

Grace lifted her phone up and took several pictures of the Venice Grand Canal painting, wondering if she should put some filters on to enhance the scene, but thought better of it as Ellis would most likely need to see the original work in all its naked glory. She repeated the process with all the paintings, and there were a dozen at least, many in the same style. They couldn't make out the marking in the bottom right corner; it wasn't even a proper signature and gave them no clues as to whether Connie herself was the artist. The thought had crossed Grace's mind, though, after reading her diaries – the imaginative style of her writing showed that she clearly had a creative talent. Perhaps painting was in her repertoire, too, and that's why she went to Italy . . . to capture its beauty on canvas.

Twenty minutes later, and Grace had photos of every painting.

'I'll email them to you,' she told Larry as he stowed the last painting back in its place.

'Thank you, Grace. I'm so pleased we have you here with all the good ideas,' he said kindly.

'Really?' she said without thinking, unused to impromptu praise.

'Of course,' he nodded. 'And don't be worrying about being late now and again, I know it's hard for you at home.' A silence hung in the air between them as Grace studied a fingernail. 'The important thing is that we have you here.'

'Thank you,' she managed quietly, fearful now that Larry being nice might make her emotional.

As if sensing this, he jovially added, 'So how about we have a lovely cup of tea?'

'I'd like that,' she breathed, grateful to be talking about something else. 'And Larry . . .' She hesitated, wondering if he would agree to another idea.

'Go on,' he prompted.

'Well, I was wondering if I could take some pictures of Connie's diaries and letters too? I know I can't take the originals home, but I could read through them when I'm up in the nigh—' She stopped talking. 'Um, if I get time,' she added. Larry looked at her, momentarily hesitating, as if he wanted to say something more but wasn't sure if he should.

'Grace, you can read through them here tomorrow,' he settled for a few seconds later. 'There's really no need to take on more work, I'm sure you have enough to be getting on with at home as it is . . .'

'But I'm not sure I can wait until then. Please Larry, it will give me something interesting to do . . .' She looked away, disliking how desperate she sounded. But it was the truth. The thought of delving into Connie's life gave her a sense of purpose, and it would be a break too from the monotony of her usual night-time routine of waiting for her mother to fall asleep . . . just so she could do something for herself, if only for a short while, uninterrupted, and

81

without fear of being bellowed at and then chastised for not coming to her aid fast enough.

'Well, in that case, I'll get the jewellery box into the safe while you get cracking on reading more of that diary to see if you can spot some clues.'

A little while later, Larry returned with two mugs of tea.

'Betty made it just how you like it,' he said, handing a mug to her. 'And said to give you this too.' He pulled a bundle wrapped in kitchen towel from his pocket. Inside was another generous slice of Betty's delicious babka. 'She also said I was to give you a hand with going through Mrs Donato's things and she'll take care of the invoice letters.'

'Oh, that's kind of her. And thank you, Larry.' Her eyes lit up as she took the cake. She hadn't had time again to eat a proper lunch, just half a homemade ham sandwich on the bus back to work. But at least Cora had agreed to serving herself a cheese plough-man's with a big buttered baguette and tomato soup from a flask while Grace had Googled local engin-eers in the hope that one could come and take a look at the washing machine that was now playing up. She devoured the cake and took a slurp of tea while Larry lifted the first suitcase from the pile and flipped open the lid.

'Well I never! There must be dozens of diaries, letters and papers in here,' he said, placing his hands on his hips in preparation for the mammoth task ahead. 'Right, let's make a start. I'll open and place each one on the chaise longue while you snap a pic, and then I'll put it all back in the suitcase afterwards. If we get a system going then we might be done by home time . . .'

My truelove is never coming home! I swear my heart shattered into a thousand tiny pieces as my knees buckled and I grasped the back of an armchair on hearing the news. Mother and Father travelled all the way here on the train to Tindledale especially to tell me themselves. Killed in a training exercise is what Father explained, with his head bowed and black fedora hat pressed to his chest as he imparted the terribly sad news in the middle of Aunt Maud's sitting room. Mother put a steadying hand on my arm as she passed her best embroidered hanky towards me. I managed to control my emotions, though, and didn't cry until I was alone upstairs in the bedroom.

Hitler has a lot to answer for!

This world is so cruel.

Poor Jimmy will never see the baby that is kicking its tiny feet as it grows within me, and this darling soul will never feel the love of the marvellous father that I know Jimmy would have been. The father that poor Jimmy could and should have had the chance to be if he hadn't gone off to learn how to fight in Hitler's phoney war! Not even a proper war.

Mother says adoption is the only option now, especially as I'm unmarried and will not be in any fit state to deal with the grief as well as look after a new baby all on my own. Because that is what I shall be: alone! An unwed mother. Not even my best friend, Kitty, knows of my predicament. There was no time for me to even get a message to her before I was sent away, and Mother says she saw her at the station going off to join the Land Army in Oxfordshire, so I can't burden her with my troubles when she needs to concentrate on doing her bit for the war effort. Mother also says it won't be long now until baby arrives. But how can I bear to be parted from Jimmy's child when it is all I have left in the world? And this poor mite doesn't deserve to be abandoned to strangers who never even knew Jimmy. How will they ever be able to tell our child what a marvellous man he was?

In the lounge below her mother's bedroom, with her laptop on her knees, having transferred the pictures of Connie's paperwork from her mobile, Grace felt a solitary tear trickle down the side of her nose as she wished she could reach into poor Connie's diary and sweep her up into an enormous hug. Although Jimmy had died a lifetime ago, Grace knew the sense of loss for a life you thought you were going to have never really goes away, and she wondered if Connie still felt it after all these years . . . if it turned out that she was still alive. And Grace was even more hopeful now that her instinct was wrong and Connie was still here.

She would love to meet her, to see a glimpse of the young woman she was reading about back in . . . she paused to click through her photo stream to find the date of the diary she was reading from . . . ah, January 1940. During the Second World War. So Jimmy served his country and courageously gave his young life so that others could live on in peace. But not for poor Connie; Grace imagined her life was shattered on losing her love, and therefore so very far from peaceful.

Grace made a note in the pad on the coffee table in front of her. 'Jimmy died – 1940. Connie's baby born 1940.' So the baby would be in her seventies if she were still alive today, thought Grace, assuming the child was a girl on remembering the delicate pink hand-knitted matinee jacket and bootees. She vowed to read on and see if she could find the name of Connie's daughter, as that would probably be the easiest and quickest way to find her mother, Constance di Donato, now that she knew the truelove mentioned in the later diary extract in Italy clearly wasn't Jimmy. 'Another man' . . . Grace wrote on the pad, followed by, 'Italian? Connie's husband? Mr di Donato.' And then she made a list of questions she would look for answers to in amongst Connie's paperwork inside the unit.

1. Who is he?
2. Where did they meet?
3. Where is he now?
4. Was Connie's baby (a girl?) adopted?
5. If not adopted, did the baby take Mr Donato's surname?
6. Ask Betty to ask Maggie for advice on how we can look up the name 'Donato' on the ancestry websites that she uses to make her family trees.
7. Or, better still, how do we go about looking on the electoral roll?

Donato is an unusual name; there can't be that many people with it, surely, and if Connie's daughter did take her stepfather's name and then never married, or even if she did, she may have kept her name in any case, so we could find her that way. Grace's head was spinning as she went through all the possible options.

She placed her laptop and pen on the sofa beside her and sat back, still and numb for a while, letting the silent tears flow for Jimmy and the heartbroken, lonely young woman from the past who had been left behind with Jimmy's unborn baby. Loneliness was a terrible thing, Grace knew; she had endured it when Matthew first left and before she'd conceded and had given up the flat, unwillingly moving back in with her controlling mother. And, from the sounds of it, Connie had a controlling, unfeeling mother too! Who tells their grieving young daughter that giving their unborn baby away is the only option? Grace knew things had been different for unmarried mothers back in those days when Connie was a young woman, but still, it felt so heartless, and why was she far away in the countryside and not with her parents when she most likely needed them the most?

Grace wiped her tears. Determined to find something or some way of helping Connie, she picked her laptop up and read on. The next few pages were blank as she tapped through on the mouse pad, but then something familiar caught her eye. After tapping back a page, she took a proper look.

If only I had kept my passion and love for Jimmy intact a little longer, certainly until my eighteenth birthday on 20 June, and then we could have married and . . .

Grace sat bolt upright. The twentieth of June. That was her birthday too. Her pulse quickened. What were the chances of that? It had to be a sign. She liked signs, and wasn't sure why exactly, other than that they tended to feel comforting, reassuring somehow. As the similarity sank in, drawing her and Connie together over the decades, a fresh batch of tears came as she picked up her pen and pad and tried to write.

8. 20 June. Mine and Connie's birthdays!!!

Grace let all the feelings flood through her until, moments later, she became aware of a colourful flash at the window. A Hawaiian shirt in petrol blue with vibrant green parrots all over it was jigging up and down. Jamie from next door was tapping on the front-room window and waving exuberantly with his other hand. Grace quickly swiped at the tears with the sleeve of her top and leapt up, motioning to him that she was coming to the front door. After taking a brief moment to gather herself, she let him in.

'How are you, Grace? A million miles away you were then. Everything OK?' he asked, folding his tattoo-covered forearms and staring at her intently. 'You looked like you were crying. Not that I was spying on you or anything – I had barely glimpsed in before I tapped on the window. Promise.' And he enveloped her in an enormous embrace, the waft of his coconut hair gel engulfing her. Grace let herself lean into his gym-honed chest, grateful for the moment of comfort. 'Ah, that's it, love, you let it all out,' he added, when she couldn't help her shoulders from heaving up and down. The last few months had been so exhausting, what with caring for Cora and then on reading and absorbing Connie's pain . . . well, it all felt so overwhelming right now and Grace realised she was crying again. An ugly cry with the tears sprinkling all over the shoulder part of Jamie's cheery parrot shirt.

'*Is that you, Jamie?*' Cora's voice bellowed, breaking in to Grace's moment of comfort from her friend. Jamie lifted his chin from where it had been resting gently on top of Grace's head and responded.

'Yes it is, Cora. I'll be up to see you after I've spent some time with Grace, OK?' he called out, firmly, never one to take any nonsense from her mother.

'Of course, love. No rush, I know how busy you are at the hospital . . . get Grace to make you a cup of tea, I'm sure you could do with one.' And her voice faded as she turned the volume of the TV up even higher.

'Can you turn that down, please, Cora? It's very loud,' Jamie added, giving Grace a look as he let out a sigh and rolled his eyes.

'Oh, yes, sorry. I didn't realise,' Cora acquiesced sweetly, and the TV volume instantly lowered.

'How do you do that?' Grace whispered, shaking her head as she went to pull away. 'Oh God, I'm sorry,' she added, on seeing the state of his parrot-print shirt. But he gave her another squeeze before taking her hand in his and leading her into the lounge.

'Oh don't worry about a few tears, they will all come out in the wash,' he said, gently.

'There you go.' He steered her to the sofa. 'Now sit down and I'll make *you* a nice mug of tea and you can tell me all about it. Better out than in.' He squeezed her hands in his before turning on his heel and heading towards the kitchen.

Half an hour later, and Grace had told Jamie

all about unit 28 and Constance di Donato's diaries and beautiful belongings.

'Blimey! How intriguing,' Jamie exclaimed through a mouthful of strawberry jam on extremely buttery toast – he had made several rounds to go with their tea, declaring this a very justified moment for some good comfort food. 'But desperately sad too. Do we know what happened to the baby yet? Was she adopted?'

'I honestly don't know. Maybe Connie will tell us soon. There are lots more diary pages and scraps of paper to look at, but it's slow going trying to piece a proper timeline together as they don't seem to be in a logical order.' Grace took another mouthful of tea as she nodded towards her laptop.

'But you already have clues to investigate,' Jamie suggested.

'Such as?' Grace put down the mug and lifted her pad and pen, poised to note any ideas that Jamie might have.

'Well, her address in London for starters.'

'What do you mean? The post from there was all returned with "Not known at this address", so we know that she doesn't live there any more.'

'Fair enough. But a neighbour might know where she moved to, or how about the person who does live there now? Somebody wrote on the envelopes and put them back in the post. Somebody kind. Somebody who cares. I couldn't be bothered with all that.' He let out a long sigh before cramming a jammy crust into his mouth.

'Really?' Grace quizzed as she turned to study her best friend. She was surprised by his attitude, as she thought Jamie was the kindest and most caring person she knew, alongside Larry and Betty of course. 'So what would you do then if post arrived for someone who used to live at your house?'

'That's highly unlikely – you know we've lived next door for as long as I can remember. But I guess I'd chuck it in the bin,' he said and shrugged.

'That's terrible.' She batted his arm. 'You can't do that.'

'Why not? Of course you can. Unless it had a credit card inside or something like that . . . then I'd open it and pocket the card ready for some seriously fraudulent online spending. Card and address details right there. Bingo!' He rubbed his hands together in glee.

Silence followed.

'You idiot!' Grace proclaimed, when the penny dropped that he was messing around and teasing her.

'What?' He pretended to cower as she batted him with her pad. 'Oh Grace, as if I would do a thing like that! You are so gullible. Always have been.'

'No I'm not!'

'Ouch. That hurt,' he laughed, going to grab the pad away from her grasp.

'Sorry,' she mouthed, halfheartedly.

'Ah, don't be. It's just nice to see you smile, Grace. You can't blame me for pulling your leg . . . I had to do something to lift your mood as you looked so down when I was staring at you through the window.' He grinned, cheekily.

'Oi, but I thought you said you weren't stalking me,' she retaliated, jabbing him with her pen which he swiped out of her hand and tossed across the room.

'Here. Have the last piece of toast,' he said, changing the subject as he lifted the plate and put it in Grace's lap.

'Oh no thanks, I'm full up.' She went to push the plate away.

'Nonsense. You've barely eaten anything and sometimes you need to feed the soul, my sweet. And I'd say that time is now. Grace, my darling, you are withering away and those circles under your eyes tell me you aren't sleeping at all. Come on, what's really going on? Your gorgeous green eyes used to sparkle . . . is Cora being horrendous?' He lowered his voice and lifted his eyes upwards to the ceiling. 'You must be firmer with her. The no-nonsense approach is the only way, I'm afraid.'

'Oh, Jamie. I'm fine. I'm tired, that's all. A few late nights . . .' She looked away, knowing it was so much more than that and Jamie was her oldest and closest friend, but she also knew that if she went into it all now – Cora and the full extent of her care needs, what had happened with Phil – then there was no saying how she'd feel . . . she'd cry again for sure, and that wasn't really fair on him. No, now was not the time for a pity party for one. In any case, she just didn't have the energy for any more emotion.

'But you're not fine, Grace. Look, why don't you put your feet up for an hour here on the sofa and I'll go and keep your mother company for a bit. I can get her scratchcards and then encourage her to take a while going through them. You never know, she might hit the jackpot and you'll have your ticket out of here . . . they do a very nice care package at the Treetops Residential Home over in Bromley on the outskirts of London. Costs a bomb, but why not if you can afford it?' He nonchalantly lifted one shoulder to punctuate his point.

'Honestly, you don't need to do that.'

'Yes I do! Grace, how long have we been friends?' Jamie looked her square in the eyes with a determined look on his face.

'Um, for ever,' she said, 'since we were children and you stole my dress-up shoes that time. I got them from a charity shop and had managed to hide them from Bernie and Sinead for ages . . . and then I caught you dancing around in the garden in them. Covered in grass stains they were when I got them back.' She shook her head and laughed.

'Exactly! And what gorgeous shoes they were. I would have died for those heels – silver crystal platforms.' He shook his head and made dreamy eyes, clearly in shoe heaven.

'Well, you nearly did die that time when your dad caught you and whacked your backside for dressing up like a "big girl's blouse",' Grace said bluntly, and instantly regretted it on seeing a flicker of a flinch on Jamie's face. 'Sorry, that was insensitive of me,' she swiftly added, touching her friend's arm.

'Ah, don't be. I'm over it. Dad was a dinosaur. He was never cut out for having a son like me. A big pansy!' Jamie rolled his eyes. 'Anyway, back to the point . . . you and I have been friends for donkey's years and there has been many an occasion when you've helped me out. Like when you let me stash my eyeliner in your school bag, not to mention when I used to go on dates with boys and you pretended that I was with you when Dad came round here shouting the odds the next day. So, let me help you out now, please. Plus, you have to trust me . . . I'm a nurse! So I'm ordering you to get some rest.' And he lifted her feet up and swung her legs round so she was now lying on the sofa.

'But . . .' She went to sit back up.

'Nope! I shan't take no for an answer. Stay there and I will see to Cora. And then later on we can work out a plan for you to play detective and go and visit the address you have for Connie, to see what you can discover about her whereabouts.'

'I can't do that!' Grace said, immediately panicked. She couldn't remember Mrs Donato's address off the top of her head, but she was quite certain a trip there would involve going on a bus that took a different route to the one she was used to, or worse still, a train journey involving many, many steps just to get to the station before even boarding the train.

'Yes you can.' Silence followed. 'Come on, Grace . . . where's your fire?' He crouched down in front of her and placed one hand on her shoulder, then in a gentler voice he added, 'OK, I know it's not easy, my love. But look how far you've already come. You can do this. You really can. I know you can, I promise you.'

'Hmm, maybe,' Grace ventured, placing her hand on top of his.

'Maybe what?' Jamie tilted his head to one side and smiled tenderly. She moved her hand to the side of his face. He was such a kind and thoughtful man.

'Well, it depends . . .'

'Depends on what?'

'If you come with me?' Grace stared him in the eye, hoping he'd agree as she very much liked the idea of investigating Connie's whereabouts. Not to mention seeing where she had actually lived here in London. But the thought of travelling there on her own filled her with fear.

'Sure. I can do that.' He nodded like it was no big deal.

'Really?' Her eyes widened.

'Yes, really.' He smiled. 'And the next time you venture out somewhere new by yourself, I'll come with you halfway, and then the time after that I'll come a quarter of the way and then, before you know it, you will be going all the way by yourself and you'll be absolutely golden!' And he clapped his hands together, seemingly having it all worked out. 'Ooh, it's so exciting, like a proper TV detective drama. Larry might even let you go there during work hours . . . it is a work matter, after all. So you won't have to worry about her ladyship upstairs,' he paused to point a finger at the ceiling, 'and I will figure something out with my shifts. We'll be like Cagney and Lacey!'

And, seemingly content with this plan, Grace nodded off before Jamie had even reached the stairs leading up to Cora's bedroom.

6

Constance di Donato's address in London was the garden flat of a handsome, double-fronted Georgian townhouse overlooking the grassy heath in the centre of Blackheath village. Vibrant purple begonias tumbled from the tall pots on either side of the majestically arched front door, and a brass plaque listed the apartment numbers above their respective bells.

Grace pressed her index finger on to the Garden Flat bell for the second time and then waited. Still no answer. But if by some chance Mrs Donato was still alive, then she would be very elderly – in her nineties, if she had a baby born in 1940 – so it might take her a while to come to the door. Should she press the bell again? Grace wasn't sure it would be polite to, so she pulled her phone from her pocket and, after shielding the screen from the dazzling afternoon sunshine, she looked in her notes app to double-check that she had the right address. *Garden Flat, 1 Montpelier Row, Blackheath, London SE3.*

Yes, it was definitely correct. But then, on glancing at the time at the top of the screen she felt anxious on realising she needed to be back home very soon to give Cora her tea. Larry had agreed she could leave work early to come here and look for Connie, and Jamie had kept his promise to come along too, even though Blackheath wasn't very far from where she worked in Greenwich. He had been true to his word and had come to Cohen's to meet her, having arrived half an hour early, so had sat and chatted to Betty in the office while he waited for Grace to finish up checking in a new customer and teaching them how to operate the electric trolley, which really did seem to have a mind of its own, veering off in all directions apart from the one it was actually supposed to go in.

Jamie was currently bobbing up and down with his hands pressed up to the sides of his head as he tried to get a look through one of the big sash windows on the ground floor.

'Come on, it's obviously a dead end,' Grace said, slotting the phone back into her pocket, resigned to not finding Mrs Donato after all, which was a shame as she had hoped to meet the glamorous lady. But she knew that it was highly unlikely given that Larry's payment reminder letters had been ignored for all this time. From what Grace already knew about Connie, from the impeccably organised storage unit and her compassionate diary entries and notes, she had formed an impression of a meticulous lady of considerable substance, and not the kind of person who would just stop paying their bills and then ignore reminders. No, Grace knew deep down that her initial hunch must have been right and that Connie had died. It was just fanciful thinking to get her hopes up of a different outcome.

'Not so fast. We can't give up now,' Jamie said, over his shoulder. 'Try ringing one of the other bells.'

'I can't do that. And I'm not sure you should have your face pressed up to that window . . . what if someone is in there? And we don't even know if that is the garden flat you're peering in to. They might think you're staking out the place with a view to burgling it!'

'Don't be daft!' he hissed in an exaggerated stage-whisper voice. 'They're hardly going to think that with me in this get-up now, are they?' And he ran a hand over his bright pink T-shirt with a bold white flamingo print splashed all over it.

'Hmm, I guess not.' Grace had to agree, as with his mirrored petrol-blue sunglasses and flamboyant fluoro-lime trainers, he wasn't exactly blending in with the genteel top-drawer set who lived in an exclusive place like this. 'But there's still nobody in, Jamie.' And she went to walk off.

'Hang on, I think I just saw someone moving around inside . . .' And he tapped on the window. A little while later, the big front door was slowly opening, and a very elderly woman was standing before them, wearing a smart, pink tweed Chanel jacket and pearls, with coiffured snowy hair and pensive eyes.

Grace inhaled sharply and then held her breath as she scanned the woman's papery, age-lined face, wondering if this frail old lady really could be Connie? Maybe her hunch was wrong after all and Connie was still alive. The woman standing in front of her looked to be at least in her nineties, so it was possible she could have a daughter who was in her seventies.

Jamie darted away from the window and towards the front door.

'Hello, I hope I didn't startle you. It's just that my friend here is looking for someone . . . A friend. Yes, a long-lost friend,' he quickly reassured as the woman clasped her hands together in worry, her eyes flitting left and right along the street and then gazing out over the grassy heath behind them, as if trying to fathom the situation with these two strangers.

Grace smiled and stepped forward so she was standing alongside Jamie.

'I'm so sorry to bother you,' she said and held out her hand, resisting a sudden urge to dip into some kind of curtsey, such was her feeling of reverence for the elegant woman standing before her . . . or was it in hope of meeting Connie after all.

'Who are you?' the elderly woman asked tentatively.

'Um, my name is Grace Quinn,' she said, briefly holding the lady's tiny soft hand in hers. 'And this is my best friend, Jamie.'

'Hello.' Jamie did a little wave by way of introduction before folding his arms and stepping back to allow Grace to carry on.

'We've come here to find a long-lost friend—'

'You'll have to speak up, my dear,' and the old lady moved in a little closer, placing her hand on Grace's arm. 'My hearing isn't what it used to be, you see. It comes to us all in the end, I'm afraid. Pleased to meet you . . . you can call me Lady Bee

. . . everyone does. Now, what is it you were saying?'
And with her free hand she patted her immaculate
hair while Grace wondered if this meant that she
really was a bona-fide Lady . . . she certainly had
an air of nobility about her.

'Nice to meet you too.' Grace smiled gently and
rested her hand on top of Lady Bee's before speaking
each word more precisely. 'I said, I have come here
to today to look for a friend . . .'

'A friend you say? What is your friend's name?'

'Con . . .' Grace paused and then continued with,
'Mrs Donato.'

'Constance?

'Yes, that's right.'

'Oh dear.' Lady Bee suddenly looked agitated as
she patted Grace's arm before withdrawing her hand.
'That can't be right . . .' Her voice trailed off as she
shook her head.

'Why is that?' Grace enunciated carefully to make
it easier for Lady Bee to lip-read.

'Mrs Donato didn't have any friends, my dear, so
that's why. She kept herself to herself when she lived
here. I never saw anyone visit her, and my apartment
is right across the hallway. I did say hello on occasion if I saw her in the hall when she first moved
in and we made polite conversation . . . you know,

she told me once that she had lived in this very house as a child before having to leave when she was only seventeen. It wasn't converted into flats in those days, though ... she said it was a grand Georgian house with servants' quarters in the attic rooms and a magnificent kitchen with an enormous Aga in the basement, so I imagine her family must have been very wealthy indeed.' Lady Bee widened her eyes and tilted her head.

'Did she say why she had to leave?' Grace asked, wondering if it was because Connie was pregnant – the diary entry had mentioned her parents visiting her in a rural village called Tindledale to break the news of Jimmy's death.

'No, she didn't, and I did ask as I thought it an opportunity to find out a bit more about her, but she clammed up. She was very distant. Quiet and reserved. "A recluse" is what they call people like her. And then she moved on.'

'Moved on?' Jamie intervened. 'Do you by any chance have a new address for her?' The woman looked at him and then back at Grace, who was trying not to feel disappointed that she definitely wasn't Connie.

'Oh dear, there's no easy way to tell you this ... so I'll just get on with it and then it's out of the way.' Lady Bee straightened her back and fixed her eyes on Grace. 'I'm afraid your friend passed away some time ago. She had a fall in the street and an ambulance took her to hospital where she later died. I'm so very sorry for your loss,' she stated, stoically. Grace gulped and felt grateful for the sunglasses she was wearing as she could feel her eyes stinging with the threat of tears, which was ridiculous really as she hadn't even known Connie in real life. But she had felt a connection. She identified with Connie, knowing she had a controlling mother and that they shared the same birthday as well; she felt as if she knew Connie intimately, too, through reading her personal diaries and notes. So now Grace felt a loss on realising that she really would never get to talk to the woman whose life she was piecing together.

A short silence followed.

It was Jamie who spoke next.

'I'm so sorry,' he soothed, looking at the elderly woman before placing his arm around Grace's shoulders. 'Do you know when she, um . . . moved on?'

'I'm afraid I do. You see, I was away when it happened.' She glanced apprehensively at Grace. 'When it's winter time here I stay with my son at his villa in Spain every year . . . the sunshine, you see; it helps with my joints. But when I came home in the springtime, poor Constance had already gone. This would have been nearly two years ago now.'

'I'm so sorry, it must have been a shock for you,' Jamie said.

'It was. Yes, it really was. A dreadful business.'

'Do you remember meeting any of her family? Did anyone visit here perhaps?' he asked carefully.

'On no, dear. Like I said, there was no one, and I don't even think there was a proper funeral. It was certainly all over by the time I came home. You see, I would have gone to her funeral if I had known about it. It's not nice to think of anyone going without any loved ones to give them a bit of a send-off now, is it?' Grace shook her head emphatically. 'And then her apartment was cleared out and the contents collected by one of those house clearance companies – I saw their van come here; not that there was very much to take away. Such a shame . . . there wasn't any furniture to speak of – just a rusty old metal bed frame with a worn-out mattress and a few bags of clothes. One of the men said all her kitchen cupboards were empty and there was only a carton of sour milk in the fridge.' Lady Bee shook her head and Grace's heart sank further as she processed all this information.

'I wish I had known she wasn't coping, but she

never invited me into her home. If she had, I would have helped her. I could have fetched her groceries – my son sorts out the supermarket delivery for me and he wouldn't have minded at all if I'd added in a few extras for Constance.' She clasped her hands together in anguish. 'Ooh, here comes Mr Conway, maybe he can shed some light on what happened to poor Constance.'

They all turned to see a dapper gentleman exiting a silver Mercedes that had just pulled up behind them; he was wearing a smart suit with a vibrant pink handkerchief popping out of a top pocket. 'He lives in Connie's flat now,' Lady Bee informed them. 'But don't mention what I said about her,' she quickly mouthed. 'It might upset him to know she was living so frugally, in what is his home, now.'

Grace and Jamie quickly nodded in unison as they were introduced to Mr Conway and Lady Bee explained, bringing him up to speed.

'I'm afraid I have little more to tell you,' he nodded, 'other than the occasional items of post arriving for your dear deceased friend . . . Of course, if there's a return address then I always write the obligatory "Not known at this address", etc. on the envelope before popping it back into a letter box.'

'Ah, I see,' Grace interjected, remembering the

flamboyant handwriting on the payment reminder letters that Larry had received back in the office. 'Do you mind me asking if there is still very much post for Mrs Donato? Any handwritten envelopes that could be a birthday card, or Christmas card, from a family member or friend perhaps? Anything you can tell us would be very much appreciated. You see, I work at Cohen's Convenient Storage Company – it's past the heath and down the hill in Greenwich – and we have some items belonging to her that really need to be passed on to a next of kin.'

'Ah, I see.' Mr Conway cupped his chin in his hands as if momentarily deep in thought. 'Hmm, not that I recall. Just brown envelopes – the type that usually contain bills. I don't think she had any next of kin as I bought the flat from solicitors acting on behalf of the Crown.'

'The Crown?' Grace asked.

'Yes, as in the State. There's a government legal department called Bona Vacantia and they deal with the estates of people who die without leaving a will or having any known living relatives.'

'Oh dear.' Lady Bee stepped in and looked at Grace. 'Perhaps you could get in touch with the special department, my dear, and then you could let them know about the items you have in your storage facility.'

'And a relative could have come forward; perhaps they were estranged from your friend and didn't know about her passing until more recently,' Mr Conway suggested. 'I assume the proceeds from the sale of the flat will be sitting in a government account somewhere, waiting to be claimed.' He nodded again and apologised for not being able to help further before saying goodbye.

So it seemed Connie died in poverty and all alone in what used to be her childhood home. Grace knew they could probably check about the funeral arrangements with Betty's friend, Maggie, at the coroner's office of course, just in case a family member had surfaced to organise everything. But even so, why had poor Connie been alone with only a bed and some bags of clothes when she had a lifetime of belongings in storage, some items of which were clearly of considerable value? She could have sold them and made her life a little more comfortable. It just didn't make sense, especially when Grace remembered the glamorous woman in the picture taken by the harbour in Portofino during the 1950s. The woman with a treasure trove of jewellery and fine art and a collection of vintage gowns seemingly from another, more affluent time . . . a golden era of gaiety and prosperity for Connie. In stark contrast to the way she lived at the end of her life.

And in that moment, and with tears still smarting in her eyes, Grace made a decision: she was going to do whatever it took to find out what had become of Connie. How had her life spiralled into one of such obscurity where her next-door neighbour didn't even know how she was living, so desperate and alone with her shabby bed and empty food cupboards? It broke Grace's heart and she couldn't imagine her own life coming to an end in that way, or indeed her mother's life. What would become of Cora if she stopped caring for her? Would she end up like Connie? Lonely and hungry? It could so easily happen. No. Having forged a connection with Connie through her diaries and notes, Grace now felt even more compelled to find out the truth. It was the least she could do for a woman in time who fell in love, only to have her heart broken, and who lived a glamorous life in Italy . . . but then somehow ended up all alone back here in her childhood home in very different circumstances to the ones she had enjoyed all those years previously.

7

'Where have you been?' Cora bellowed the very second Grace turned the key in the lock and pushed open the front door. After slipping off her ballet pumps, Grace glanced at her watch to see that she had arrived home fifteen minutes later than usual, so grasped the banister and quickly made her way up the stairs to her mother's bedroom. A trio of sudden thuds made her stop short. *Surely Mum hasn't tried to get out of bed by herself? Her legs aren't up to it. What if she's fallen?*

'Are you OK, Mum?' Grace yelled out, rushing up the rest of the stairs and into the bedroom, her heart rate quickening on fully expecting to see her mother lying prone on the floor following a nasty fall. And given Cora's considerable weight, there was no way Grace would be able to get her back up off the floor and into bed all by herself. If Jamie wasn't at home to lend a hand, then Cora could end up being on the floor for hours.

'Yes! And no thanks to you though!' Cora was lying in bed with a pained look on her face. Grace breathed a sigh of relief. 'Why would you leave me all alone for so long? I'm near dying of thirst here.' Grace opened her mouth to answer as she saw a glass rolling across the carpet, stopping short when it hit the wheel of the commode which was now over by the wardrobe in the corner. Grace wondered how it had got so far away across the room and was certain it hadn't been there when she was last in her mother's bedroom. 'I tried to help myself. Like you told me to,' Cora said pointedly, looking the other way.

'I'm sorry, Mum. But when we had the chat about you doing more for yourself, I didn—'

'So you should be,' Cora cut in. 'I tried to lift the heavy jug to pour myself some water into the glass but my poor weak arms just aren't up to it.'

'Did you actually manage to get to the edge of the bed then, and sit up and lean over to lift the jug, by yourself?' Grace asked.

'How else do you think it ended up over there?' Cora indicated with her head towards the glass. 'I tried, Grace, but it must have spun away from my hand as I went to grasp it.'

'I see. And how did the commode get over there?'

'How should I know?'

'And what were those thuds?'

'What thuds?' Cora asked evasively.

'The thuds I heard when I was coming up the stairs?' Grace asked again.

'What is this? Twenty questions!' Cora tutted, shaking her head. 'You always were a nosey one. Even as a child, with your constant questioning. Drove your father mad, sure it did. Why don't you concentrate on getting me a drink instead of inter-rogating me? And I've got a tummy ache too so don't be trying to feed me that foreign muck again . . . Lasagne doesn't agree with me.'

Grace went to explain that Cora hadn't actually eaten any of the lasagne, and besides, that meal had been well over a week ago. But thought better of it and swiftly obliged by fetching a fresh glass and pouring some water. It was only after she had gone back downstairs to make the dinner that she realised Cora hadn't actually given her a proper explanation as to how things in the room had seemed to move around by themselves.

8

The deed is done. Mother and Father have visited me here in Tindledale and have taken my darling baby, Lara, to live with them. They are going to care for her until I am stronger. Mother was most disappointed when I refused the adoption, and said she wants nothing more to do with me if I'm going to be selfish and put my own needs before those of a poor, helpless infant. But Father stepped in and agreed that this is a suitable solution for now, so they have taken a cottage here in the countryside for the duration of the war. The cottage is in the grounds of a country estate on the outskirts of Tindledale which belongs to a friend of Father's who works for the Home Office so is away much of the time doing important work for the war effort. It's for the best all round, he says. Lara will be safe there away from Hitler's bombs in London –

Father says it's only a matter of time before they come and rip the heart out of the capital – and this way, their society friends will be none the wiser as to my predicament.

Losing Jimmy has knocked the wind right out of me, so it is probably for the best to let Lara have the proper care that she needs. She is too tiny to be left crying for milk in her crib all morning while I lie in bed and stare listlessly at the ceiling. But what is the point of living without Jimmy? Lara deserves far better than me. I'm a terrible mother, who cannot even muster up enough energy to feed her own baby, let alone leave my bed and get dressed to take her outside for some fresh air. And Mother says babies must have fresh air if they are to thrive.

Oh Jimmy, I'm so frightfully sorry for abandoning our beautiful daughter. But it won't be for long, my darling, I promise. Just until my energy returns and I'm back on my feet, and Mother will love her for me. For both of us. Of that I'm certain after seeing the tenderness in her eyes as she lifted tiny Lara from the crib and into her own arms. But my darling, our little Lara will always have a part of us with her, for she has the fluffy pink teddy bear now, a gift from her *daddy to go with the hand-knitted baby set her mummy managed to make, using pink wool from an old cardigan, before she became too fatigued. A dreadful dark cloud descended shortly after Lara was born and I simply can't shake it off. It's as if the light in my life has disappeared and I can't find a way through the tunnel to see it shine again . . .*

Grace was in the office at work, reading through more of Connie's diary entries and notes. Betty was sitting beside her in an armchair, busy crocheting Hannah's dolly blanket.

'Oh dear.' Grace shook her head and turned the page of Connie's diary dated 1940.

'What it is, Grace?' Betty looked up from her crochet.

'It's just so sad.'

'Ah, come on, lovey, please don't be upsetting yourself now . . . I know it was a terrible blow to have Mrs Donato's death confirmed, but we always knew it was the most likely explanation.'

'Sure, we knew it deep down,' Grace said quietly, 'but I can't stop reading these diaries and finding out more about Connie. It's as if she's my friend, and I care about her . . . she honestly feels alive to me. And did you know that we share the same birthday?'

'Well, fancy that! No wonder you feel an affinity with her,' Betty said kindly.

'Yes, it's such a coincidence, and then there's the similarity . . .' Grace let her voice tail off on realising that she didn't really want to talk about her and Connie's overbearing mothers, and so instead she lifted the leather-bound notebook up to show Betty. 'Poor Connie. She's now lost her sweetheart, Jimmy – Connie's parents have visited her to break the news that he died in the war and her parents have taken her baby, along with the pink teddy bear and knitted baby set that I found in a suitcase inside the storage unit. And now Connie is just so desperately sad and alone. And if that wasn't sad enough, I think she was also suffering with postnatal depression after Lara was born.'

'Oh my, that is dreadful,' Betty said and stopped her crocheting. 'My sister suffered with depression after her fourth child and it was just awful for her. And her husband, too. She couldn't leave the house for a good few months and near became a zombie until the doctor prescribed some antidepressants to get her through the worst of it. And then she overhauled her diet and took up aerobics and got involved in all kinds of self-help therapies until she felt like her old self again.'

'Oh dear.' Grace shook her head, thinking of her own battle with depression after the split from Matthew. 'I wonder if Connie was prescribed anti-depressants too?'

'I doubt it, dear. I don't think there was as much awareness of PND – or any kind of mental illness – in those days. Folks tended to get on with it, best foot forward and all that, or at least they tried to. They didn't have the kinds of therapies that they do these days. And with a war on, it would have been even more difficult for poor Connie. With no family to fall back on, she would have been all alone. I can't imagine she would have been able to support herself and a baby without financial assistance. And who was going to give an unmarried mother of seventeen a job with a young baby in tow?' Betty sighed despondently at the harshness of the situation for Connie. 'They didn't have the NHS or social housing or even any social security benefits back then,' she added.

'It's terrible,' Grace let out a long breath, 'that she was punished for falling in love and just being young and naïve.'

A short silence followed as both women

contemplated the heartache and loneliness that Connie must have endured, with nobody to turn to for help or advice.

'So, just a thought . . . how come the teddy bear and knitted baby set are in the unit then?' It was Betty that broke the silence.

'I don't know, but that's a very good point. Surely they would have stayed with the baby,' Grace said, turning more pages to see if there was another mention of baby Lara or the pink teddy bear, but the rest of the diary for 1940 was empty. So it was as if Connie's life had stopped when the postnatal depression took hold and her parents coerced her into relinquishing the baby.

'Well, let's hope Maggie can shed some light on what happened next, where the baby is, and find out why Mrs Donato was all alone when she died. She can then help us decide what to do next. But from what you've said that Lady Bee and Mr Conway told you, it doesn't sound as if poor Mrs Donato had any family around her at the end. Can't have done, can she, poor dear? And that's a terrible shame.' Grace sighed and shook her head in agreement, wishing things had been different, as then she might have met Connie, and maybe been able to be there for her, if only to pop in and see her now and again, so she wasn't all alone. Grace felt that she would have liked to have done that – made her a cup of tea and had a good chat. To have found out about her life and been a friend to her, because it seemed that they had much in common. Connie had loved to dance, too; she had written about it with such passion in her earlier diaries, only to abandon it when she had to leave London and go to the countryside, parted from her truelove and with a broken heart. In much the same way that Grace had lost sight of her own passion for dancing when Matthew broke her heart. And she was aware that her only friend was Jamie, and she had to admit that she also felt lonely sometimes. 'Because surely if she'd family around her,' Betty continued, 'then they wouldn't have left her to live like that . . . with just a carton of milk in the fridge, I ask you!' And Betty let out a long puff of disapproval.

'Yes, it's so very sad,' Grace nodded, knowing how important family was to Betty. Her too, had to be . . . why else would she take care of her mother?

'It sure is!' Betty agreed. 'And that's why it's commendable of you to stay with your own mother. I know it's very hard for you, dear, but she's also very lucky to have you looking after her like you do . . . not many young women of your age would do it, and nobody would think less of you if you got in some help, you know, dear . . . or even put her in a home. There are some very nice ones now and she might be much more comfortable . . .'

Before Grace could respond, Larry appeared holding out his mobile phone to Betty, his face all flushed.

'It's Ellis. Our favourite nephew! He's here in London,' he said, quickly.

'London?' Betty put down her crochet and took the phone from him with a baffled look on her face. 'What on earth do you mean? He lives in America.'

'Yes I know that, dear. But he's at Heathrow Airport,' Larry stated, animatedly. 'He's just arrived. Talk to him, love, he wants to know about the train, the fast one – what's it called? The express. Or is he better in a black cab? I've told him not to go in one of those Uber ones, but—'

'Shush. I won't be able hear him,' Betty chided softly, waving a hand in the air as she lifted the phone to her ear. 'Hello, love. Are you really here, in London, in England?' A short silence followed. 'Well, I never.' She lifted her eyebrows and pulled an impressed face. 'On business, you say. Fancy that.' Another silence. 'That's nice of you to take the time to visit us. Really? How exciting. Yes.' She looked deep in thought now. 'Yes. Yes. That's right. Oh I don't know. Here, let me pass you over to Grace. She'll be able to help you, I'm sure. See you soon, Ellis. Safe journey.'

Grace immediately sat upright and closed Connie's diary. A dart of anxiety flitted into her stomach. She'd never actually met Ellis, only heard about him from Larry and Betty – about how successful he was at the auction house where he worked in New York and lived in a penthouse apartment with its own lift 'that goes right into the lounge' is what Betty had told her. And the apartment was in the trendy Tribeca area where lots of cool celebrities lived – and he was American, so bound to be assured and confident. Certainly more so than she was. So Grace already felt way out of her depth. After swallowing hard she managed to speak.

'Um . . . hello.'

'Hello, Grace, this is Ellis,' he said, his accent smooth and a little drawly and just as she imagined a native New Yorker to sound. 'Can you tell me if Paddington is near, err . . . Greenwich?' he asked, getting straight to the point.

'Oh, um . . . no, not really. Um, no I didn't mean that I can't tell you . . . just that Paddington isn't near—' she started, getting flustered and racking her brains to think of the best way for him travel. But then Larry cut in, making her anxiety escalate further when he said, 'Grace, you could go and meet him. Show him the way here . . . it's only early and you'd easily be back by lunchtime,' he boomed.

Silence followed.

Grace could feel a rivulet of sweat snaking a path down her back. There's no way she'd make it all the way to Heathrow on her own. No way. In her addled state, she instantly wondered if Jamie was working today and, if not, if he might come with her. It was worth asking. But she knew in reality she was clutching at straws – a decision had to be made right this very second as Ellis was waiting on the other end of the phone that was trembling slightly in her left hand.

'Oh, don't be daft, Larry.' It was Betty who stepped in to save Grace. 'She doesn't want to be trekking all the way across London on the tube now in this hot weather, do you, love? Besides, she needs to get on and catalogue the rest of all the items in Mrs Donato's unit,' and she gave Grace a look of motherly concern. 'No, Grace, tell Ellis to get a black cab straight here. Our treat! Larry will scoot out when it arrives and pay the bill, won't you, dear?' Larry swivelled his head from Betty to Grace and back again before mumbling something about money trees. 'Ellis doesn't want to be bothering with going to cash machines and all that,' Betty finished, and that was that, the decision was made.

After politely conveying Betty's instructions to Ellis, Grace ended the call, surreptitiously wiping the phone on the side of her skirt before handing it back to Larry.

'Well, this is going to be a nice surprise,' Betty chuckled, gently patting Grace on the back as she went into the little kitchenette area to put the kettle on.

'I wasn't expecting him to drop everything and come rushing over here when I emailed the pictures to him,' Larry said, looking concerned. 'He's very busy and I don't want to get him into trouble at work by taking time off to come and look at some paintings that probably aren't even worth tuppence ha'penny.'

'But he isn't rushing over here just because you sent the pictures, you silly old fool,' Betty chuckled. 'No, he has some business to attend to in Europe.'

'Europe? Where in Europe?' Larry puffed, straightening his jacket. 'And why didn't he let us know he was coming?'

'I don't know where exactly, he just said some business in Europe. You know how it's all the same place to the Americans,' Betty told him. 'Anyway, the important bit is that the business he has to deal with is over the next month or so – meetings with a client, he said, and so he thought why not start the trip a bit earlier so he could call in and see us while he's here. Isn't that kind of him? And then he can take a proper look at the paintings and all the other stuff in Mrs Donato's unit too. He said he's quite intrigued and thinks some of the paintings might be worth a few bob . . . well, he didn't say that *exactly*, but you know what I mean. He wants to cast a proper eye over them to see if they are genuine. And if they are, well . . .' Betty nodded impressively, 'then we could be sitting on a bit of a gold mine, you know.'

'Oh?' Larry perked up. 'Well, in that case you had better get the babka tin out as Ellis is bound to be hungry when he gets here after such a long journey.'

9

Grace had missed meeting Ellis the day before as she'd had to get home to see to Cora rather than get another telling off for being late again. Now, the next morning, Grace had just arrived at work and could hear him talking in the office. After smoothing her top down, she stuffed her cardigan (it had a snag in the sleeve from catching on the corner of the kitchen counter as she'd rushed out to get the bus) into her handbag and pushed open the door with a big smile on her face to mask the anxiety she was feeling inside. Meeting new people was on a par with going to new places as far as she was concerned – fraught with uncertainty and something she'd rather avoid if possible. And last night had been another trying one, so she was now exhausted, and that never helped. Cora had hardly slept, calling out for drinks followed by demands for the lamp to be switched on, or indeed off, as the mood took her, and making Grace feel murderous. At about midnight Grace could have sworn she'd seen a smirk on her mother's face when she'd bellowed for the lamp to be switched on again so she could read. It was all Grace could do not to bop her mother over the head with the flaming book, she was that worn out.

When she had eventually managed to get her mother settled, Grace had then been so wired that she hadn't been able to sleep at all. Instead her thoughts had meandered into a destructive spiral of self-loathing brought on by going over all the little digs Cora had given her recently. Forgetful. Nosey. Rough-handed. Lazy – this had been shortly after 2 a.m. when Grace hadn't come into Cora's bedroom quickly enough to check out the noise coming from the street outside that had woken her mother up. When Grace had then got back into her own bed she had analysed each of Cora's criticisms, turning them over inside her head, searching her memory for all the shreds of evidence that corroborated the words, so they were now hanging around her like a millstone dragging her down and making her feel quite useless.

Grace looped her bag over the back of the chair by her desk, then straightened her hair and inwardly rallied herself so as to appear outwardly poised and breezy. Mindfulness. Or 'in the moment' as her counsellor called it. A strategy he had taught her to help her focus and to not let her mind wander away with self-sabotaging thoughts.

'Here she is! Our wonderful Girl Friday.' Betty came bustling towards Grace and put an arm around her shoulders, giving them a little reassuring jiggle as she propelled Grace forward. 'Ellis, this is our Grace. She keeps the whole place going and we'd be absolutely lost without her,' Betty said kindly, lifting Grace's spirit. Blushing, she said, 'Hello,' and put out her hand. Ellis wasn't at all how she had imagined he might be – big and brash and dressed in long baggy shorts and a baseball cap with a Yankees logo on; she realised now that this stereotypical image was way off. He was younger too, late thirties perhaps, and wearing a dark navy, impeccably cut suit and a crisp white open-necked shirt. He was also very attractive; tall, athletic, with a natural tan that accentuated his toffee-coloured eyes and dark brown hair.

'Hello. Pleased to meet you, Grace.' He shook her hand, firm and self-assured. 'And thank you for thinking to email the images of the artwork over to me. I'm very excited to see them in real life, as it were.' He smiled, showing perfect white teeth and making his eyes crinkle at the edges.

'Oh, it's no trouble.' She looked away and downwards. 'Thank you for coming to see them. Shall I take you to the unit now?' she then asked, realising that she still had hold of his hand as she stole another quick look at him. She promptly dropped his hand and folded her arms instead, wishing she'd kept the cardigan on now to wrap around as a comfort to mask her feelings of inadequacy. 'Um, that is if you have time, you might want to . . . do other stuff first, or get a drink or something . . . I'm not sure what the plan is . . .' She let her voice fade away, knowing she was talking too much.

'Let's get you both a cup of tea first, love, and then you can show him everything,' Betty said, chivvying Ellis towards an armchair in the customer waiting area and beckoning for Grace to come along too. 'Or would you prefer one of those posh coffees you like, Ellis?' Before he could answer, Betty bellowed over her shoulder to Larry: 'Can you go to the café on the corner and see if they do that macchiowotsit coffee that Ellis likes?'

'Aunty, it's fine. Please don't put yourself to any trouble on my account. A cup of quintessential British tea would be perfect.' Ellis smiled, placing a grateful hand on Betty's arm as he saw the bewildered look on Larry's face.

'It's no trouble,' Betty said.

'I could go for the coffee, if you like.' Grace quickly intervened to save Larry having to go, and thinking it best to offer in case Ellis was just being polite and really did want a macchiowotsit. He was their guest, after all, and had come to help them find out more about Connie, for which she was very grateful, so it was the least she could do. But as soon as the words were out of her mouth, Grace started to panic. Where was the café? It wasn't between here and the bus stop, that was for sure. But it couldn't be that far if Betty said it was on the corner, and she had asked Larry to go, and she knows he can't walk a long way with his knee . . . so maybe it would be OK.

'That's really kind of you, Grace, but I'm sure you have better things to do than fetch coffee,' Ellis said.

'Honestly, it's no bother,' she replied on autopilot, missing her chance to quell the panic at the prospect of going somewhere new. 'I'm used to . . .' She stopped talking.

'How about you both go to the café?' Betty stepped in again and saved Grace from floundering even further.

'Sure. Let's do that,' Ellis said. 'We can grab a coffee and you can bring me up to speed on what you know so far about Mrs . . .' He paused before pulling his phone from a pocket and going to check.

'Donato,' Grace prompted. 'Mrs Constance di Donato. Although, from what I can gather in her diaries, she liked to be called Connie.'

'Then Connie it is! I like that too . . . brings her alive and makes it more personal.' He beamed, his eyes dancing with curiosity. 'And Uncle Larry says you've already found out lots about her from some old diaries?'

'That's right. I have.' Grace nodded, the panic subsiding slightly now. But she still had to go to the café. With Ellis. A stranger.

'Well, I'm intrigued to know more.' And Ellis headed towards the door. So without any time to deliberate further, Grace grabbed her bag and caught up with him. 'After you . . .' He pulled open the door and held it ajar for her.

*

Twenty minutes later, and Grace had shared everything she knew so far about Connie with Ellis. They were sitting in a booth in the café and, having finished his macchiwotsit, as he had now renamed it in honour of Betty, he'd asked for a glass of orange juice, and persuaded Grace to go for a hot chocolate topped with whipped cream and marsh-mallows. Insisting it was absolutely necessary, even though she had initially chosen just a plain hot chocolate to have after her glass of water as, 'Hot chocolate isn't hot chocolate without all the pizazz!' he'd said. And so she had decided to go for it. And now Grace was inwardly marvelling at herself for actually feeling fairly relaxed in his company. Although Ellis had made it very easy. There had been no time for her to feel anxious over the number of steps to the café as he had walked fast and chatted nonstop all the way. He was so upbeat and cheery and it was rubbing off on her, making the millstone from earlier seem so much lighter.

She leant forward to see Ellis's phone – he had found the email that Larry had sent to him and was scrolling through the images.

'See this one here . . .' He pointed to the screen.

'Yes, it's beautiful, my favourite of all the paint-ings,' she said to him, then thanked the waitress when she placed the hot chocolate with an enormous tower of swirly cream on to the table.

'Wow, that looks good,' Ellis looked up from his phone.'

'Sure does, don't know what I was thinking going for the plain one at first,' she grinned. Ellis grinned back before he turning his attention to the waitress. 'Can I get another coffee please? The strongest you have, to help stave off this jetlag.'

'Sure, you can get whatever you like.' The waitress beamed at him, fiddling with her hair coquettishly, then added, 'Are you American?' in a coy little girl voice.

'Yes I am,' he smiled politely. 'Pleased to meet you,' and Grace was intrigued when he put out his hand to the waitress, never having seen anyone do that before in a café or restaurant. Maybe it was an American thing . . . to strike up a conversation with a complete stranger, as it definitely wasn't a British thing, where people mostly avoided conversations with anyone they didn't know. And part of her wished it wasn't this way; she reckoned it must be nice to be that self-assured and friendly instead of anxious and inward-thinking. 'I'm Ellis, what's your name?'

'Cheryl,' the waitress giggled, followed by, 'pleased to meet you, Ellis.' Then, after wiping a hand on her apron, she shook his hand. 'Where are you from?'

'America.' Ellis glanced at Grace, a flicker of confusion on his face.

'He's from New York,' she prompted.

'New York! Wow. Oh, I've always wanted to go to New York, would you show me around if I came to New York?'

'Oh, err . . . probably best not to. My girlfriend is the jealous type you see, so . . . I'm very sorry.'

'Oh, no, I didn't mean anything by it, sorry, I—' Cheryl stopped talking and glanced nervously at Grace.

'It's fine,' Grace smiled at the younger girl, 'I'm not his girlfriend.'

'Phew, that's a relief. Me and my big mouth.' And she scooted off quickly.

Grace picked up a teaspoon and busied herself by scooping whipped cream into her mouth as she wondered what Ellis's girlfriend was like. Jealous type! A mean-girl cheerleader perhaps, all blonde hair and bouncy like the Perky Yoga One; or a power type, perhaps, working on Wall Street and wearing suits and super-spikey stilettos that she could power-walk really fast in – something Grace had never managed to master.

'Are you always so polite to waitresses?' she asked, to open the conversation again.

'Sure. If they're friendly, why not?' he shrugged easily.

'It's just not something we tend to do here . . . not that I'm criticising, far from it. It's nice, you know . . . to be kind,' Grace grinned.

'Well, kindness matters! That's what they say.' And he chinked the side of his coffee cup against her mug in agreement. 'And I know you Brits are more reserved so I probably should take note of that, or I could end up in trouble with women like Cheryl looking to hook up when they come to visit the Big Apple.'

Grace laughed and was about to ask what his girlfriend's name was when her mobile rang. She glanced at the screen, surprised on seeing that it was Phil.

He never rang her.

'Do you mind?' She waggled the phone in the air, figuring it the polite thing to do before answering. It was such a long time since she'd been out in a social situation that she wasn't even really sure what the protocol was these days.

'Sure,' Ellis nodded, 'go right ahead.'

'Hello,' Grace said tentatively, racking her brain as to why Phil would be calling her in the middle of the day.

'Listen, Grace,' he said to open the conversation. 'I've been thinking . . . about our chat the other night.'

'Oh, I see,' she said softly, bracing herself for what was to come but wishing she hadn't answered now as nobody wanted to be dumped in public. Maybe he'd had a rethink and seen that what she had said made some sense. She'd be sad, of course, as he had been kind to her in the beginning, but recently . . . well, it was inevitable that he'd go the same way that Matthew had. Having a demanding mother like Cora would certainly put a damper on any relationship. She knew that, and Phil had said Cora was ruining his life . . .

'Yeah. About the spa break. And I really need to know if you're properly up for it because I know a bloke who can get me a deal. His missus has bailed out on him so he wants to shift the booking asap.'

'Oh, I see. Did he say when the booking was for?' she said, mentally crossing her fingers that it was sufficiently far away to give her enough time to see if it was even possible to sort out care for Cora. That's if she'd even consider letting Grace have a weekend away for her birthday.

'Err, don't know off the top of my head. A few weeks' time I think. But what does it matter?'

'Um . . .' she stalled.

'We don't want to miss out and end up having to pay full whack. If we go halves it'll be a right bargain.'

'Can we talk about it later?' she asked, feeling flummoxed at being put on the spot, let alone how they'd suddenly gone from him treating her, to them going halves on her own birthday trip. But then this was typical of Phil; on Valentine's Day they had gone to the Indian restaurant round the corner for a curry. It was to be his treat. Only he discovered he'd left his wallet in the pocket of his other jeans when the waiter brought the bill . . . and so she had paid. And he still hadn't 'sorted her out' for the pizza she paid for the other night. Not that she minded paying, but it would be nice if he took a turn now and again, especially if he had promised up front to treat her. And she didn't have enough money to spend on spa weekends in any case. But she wasn't about to debate all of this in front of Ellis.

'Where are you then?' Phil asked. 'I thought you were just at work.'

'I am,' she quickly told him, 'well, I'm actually in a café—'

'What are you doing there? You don't even like going out.'

'Oh, I'm drinking hot chocolate.'

'What? On your own?'

'No, I'm with Ellis. He's Betty and Larry's nephew, he's come over from America to help us—'

'I see.'

'Phil, I can't really talk right now,' she said quietly into the phone, conscious of Ellis stirring his coffee. He was seemingly not listening to the conversation out of politeness, but how could he not hear what was being said when he was sitting right opposite her?

'Whatever.' And Phil ended the call.

Grace slipped her phone inside her bag and went back to the cream on her hot chocolate.

'Everything OK?' Ellis asked gently.

'Oh, yes, sure. That was . . .' Grace hesitated on realising that she hadn't actually ever said that Phil was her boyfriend out loud to anyone before now. Not even to Jamie. In fact, she wasn't even sure if she had ever spoken properly about Phil to him. Maybe she should. It might be useful to get another perspective on their relationship . . . but then, possibly not, for she knew Jamie probably wouldn't like Phil. He hadn't been impressed when she'd mentioned about having to pay at the last minute for the curry on Valentines Day . . . 'A friend,' she settled on.

'A friend.' Ellis nodded, taking a sip of his coffee.

'You were showing me the pictures . . .'

'Oh yes, see this one here . . .' He put the cup down, picked up his phone and tapped the screen to bring the image of the Venice waterway and the Salute into view.

'Ah, that's my favourite one,' said Grace, licking a speck of cream that had fallen from the spoon onto her index finger.

'In that case you have an excellent eye for art.'

'Really?' she smiled, leaning in closer, but then quickly sitting back on realising she sounded overly effusive.

'You sure do. Because this is the image that made me want to tag on some extra days to my trip and come to London right away!'

'Oh?'

'Sure did. You see, this could be an original by a recently discovered artist. Is there a mention of the paintings – or indeed an artist – in Connie's diaries by any chance?' he asked, looking up from the phone.

'No. Not that I've come across so far. But I did wonder if Connie was actually the artist, as she's certainly very creative in her prose . . . maybe she had a flair for painting too.'

'Hmm, interesting theory. But I don't think so. You see, I've seen the marking on the bottom right-hand corner of these paintings before. The first time was on a collection of three American landscapes which were recently acquired by the Guggenheim Museum in New York. Then a miniature watercolour dated 1943 was discovered here in England, in the attic of a house in Woolwich,' he said.

'That's such a coincidence, as I actually live in Woolwich.'

'Really? Well, I never,' Ellis said, lifting his arms and turning his palms upward in a gesture of incredulity. 'Perhaps you know the street where the house was. I have the details right here.' And he quickly searched his phone, explaining that he'd made a note of all the information they held about the miniature watercolour on the auction house computer systems, just in case it proved useful while he was here. 'Repository Road.'

'Oh, that's where the army barracks is. Maybe the artist was a soldier if the painting is dated 1943.'

'Could be. A bundle of pencil drawings were also found there too . . . all with the same marking on, so we will need to work out how they're all connected.' Grace liked how he said 'we', as if they were already a team bound together in their quest to unravel the mystery of the forgotten items in unit 28. 'Little is known about the artist, other than that they were reclusive and most prolific in the 1950s and 60s, as there are more pieces with the same marking on in private collections around the world, each one commanding significant sums at auction. But some of those paintings surfaced in America and then some later works were found in Italy. George Clooney is a big fan, which of course has helped drive collectability of the paintings.'

'Wow! So you think the paintings in our storage unit are by the same artist?'

'Well, I need to take a close look, but I'm hopeful,' Ellis grinned, lifting his eyebrows.

'And a recluse, you say.' Grace was intrigued. 'Does that mean nobody knows who the artist is? Rather like a Banksy of olden days?'

'Yes. I guess so,' he nodded. 'Although there was rumour of the artist being of noble descent – a count, or was it a lord? It was definitely a title or prominence of some kind, but nothing has ever been proven so it could all be hearsay. But mystery surrounding an artist always adds a certain intrigue and premium to the value of each piece as it surfaces.'

'How exciting. And Connie did live in Italy,' Grace

added. 'I know that for sure from her diary which is dated 1955 . . . so the timing fits. Maybe she knew the artist and bought the paintings before they became valuable.' Ellis nodded slowly, as if mooting the idea as a possible answer to the conundrum.

'But how come the collection is here in the UK?' he asked. 'Why would she bring them all the way from Italy and put them in a storage unit in Greenwich, England? Surely she'd hang them on the walls of her home . . . don't you think it seems odd to hide them away for all these years? Call me biased, but to me art is a joyful thing. Something to be treasured and enjoyed, not banished away.' He shook his head, deep in thought.

'I agree. But I've seen all sorts of things hidden away inside our storage units.' She smiled, remembering the medals and the fossils.

'Oh, I bet you have! So come on, tell me what's the most bizarre thing you've ever found?' he asked, putting his phone away in a pocket so as to give her his full attention.

'Well, this isn't bizarre, exactly, but it did make Larry and me stare in silence for a few minutes after unlocking the door to this particular unit . . . number 211. It's stuck in my head ever since.'

'Go on . . . what was in number 211?' he

prompted, widening his eyes and hanging on her every word.

'A collection of prosthetic limbs! Which isn't that unusual; but all of these ones were right legs, and in various sizes from tiny baby ones right up to adult man-size ones – luckily the owner turned up, after Larry sent the third payment reminder notice, and took them away, as we had no idea what we were going to do with them.' They laughed together, and Grace liked how being here with Ellis made her feel. Light and relaxed. And she wondered if she might get to come to the café again before he had to leave for the next part of his European trip.

'That's too funny! I can just imagine Uncle Larry's face on seeing all the legs. I bet it was a picture.' And they laughed some more. 'Well, thankfully it didn't put you off opening abandoned units for ever more or we would never have discovered Connie's intriguing collection. And I can't wait to get inside the unit and take a look.'

'Well, it's very kind of you to come here and see for yourself,' Grace said in a moment of exuberance. 'I've grown quite fond of Connie, so it would mean a great deal to me to find out more about her life and what happened to her.'

'Then it means a great deal to me too, Grace! I've

really enjoyed being here in the café with you and I'm looking forward to us spending more time together on this.' He nodded as if to punctuate his point, making Grace blush as she looked down into her now empty mug.

Was he flirting?

She'd been out of the loop for so long that she couldn't really tell. And her and Phil had just kind of become a thing. There had never been any flirting as such . . . more a casual acceptance of two people walking home from the bus stop together. But then, suddenly, Cora's words from last night were flying around inside her head again . . . Forgetful. Nosey. Rough-handed. Lazy. And then: *he has a girlfriend, in America, you fool, and she's bound to be smart and vivacious and beautiful so he's hardly going to flirt with someone like me now, is he?*

She inhaled sharply and let out a quick breath to clear her head, determined to not let the millstone drag her down again and spoil the moment, for right now she did actually feel normal. She was out in a café with someone who knew nothing about her difficulties with anxiety and the challenges she dealt with at home, and it felt nice. In fact, it felt very nice indeed to be enjoying herself and participating in her own life for a change. And not waiting for Cora

146

to bang on the flaming ceiling any minute now and bellow her demands.

'Me too,' she said softly, 'I'm looking forward to it as well.' She didn't look him in the eye, but she'd work up to it for sure. Today was just the beginning as, in that moment, she made a promise to herself to make more of an effort, knowing that she was ready to break out of her self-imposed confinement. Even if it was only to come to the café now and again for a hot chocolate, and maybe Larry would be OK with her bringing her laptop and doing the invoicing spreadsheet while she was here? It would make a change from just being at home or at work, plus she couldn't really see another way as she could hardly stop going home at lunchtimes to give Cora her lunch and a comfort break. And she was also going to broach the topic with Cora of having a weekend off to go to the spa with Phil. After all, her mother had said she should make more of an effort with this one . . .

'Awesome,' Ellis said, then after clearing his throat he carried on. 'Unravelling the provenance of an interesting piece of art is the very best part of my job. And there are ten paintings in Larry's email, so if they are all genuine . . . then we need to hurry up and find Connie's next of kin, however far removed, and break the good news, because the Guggenheim – and George Clooney – are bound to be interested for sure.'

'Good news?'

'That's right. The collection could be worth a considerable amount of money if sold to the right buyer. Of course, I'll need to establish authenticity and ownership of title.'

'Title?'

'Yes, we need to be sure the paintings were Connie's . . . that they are her possessions to be inherited, and weren't stolen or acquired by some other criminal activity.'

'Oh, I'm sure that isn't the case,' Grace quickly intervened, 'Connie doesn't strike me as being that kind of person; her diary is so open and honest, and well . . . it's very romantic. Romantic people aren't usually criminals, are they?' Ellis smiled at her, as if amused by her rationale. 'And we know now that she had a daughter, Lara. I wonder what happened to her?'

'I guess we have to assume that she died,' Ellis said, 'and that's why the Bona Vacantia department got involved. Although, strictly speaking, everything in the unit belongs to the storage company now – it's in the Ts and Cs of the contract in the event of non-payment – but I'm sure Larry wouldn't want to deny someone their rightful inheritance, if it turns out that there is a long-lost living relative somewhere.'

'Which, unfortunately, is looking unlikely.' Grace sighed. Betty's friend, Maggie, had managed to find out that Connie did indeed die intestate and with no living relatives that anyone was aware of. And adverts had been placed in newspapers but nobody had come forward, not even to contribute to the cost of the funeral. That had been paid for by the state and then recouped from the proceeds of the sale of Connie's home. The balance of which, some £750,000, was sitting in a government bank account somewhere, waiting to be claimed. Apparently, the funds would be paid out, with interest added, if they were successfully claimed by a relative within twelve years.

'But not impossible!' Ellis said. 'We know that Connie lived in Italy for a while so there could be family members there who she didn't keep in touch with when she came back to London. If the paintings are genuine, then there are other ways to search for relatives. We have specialist law firms back home that hunt for heirs, especially if there is a large inheritance at stake. And £750,000 is a lot of money! I'm sure you have the same here in the UK.'

'Ah, yes my mother watches that *Heir Hunters* TV programme,' Grace told him, remembering when Cora went through a phase of sitting up all night watching back-to-back episodes with the volume up so high that she'd had to wear earplugs when trying to get some sleep.

'That's it.'

'So how will we know if the paintings – or indeed all the possessions – truly belonged to Connie?' she asked.

'Well, it's tricky without a will that specifically mentions each item in the storage unit, but if we can find some mention of them in her papers or diaries, and receipts would be useful, you know, if she bought them from a gallery perhaps . . . Or photos of her with the items showing in the background. Some connection is always helpful.' He creased his forehead, as if pondering on all the possibilities.

Grace thought about what he had said as she took a mouthful of her hot chocolate. 'Penny for them?' Ellis asked, 'that's what you say here, don't you?'

'Ah, yes, we do,' she laughed, touched by his efforts at Britishisms, 'although I haven't heard anyone say it for a long time . . . I was just thinking about

Connie, and wondering why she didn't sell the paintings, if they are worth a lot of money? Her neighbour told us that she died alone and in poverty . . .' Grace shook her head. 'Why would she struggle like that when she had all those valuable possessions in the storage unit right there at her disposal?'

'Yes, it's very sad, but not uncommon. I've seen it several times . . . usually the older person is reluctant to dip into their relatives' inheritance, taking pride in being able to leave as much as possible to their children or grandchildren.'

'Interesting. Then perhaps Connie was doing just that . . . kindly leaving everything for someone else to benefit from, at the expense of her own wellbeing.'

'It's odd then, that she didn't leave a will. Maybe she simply didn't know the true value of the paintings?' he suggested. 'It could be as you said, that she bought them back in the 1950s or 1960s and really had no idea . . . it is possible, and I'm looking forward to finding out.'

'And what about the jewels? They could be costume and worth nothing at all, of course, but they are very realistic looking . . . what if the stones are precious diamonds and rubies? Wouldn't they be worth a lot of money too?' Grace wiped her mouth on a napkin before summoning a modicum of courage to look Ellis directly in the eyes. He smiled and held her gaze momentarily.

'Jewels?' He lifted one eyebrow.

'Yes, there was a big leather jewellery box in the unit, crammed full of exquisite bangles, necklaces, earrings and brooches.'

'And where is the box now?' Ellis leant forward eagerly.

'Larry locked it away, to be on the safe side.'

'I'd like to take a look, if I may?'

'Sure . . . do you know much about jewellery then?' she asked, remembering what Larry had said.

'Well, I'm no expert; art is my thing. But I did spend some time covering for a colleague a few years back in the Fine and Antique Jewel department.'

'Oh, does that mean you have a contact who might be able to help us with the jewellery too?'

'Yep. It sure does,' he nodded enthusiastically, and then quickly drained the last of his coffee. 'So I think it's about time we finished up here and headed back . . . because the mystery of unit 28 just got a whole lot more intriguing.'

10

'So, tell me again what happened?' Jamie handed Grace a mug of tea before sitting in an armchair opposite her.

'Thank you,' she said, her voice wobbly as she took the mug and cupped her hands around it, drawing comfort from the heat. She glanced up at the ceiling above them where Cora was watching a game show on the TV with the volume at such a deafening level that Jamie had heard it through the adjoining wall and had come round to see what was going on. She had told him about Phil and the spa weekend and how she had broached the subject with Cora, who had flatly refused to even consider it before launching into a long tirade about how selfish Grace was. How she always had been and so, 'It's no surprise you'd be wanting to go off gallivanting with that poor man of yours and abandon me without so much as a backward glance to fend for myself for a whole weekend.' When Grace had tried to point out that it had been Cora who had said she must make more effort with this one or risk being all alone, Cora had screeched, 'Dropping your knickers in a cheap hotel like a common slut isn't making an effort. Sure it isn't.'

Grace took another sip of the tea.

'Do you mind if we don't go over it all again?' She glanced at Jamie, her cheeks still flaming with the humiliation of what her mother had called her.

'Of course not, love.' He glanced up at the ceiling before adding, 'Hang on a moment,' and after going out to the hallway he yelled, 'Cora, that's enough. Turn it down now. Please.' And as if by magic, she did. 'Right, that's better. I can actually hear what you are saying now,' Jamie continued, turning his attention back to Grace. 'I just thought it might help to let it all out. You looked pretty shaken up when you answered the door to let me in; your face was ashen,' he said, coming over to sit next to her on the sofa. He placed a reassuring hand on her arm.

'That's because after the bust-up with Mum, I had just come off the phone from calling Phil back to let him know that it wasn't going to be possible for me to go on the spa weekend. You know, I had even made my mind up to make some changes in my life.

I was actually feeling excited at the prospect of a weekend off and going somewhere new . . . that's a massive deal for me!'

'I know it is, darling. And I'm proud of you . . . when I said you'd be golden in no time, I never imagined you'd be jaunting off to swanky spa hotels at the drop of a hat,' he laughed, kindly. 'So good for you! Sounds like the old Grace that we know and love is coming back sooner than we anticipated.'

'Hmm, well she would have been if that . . .' she paused and raised a pointed index finger at the ceiling before adding, 'rude, ungrateful . . . cow-bag hadn't ruined it all,' in a whisper.

'Ooooh, Grace! You are definitely coming back to us . . . I haven't heard you use the "c" word in ages,' he laughed, shaking his head in mock disapproval. 'Go on, say it again . . . it'll make you feel a whole lot better, I promise.'

'Oh don't.' She tried not to smile. 'I really shouldn't complain about her, I wouldn't even have anywhere to live if she hadn't let me come back home when I needed to after what happened with Matthew.'

'Yes you would!' Jamie nodded firmly. 'I have a perfectly good spare bedroom next door that you could have moved into.'

'The one with a lodger in?'

'Well, err . . . yes . . .' He stalled and then quickly added, 'But he could easily sleep on the sofa.'

'No he couldn't, not when he's paying you rent. I couldn't do that; it wouldn't have been fair. Anyway, it doesn't change the fact that I can't have one lousy weekend off.'

'True. And when were you supposed to be going?'

'Quite soon, it was going to be a treat for my birthday,' she told him, and then added, 'Well, one I'd have to pay for myself,' letting her voice fade away on remembering Phil's 'if we go halves' statement.

'Your birthday?' Jamie said, sounding surprised, but with a dash of confusion on his face.

'Don't tell me you've forgotten,' Grace sighed and looked upwards in mock despair. 'We always get pizza and play charades and drink cheap cider. Not that we have to do that, of course. I guess it is a bit childish with us being actual adults now, and not geeky teenagers any more, with no other friends apart from each other.'

'Stop it,' Jamie said abruptly. 'Of course I haven't forgotten, so don't be talking yourself down. Your birthday is important. It'll be wonderful, I promise you.'

'Wonderful is pushing it a bit . . . it's only pizza from Gino's round the corner with cheap cider, but thanks. You know, I'd be lost without you.' And she smiled ruefully.

'And stop that too, Grace. You have a lot to contend with,' he motioned with his head up at the ceiling, 'and I reckon you're doing pretty well keeping on top of it all by yourself.' Silence between them followed. 'And what was that thwack on the wall earlier?' he added to change the subject.

'Oh, that must have been when she threw the TV remote control at me – it narrowly missed my head and hit the wall,' she told him, staring at the swirly patterned carpet that had been on the floor since she was a small child. The same carpet she had stared at when Mum was frequently giving Dad what for . . . screaming at him for whatever perceived misde-meanour he had committed that day.

'Grace, I'm so sorry. Come here.' And he moved closer to give her a hug. 'I'll talk to her,' he said, rubbing her back.

'I don't think there's any point in doing that, Jamie. She was adamant. I didn't even get as far as discussing possible care options, or telling her that Bernie, Sinead and Mikey have all offered to pay for someone to help out. And I didn't dare tell her about Mikey's suggestion to put her in a home . . . as that would have tipped her over the edge for sure.'

'Well, maybe you should have told her!' Jamie said, fired up. 'It might make her realise just how lucky she is to have you . . .'

11

I'm going to do my bit for the war effort and give Hitler what for. I can't sit around in the countryside any longer doing nothing when Jimmy has sacrificed his life. The dark cloud still lingers and I'm really not much use to anyone these days. Certainly not little Lara, who to my shame has been neglected of my love and attention and instead looks to Mother to care for her. I have tried to feed her and bathe her but I feel she senses my sadness and becomes fretful, until Mother lifts her from my arms to soothe her. Mother says I must pull myself together and find something useful to do now that Lara is nearly a year old, so I'm returning to London to work in the factory where Jimmy used to sweep the floors. Only I shan't be sweeping floors, I'm going to make parachutes and inflatable dinghies, and all sorts of other useful things to help the soldiers who are still fighting. I couldn't do anything to help my darling Jimmy, so this will go some small way to *make up for that. My sweet baby girl, Lara, is to stay with Mother and Father here in Tindledale, as London isn't safe for her, and I will come here on the train to visit her on my days off. It's going to be such a wrench to leave her, but it really is for the best. My life would most certainly be over if she were to be taken from me too . . .*

Grace let out a long puff of air and turned the page. She was sitting on the carpet in Connie's storage unit, reading more of her diary entries and feeling very uneasy about the change in tone. It was as if Connie had hardened and packed her emotions away now that her life was wholly determined by her mother . . . something Grace could definitely identify with. Connie certainly wasn't doing what she really wanted to, as Grace had also found a piece of paper tucked inside the pages of one of the *Variety* magazines in the hatbox with the following heartbreaking words written on it in Connie's handwriting. Grace was sure that Connie had been crying when she wrote the note, as the faint outline of faded little splatter marks could still be seen down one side.

My heart is broken without you, Jimmy, and to my shame there have been times when I have contemplated joining you, my darling, for I have not an ounce of vim or vigour these days and find myself giving in to Mother's will. Although I do know that she has Lara's best interests at heart and that is what matters most. Perhaps the light will return for me when I'm in London doing my bit for the war effort – I truly hope so. I wish with all my being that I could keep Lara with me but Mother will not hear of it. She says Lara looks to her as her mother and I understand that she does because I have not been able to care for her properly. So it is probably for the best this way as nobody in London will know the shame I've brought on my family. Mother also says that if I have any love at all for Lara then she must always be kept a secret and that I should refer to her as my young sister so she is not tainted as a child born out of wedlock. I must do that for her and not put my own selfish needs before hers. But our darling Lara will never be a secret for me because she is a part of you, and I will always hold her in my heart for she's the most beautiful baby I have ever seen, and with the sweetest temperament. Her eyes are emerald green and framed with thick, dark lashes just like yours, my love, and her hair too; ebony curls, so soft and silky. I love to brush her beautiful baby hair but Mother says the curls are too long and must be cut off short if her hair is ever to thicken . . .

A week had passed since Ellis first arrived, and Grace had managed to go to the café again with him twice more before he had left to travel to Berlin for the next step of his business trip. She had really enjoyed those visits to the café. The normality of them. And his great company too, of course. It was nice to spend time with someone who didn't know anything about her real life caring for Cora, or how she had broken apart after finding Matthew in bed with the Perky Yoga One. It meant she was free to be whoever she wanted to be, if only for the short slice of time that it took to chat and for her to drink hot chocolate with a tower of whipped cream on top. And Grace was harbouring a secret, in that she had eked out that cream, spooning in really tiny mouthfuls so as to have as long as possible in the café with Ellis, because who knew when she would get to do that again? She'd made an effort to go to the café by herself too, but it really wasn't the same, with Cheryl, the waitress, pumping her for titbits about Ellis and his fabulous life in New York. And if, by any chance, he had dumped his girlfriend yet?

When Ellis had properly catalogued unit 28, he had been in awe of Connie's jewels and had carefully photographed a selection of the key pieces before he left, to email on to his contact in the Fine and

Antique Jewel department. He had also examined and confirmed that the paintings in Connie's unit were genuine, and that she was the probable owner of them too. It was a tenuous link, but Grace had stumbled across a packet of old photos in one of the suitcases, and there was a photo of Connie standing in the doorway of a veranda at the powder pink villa, with the wonderful Venice Salute painting visible on the wall behind her. So, after consulting with another art expert at the auction house to double-check the paintings' veracity, Ellis had notified the legal people in the Bona Vacantia government department, where the proceeds of Connie's unclaimed estate were held, and organised for the paintings to be securely transported to the vaults of a private bank in London for safekeeping. Because Larry had nearly had a coronary on being told they could be worth upwards of fifty thousand pounds each. And there were ten of them in unit 28!

Grace had read more of Connie's diaries and notes over the last week and had discovered that she had met an American soldier a year or so after she returned to London to do her bit for the war effort. Connie had volunteered at the American Red Cross, which held dances to boost soldiers' morale; it was at one of these dances – where she served doughnuts and coffee and offered to sew loose buttons back onto the soldiers' uniforms – that she had met him. Grace's heart had soared on finding out Connie had found some happiness in the months after her mother had forced her to part from baby Lara.

And where was baby Lara now?

If she had died, then where was she buried? Was it here in England? Or was Connie allowed to be with her, later, after the war ended? Did Connie's controlling mother relent and let her take Lara to Italy? It was a possibility . . . somewhere suitably far away so as not to embarrass her parents in front of their influential friends in London (Grace had read all about Connie's mother maligning her over this), and it would certainly have been perfectly respectable to pass Lara off as her young sister . . . so maybe that's what happened and Lara was buried in Italy. Or, Grace pondered on another scenario; it was one that she had considered already, and it could just be wishful thinking, but what if Lara was still alive? What if she was still living in Italy and simply estranged from her mother, Connie? And just didn't know that she had died? It was entirely possible.

Grace cast a glance around unit 28. Taking it all in again. The way it was set out. Like a glamorous bedroom presenting the contents in the best possible light. It was as if it had been prepared especially . . . like a stage, a showcase of a lifetime for someone to discover and, ultimately, inherit. What if Connie had made it look all lovely like this for her daughter, Lara? Grace allowed herself some time to ponder on the possible scenario, her heart lifting at the prospect of finding Lara and chatting to her about Connie. But then her heart sank on remembering that Connie hadn't left a will. Why wouldn't she? If all this was for Lara, then it just didn't make any sense for Connie not to have done so; surely she would have made sure Lara knew all these beautiful things were waiting here for her. Not to mention the valuable artwork, and Connie's home in Blackheath, for it all added up to an extremely valuable inheritance.

Grace glanced at the screen on her mobile; seeing that it was almost time for an afternoon cuppa, she put Connie's diary away and closed her unit for another day before heading over to the office. She pushed open the door and almost jumped right out of her skin when she was greeted with a rainbow stream of party poppers. Red, yellow, blue and green confetti shot high up in the air before cascading down onto her head and shoulders.

'Happy birthday to you! Happy birthday to you!

Happy birthday dear Grace, happy birthday to you,' chorused Betty and Larry, and Betty's friend, Maggie, from the knit and natter group and who worked in the coroner's office. A silver and purple hologram banner with 'Happy Birthday' on it was pinned to the wall by Grace's desk, and Betty was holding an enormous triple-layered birthday cake smothered in pastel pink icing and big 'three'- and 'five'-shaped candles on top.

'Remember to make a wish, sweetheart.' Betty put the cake down on Grace's desk and clapped her hands together in delight.

'*Wow*. Oh my goodness. Thank you,' Grace said, momentarily dazed. It was her birthday today and – until now – it had been just like any other day. Her mother had forgotten; Grace figured she must have, as she hadn't mentioned it, not even to say happy birthday. Of course, Grace appreciated that Cora wasn't mobile and so couldn't go out herself and buy a card, and she really didn't expect that, but an acknowledgment would have been nice. Phil hadn't been at the bus stop either, and she hadn't liked to arrive at work and announce it herself to Larry and Betty, so this wonderful surprise felt even more special. 'It's amazing,' she beamed, cupping her hands up under her chin and willing herself not to get teary as she looked at Larry and Betty, their kindness emanating from them and making her feel overcome with emotion.

Grace looped her hair up into a quick bun and after closing her eyes and making a wish – *Please let Mum win the scratchcard jackpot so we can both be happy – her at the Savoy, and me on a spa break with a cocktail in one hand and my feet firmly up on a lounger* – she blew out the candles. Larry, Betty and Maggie all clapped, and after Betty had handed them each an exceedingly generous slice of cake on a pink paper plate with a matching napkin, she fished in her handbag and pulled out an envelope.

'A present from Larry and me,' she said, handing the envelope to Grace.

'Oh, thank you so much,' Grace said, swallowing her mouthful of cake and then putting the plate on her desk. 'But you really didn't need—'

'Nonsense!' Larry stepped in to give her a hug. 'You're our Girl Friday, a breath of fresh air around here, and we really appreciate all the work that you do.'

'And we are very fond of you, love,' Betty added, bustling Larry out of the way so that she could give Grace a hug. 'Now, open the envelope.'

Grace did as she was told. Inside the envelope

was a gorgeous birthday card with a picture on the front of a glistening Mediterranean sea beside a terracotta-coloured brick cottage with pretty pink bougainvillea tumbling all over one side of it.

Grace opened the card and unfolded an A4 piece of paper that was tucked inside. Scanning the words, her pulse quickened as she took it all in.

Italy!

A holiday to Italy.

She stared at the boarding pass and itinerary in her hand.

'I can't go to Italy.'

'Oh yes you can, sweetheart.' It was Jamie coming through the office door with a smile on his face the size of a slice of watermelon.

'What are you doing here?' she beamed, dashing forward to give him a big hug.

'Larry and Betty invited me,' he said, pressing a big bunch of bright purple, pink and orange chrysanthemums into her hand before giving her an enormous hug.

'But how? When? You don't know Larry and Betty,' she gasped, barely able to take it all in. She glanced over at her employers to see them both now looking very conspiratorial.

'Don't blame the lad,' Larry stepped forward.

'Betty and I had been thinking for some time now that a little break would do you good. You're run off your feet working here and caring for your mother too.' He paused, and Grace glanced at the floor momentarily. 'And so when Jamie here,' he put a hand on Jamie's back, 'called in that day to go with you to check out Connie's address in Blackheath, we got chatting while he was waiting for you and—'

'Hatched a plan!' Betty took over explaining. 'We know you've found an affinity with poor Connie, and Larry saw how fascinated you were with the painting of Venice inside her unit, and then reading all about the powder pink villa on the hilltop in her diary, not to mention the other beauty spots she mentions . . . and so that got us thinking.' Smiling, she put an arm around Larry and indicated for Jamie to come and stand on the other side of her. 'You might like to experience it all for yourself first hand. Go and see where Connie lived in Italy, and also see if you can find out a bit more about her . . . talk to her friends and what have you.'

'But . . .' Grace faltered. She couldn't go to Italy on her own. Not to the airport. How would she get there? And she certainly couldn't go on an aeroplane by herself and then navigate her way around a foreign country. Just the thought of it was making her pulse quicken and her top lip glisten with anxiety sweat. *Ah, but maybe that's why Jamie is here: to let me know he's coming too.* 'It's a really kind idea,' she started, not wanting to sound ungrateful, 'but what about Mum? I can't leave her on her own.'

'Yes you can. It's all sorted. I've got loads of annual leave left and if I don't take it I'll lose it . . . so I'm looking after Cora while you're away,' Jamie nodded.

'What? But she wouldn't have it when I spoke to her about the spa weekend.'

'And thank God she wouldn't, because that would have scuppered the whole surprise if you had gone ahead and booked the spa break instead.' Jamie shook his head. 'Plus I went to a lot of trouble to find your passport. Why would you keep it at the back of your knicker drawer? And that's another thing, lady, I'm taking you knicker shopping pronto, as we need to replace those washed-out horrors you have clogging up all the space in your drawers.' He pulled a face.

'*What?* Did you actually rummage through my bedroom?' Grace asked, flabbergasted. She'd had no idea and felt a tinge of embarrassment on knowing that Jamie had now seen the extent of her apathy over self-care. She couldn't even remember the last time she had bought new knickers, or indeed anything much for herself apart from food and essential toiletries.

'Of course!' Jamie shrugged covertly. 'How else were we going to book the flights? I know your date of birth and all that, but I wanted to check you in too and get you a nice window seat, so there's no backing out now.' And he grinned so hard it made his whole face glow like a lit paper lantern about to soar right up into the air.

'I can't believe it. Nobody has ever done anything like this for me before.'

'I know. And that's another reason why we wanted to,' he said, and Betty, Larry and Maggie all nodded their agreement.

'But . . .' Grace started again, and Jamie leant forward on the pretext of giving her a hug so he could whisper in her ear.

'It'll be fine. Promise you. One step in front of the other. Golden, remember?' And he gave her shoulders a reassuring squeeze.

'And you can see for yourself where Connie lived; you never know . . . some of the neighbours might be able to tell us more about her and may even lead you to find a relative, someone to inherit all the contents in unit 28. You'd be doing me a favour if we can actually shift it all and open up the unit to another customer,' Larry said. 'So it's really a business trip in more ways than one, because Ellis's friend in the jewellery department at the auction house called me and said the items in Connie's jewellery box are very valuable – good job I've stored them in the safe.' He paused to chuckle. 'Yes, he said they are one-offs. Bespoke. They are all of Italian design and made in the 1950s and 60s. And they didn't have computer records in those days, so he said you're best off going to the actual jewellery shop yourself to see what you can find out and ask to look at the paper records. He did phone them himself and at first they got a bit worked up at the mention of an auction house and went on about client secrets and stuff, but then called him back and said that they would be happy to see you when you visited . . .'

'And Ellis is going to meet you at the airport, love,' Betty added. 'He has to visit some clients in Italy anyway, so it's easy for him to tie in some time off afterwards to spend with you on this adventure. Did you know he can speak a bit of Italian?' Grace shook her head, feeling bamboozled, for it was like a whirlwind . . . she so desperately wanted to fly off to Italy and experience another, more exciting life, if only for a short while, and with Ellis too, so she could be whoever she wanted to be again. But, well . . . was it really even possible? Jamie might have managed to persuade Cora for the time being but, knowing how her mind worked, Grace knew that could all change in an instance if she felt so inclined, so was it even worth Grace getting her hopes up?

'I didn't either, but fancy that,' Betty carried on. 'He's a dark horse, our Ellis.'

'And I've managed to find out some interesting pieces of the puzzle too.' It was Betty's friend, Maggie, who spoke next as she fished inside a lovely retro cloth knitting bag with wooden handles and a bold orange flower print.

'Ooh, really,' Grace said, trying to calm down. She couldn't deny the bubble of excitement building inside her, but did she dare take – she glanced again at the boarding pass – *six days* off from caring for Cora to actually go away to Italy? Could she really do it? And how on earth had Jamie managed to swing it with Cora? Her mother had always absolutely refused to even discuss it whenever Grace had broached the idea of taking time off with her.

'Yes, I've got a copy of Constance's marriage certificate right here,' Maggie said, patting her iron-grey bob and lifting a pair of glasses that were hanging on a colourful beaded chain around her neck, up on to her face, before unfolding a long piece of paper. 'Married in January 1946, so shortly after the end of World War II. She married Giovanni di Donato in Marylebone Register Office in London.' Maggie showed Grace the marriage certificate with the words written on in old-fashioned swirly cursive handwriting. Grace touched an index finger to it, imagining Connie doing likewise with the original certificate. 'I wasn't able to find a death certificate for Giovanni . . .'

'Oh?' Grace said hopefully.

'Ah, but don't get your hopes up as he might very well have died in Italy,' Maggie surmised.

'And Lara?'

'The same, I'm afraid. If she died in Italy too, then it isn't impossible to find out, but may take me a little longer. I'm sure you'll be able to find out more when you visit as there's bound to be someone there who knew Connie, and if she did take Lara to Italy after the war, then she would have gone to school, had friends, hung out in cafés eating gelato. You must leave no stone unturned, so I expect to hear that you've visited and sampled every gelato shop within a ten-mile radius of the powder pink villa.' They all laughed. 'Now, getting back to the certificate

– the most interesting thing on it is Giovanni's profession and address. See here.' And she pointed to the piece of paper where it said that he was a soldier and living at an address in Woolwich. Repository Road, to be precise.

'Could it be the American soldier she met at the Red Cross dance?' Grace suggested hopefully, thinking how wonderful it would have been if Connie had found happiness to help ease her pain on being parted from Lara when she returned to London to do her bit for the war effort.

'Yes, it very well could be,' Maggie nodded. 'Perhaps an Italian-American GI, given his gorgeously romantic name. They were very popular with the British women during the war,' she chuckled saucily.

'But hadn't the war ended by then? If Giovanni was an American GI, then would he have still been in Britain in 1946?' Grace checked.

'Oh yes, it's quite possible . . . some GIs weren't demobbed until well into 1946,' Maggie assured her. 'And we may be able to find out more from his army records.'

'Is it really possible to do that?' Grace asked, thinking about Jimmy too. She would like to find out how he had met his fate, as a mark of respect to honour the sacrifice he had made.

'Yes. I can certainly try.'

'And Ellis is extremely excited.' Larry dipped into the conversation. 'He's now convinced that Giovanni is the artist who painted the pictures we found in the unit, plus the ones discovered in the attic of the house in . . .'

'Repository Road in Woolwich!' Grace exclaimed in unison with Larry.

'And if he was an American GI, then that could explain the other paintings that surfaced in America – Ellis told me about them too. Maybe Mr Donato painted them before he came over to England during the Second World War,' she said, processing all the pieces to see if they fitted together, and so far they certainly seemed to. It was too much of a coincidence for the address in Woolwich near the army barracks to crop up twice with a link to the paintings.

'Well, it's certainly an exciting mystery . . . like something out of one of those true-crime documentaries on the telly,' Betty chimed.

'I certainly hope not!' Larry puffed. 'Nobody has died.'

'Apart from Connie, that we know of,' Jamie chipped in, stating the obvious.

'And Jimmy. And his mother too, she died in the Blitz,' Grace added, remembering the poignant passage that she had read in Connie's diary, written when she had first arrived back in London to work in the factory.

I went to Jimmy's home today in Deptford for old times' sake and . . . well, I don't really know why, but I guess I was hoping to see his mother, to pass on my condolences to her and maybe tell her about Lara, her granddaughter, for I feel certain she would be overjoyed by the news of her. It would have been so nice to talk about Jimmy and to feel close to him again. But I was met with the most dreadful sight. Rubble piled up high where Jimmy's home once stood. The whole of Franklin Street has disappeared. A man was there, rooting through the debris, trying to salvage whatever he could, and he told me the street took a direct hit. Poor Maureen at number 27 didn't stand a chance as she never made it to the shelter in time after doubling back to fetch her tabby cat, Mischief. It was such a sorry sight and I came away with tears in my eyes but took comfort in knowing that Jimmy will have his mother, Maureen, with him now. I then went over to the hilly field section of Greenwich Park and picked a big bunch of wild flowers, just like Jimmy did for me when we were courting. After tying a jolly yellow ribbon from the haberdashery shop around them, I went back to where

Jimmy had lived and left the flowers there, saying a silent prayer as I placed them in the rubble. A flash of bright colour in amongst all the grey, from Lara and me, for the father and grandmother that she will never meet.

'Oh, you know what I mean,' Betty said, bringing Grace's thoughts back to the present day, 'it's like the bit where they try to work out how everything happened . . . anyway, our Grace is going to have a terrific time in Italy being our very own Miss Marple. And that's the main thing.'

'Let's not get carried away, dear. Grace isn't going to investigate a murder!' Larry shook his head with a worried look on his face and then, after pondering momentarily, he looked at Grace and added, 'Maybe this isn't such a good idea. I won't live with myself if anything happens to you out there, my dear.'

'She'll be fine,' Jamie said keenly. 'Grace will have the time of her life and come back feeling all refreshed and wonderful, and with a glorious tan to boot. Plus she'll have Ellis with her, so it's not as if she'll actually be properly on her own . . .'

They all looked at Grace as if waiting for her to sanction the trip. She took a deep breath and after breaking into a big grin, she gave her verdict.

A Postcard from Italy

'Yes. A 100 per cent yes! And thank you,' she said, with far more conviction than she actually felt inside, but the thought of going to Italy for six days was just too wonderful an opportunity to miss out on. When else might she get the chance? And her mother was only going to get older and more dependent, and so this could very well be a chance of a lifetime, certainly for Grace during Cora's lifetime. And, in all honesty, Grace had been feeling for a while now that enough was enough. Bernie had been on the phone again last night complaining because Cora had called her 'in a right state', saying that Grace was 'threatening to leave me all on my own just so she can have a dirty weekend with that poor man of hers'. So Grace had had it up to here with being the family doormat, taking care of their mother single-handedly, and had told Bernie so. She had no idea how Jamie had managed to persuade Cora, though he had always had a knack of appeasing her, but what Grace did know was that she would be eternally grateful to him.

It was time.

Time for Grace to move on.

Time for Grace to take back a bit of life for herself.

And time for her to stop punishing herself for feeling that she was to blame for what Matthew did.

179

That he slept with another woman in their bed because Grace wasn't enough. Not sexy enough. Not perky enough. Or interesting enough. Funny. Cute. Or clever enough. No, he chose to cheat on Grace, shatter her love for him in the worst way possible. And that was wholly down to him. Some time away would give Grace the chance to properly clear her head and cement her new view of her life. So she was going to call her counsellor and talk through some practical strategies for the trip and then focus on packing her suitcase and feeling excited . . . because Grace Quinn was enough.

And she was going to have new knickers.

And she was going to Italy.

Fantastico! As they say in Italian . . .

12

Two weeks later, and Grace could barely believe her own eyes. The view before her as she stepped out of the aeroplane in Italy was breathtaking. On the horizon, rising majestically over the rooftop of the airport, were lush green hills dotted with traditional white brick houses nestling amongst cypress trees and olive groves. The warmth from the dazzling morning sun as it drenched the bare skin on her arms was like a balm for her soul, instantly uplifting and lightening her mood as she near glided down the staircase and onto the tarmac.

And it was incredible how she had stopped counting steps. She had first become conscious of this as she walked to the departure gate at London's Heathrow, having stopped off in duty free to treat herself to some new make-up, a pair of sunglasses, a couple of bikinis and a divine, coconutty-smelling sun cream especially formulated for redheads with fair, freckly skin, figuring she might get to do some sunbathing . . . when she wasn't busy searching for Connie's relatives, of course. Her counsellor had said this might happen: that once she was distanced from her everyday life and away from what her subconscious detected as constraint – in other words, caring full time for a controlling mother was grinding her down – then she might flourish and no longer seek the security of counting steps. And so she was delighted to discover that he had been entirely right in his prediction.

Grace felt unencumbered and free for the first time in a very, very long time, certainly since she had moved back into her childhood home after the break-up with Matthew. But that was in the past and she was determined to focus on the here and the now in glorious, sumptuous, romantic and stunningly beautiful Italy. She was here for six days and fully intended on making the most of this wonderful, generous gift that lovely, kind Larry and Betty had given her. Not to mention the generous gift that Jamie was giving her by minding Cora – which reminded her, she must call him to make sure all was OK. Or should she? Jamie had been adamant last night when he came round to wish her a good trip that she should not call, saying he wanted her to have a proper break and would be in touch if disaster struck, which was extremely unlikely given that he was an experienced nurse. And, well . . . 'I could always confiscate her telly remote control if she gives me too much grief,' he had added to lighten the mood when Grace had wobbled and very nearly started unpacking her suitcase, worried that Cora would just be too much for him with her continuous calls for attendance throughout the nights.

After collecting her suitcase, Grace headed to the arrivals section of the airport where she was due to meet Ellis before travelling with him to the little Airbnb townhouse they were to share whilst here in Venice overnight. Betty had told her all about it being right next to the water with a tiny balcony, and Grace couldn't wait to get there and see it for herself. Then tomorrow afternoon they were going to take the train to Santa Margherita to see where Connie had lived in the powder pink villa on the hillside. Betty had said the train trip looked like the nicest way for them to travel, as they'd get to sit back and enjoy a picture-postcard tour of the Italian scenery along the way.

The rest of their time in Italy would be spent talking to neighbours and going to the jeweller's in Portofino too. She had also stumbled upon the name of the powder pink villa from a photo of Connie standing by the majestic front entrance where there was a ceramic name plaque mounted on the wall. *Casa di Donato*. So they would ask around until they found somebody who knew exactly where the villa was. And there were still lots of diaries that hadn't been read yet, which Grace had painstakingly copied onto her laptop, so a long train journey would provide the perfect opportunity to read through them.

Walking through the crowd, Grace experienced a moment of anxiety when she couldn't see Ellis, but then her face broke into an enormous grin of relief on spotting him looking every inch like a suave local in shades, chino shorts, loafers and an open-necked striped polo short with the sleeves rolled up, accentuating his caramel-coloured tan. Somehow, he looked different, standing here in the airport in Italy. Sort of radiant and more handsome, but then Grace supposed somewhere as beautiful as Italy would make everyone and everything seem more attractive and airbrushed. Plus she was relaxed and happy and that always had a wonderful effect on her perception.

Ellis was holding up a piece of black card with the words *Grace Quinn Benvenuta a Venezia* printed on in purple ink.

'You made it, Grace,' he said, his American accent sounding even stronger when mingled with the lyrical Italian language being spoken all around them as the other travellers greeted their loved ones. Waggling the card in the air, Ellis stepped forward to embrace her with a kiss on each cheek. Grace reciprocated, liking the quick burst of citrusy lemon scent that emanated from him and filled her senses. It was rejuvenating and upbeat, and much like her current mood.

'I did, and thanks for the lovely welcome,' she said, touching the card in his right hand, thinking what a sweet gesture it was.

'Ah, this! Well, I figured . . . when in Rome—'

'Do as the Romans do,' she said, laughing, and then added, 'but we're not even in Rome.'

'Sure, I know that, even if I do spend most of my time in the auction house peering through a magnifying glass authenticating valuable artwork,' he laughed along, making his shoulders bob up and down and his hair flop into his toffee-coloured eyes. 'But we are near enough to Rome; it's the same land mass at least.' And as he tilted his head and gently tapped her arm with the piece of card, Grace couldn't help seeing and thinking how attractive he was, and it made her stomach do a little flip. *Do I fancy him?*

But then she quickly pushed the thought away for she wasn't one of those women. The Perky Yoga One had been one of those women. Matthew had told Grace that he had 'been honest' with the Perky Yoga One right from the start, telling her that he was in a relationship and engaged to be married, but it 'hadn't put her off'. For crying out loud. *And Ellis has a girlfriend, a very confident, trusting one, as I'm not sure how I would feel knowing he was having a holiday with another woman in Italy, aka quite possibly the most romantic place in the world.* And as if to confirm this, a man strumming a ukulele strolled up to them and started singing.

'*Per gli amanti*' and then translating in English, 'for the lovers', at which point Grace felt her whole body flush, right from the tips of her toes up to the top of her head, even making her scalp tingle. Especially when Ellis played up to the man's assumption by swiftly taking her in his arms and tilting her backwards into a classic embrace, making her left leg pop up like they do in the old movies she loved so much. And for one breathtaking moment, Grace indulged herself in a teasing role-play by smiling and laughing to the clapping crowd, who clearly thought they were a properly loved-up couple.

'Come on, you,' Ellis grinned, his face mere

millimetres from her as he eventually let her go. Then, after hoisting her suitcase onto a nearby trolley, the moment vanished, leaving Grace feeling discombobulated . . . Ellis might be out of bounds, but there was no harm in a little flirtatious fantasy inside her head, was there? 'Let's find the speed boat.'

'Speed boat?' Grace gasped, feeling another frisson of excitement. She'd never been on a speed boat. The ferry from Holyhead to Ireland as a child one cold Christmas was the extent of her sailing experience, and so there really was no comparison.

'Yep, that's right. The water taxi will take us from here to Venice. The dock is at the end of that covered walkway over there.' And he indicated with his head in the direction they needed to take.

'Well, fancy that!' Grace beamed, popping on her sunglasses and falling into step alongside Ellis as he led the way through the crowds.

13

'What an amazing place,' Grace yelled excitedly to Ellis, as the boat chugged to a slower pace, in deep contrast to the breakneck speed they had reached coming across the lagoon from the airport. Or 'water motorway', as the captain of the boat had said it was called in English.

As they sailed into a narrow canal, she could see rows of beautiful tall buildings, some of them six, maybe eight storeys high on both sides with painted shutters in pastel pink, blue and green, and geraniums in a glorious array of bright orange and red cascading from wooden window boxes. The canal was crossed with a succession of low arched bridges, and with the warm wind wafting all around them and the water frothing up in the back stream of the speedboat like prosecco fizzing from a shaken bottle, Grace felt as if she had actually stepped inside a glamorous old Hollywood film. Or one of Connie's diaries perhaps. Grace imagined Connie must have felt much the same way as she did right now, when she had sailed from Portofino to the bay of San Fruttuoso. Energised and alive. What a wonderful experience it must have been for Connie, and now for Grace too.

'It sure is,' Ellis said, leaning forward on his bench seat. They were sitting opposite each other, him travelling backwards and her forwards. 'Is it your first time here in Venice?' he asked.

'Yes, and I hope it won't be the last because it's just so incredible, I don't think you could ever tire of a place like this,' she said, gazing around in wonderment at the sights, keen not to miss a thing. Canopied cafés with people basking in the sun drinking coffee and wine. Gondolas drifting past as they sailed underneath an ancient-looking arched bridge, everyone instinctively ducking just to be sure they didn't hit their heads, even though there really was enough space, just about. The air as they cruised into another narrow waterway was filled with the scent of fresh pizza drifting towards them from a nearby pizzeria. As the boat passed by the open kitchen door, Grace glanced in to see a man in a long white apron throw a floppy lump of dough up in the air and then deftly catch it on one index finger, to spin it around before slapping it on a work bench and giving her a wave. She waved back enthusiastically, drawing in a giant waft of basil mingled with rosemary and garlic. Next, her senses were met with music, a Latin tarantella-style sound of guitars and tambourines and maracas and she swivelled her head to see where it was coming from.

'It's over there.' Ellis pointed, switching benches so he was sitting next to her now with his left arm casually slung along the panel behind her shoulders. 'It looks like a celebration of some kind.' Grace followed the direction of his pointed finger and saw a trio of men standing on a deck on the other side of the water, and then realised the boat was heading towards them.

'Ah, it's a birthday party. See there.' She pointed at a big balloon tied to a metal handrail on a length of red ribbon. 'How gorgeous, to have your birthday party somewhere as magical as this.'

'I'm glad you think so. Happy birthday, Grace.'

She swivelled her head to face him.

'What do you mean?' she asked, incredulous, before looking again at the musicians, and then upwards to where there was a sign on the brickwork above them. *Mario's Ristorante*. Was this what she thought it was? A surprise birthday meal for her?

'Come on, you'll see.' As they came to a halt, Ellis stood up; after heaving her suitcase from the boat, he offered her his hand and helped her over the side and onto the wooden deck at the entrance to the restaurant.

'I thought you might be hungry after your journey, and this place serves the best pasta in the whole of Venice. Plus Aunty Betty will never forgive me if I don't make sure you are fed and watered well. She was very insistent that I look after you properly . . . you know how she is,' he shrugged and grinned.

'*Sono arrivati*,' one of the musicians yelled over his shoulder, cueing much frenetic arm-waving from an older, plump man with slicked-back thinning hair wearing a white shirt and black trousers who appeared as if from nowhere and came bustling towards them.

'They've arrived,' Ellis quickly translated in a hushed voice, leaning his head sideways into hers before taking the man's outstretched hand. 'Grace, this is Mario, he's one of my clients.'

'He means his *favourite* client!' Mario boomed in a deep baritone voice with a strong Italian accent as he raised his free hand and slapped Ellis on the back, near winding him with sheer enthusiasm. 'And his *numero uno* friend,' he laughed. Turning to Grace, he said, '*Benvenuta, signorina,*' and gently took her hand, planted a quick kiss on the back of it and then shrugged dramatically, as if he was in an opera playing Romeo, with his heart yearning for Juliet on that balcony before adding, '*Bellissima. Come un bel fiore.*' And then in English, 'Like a beautiful flower. My life was nothing until this moment,' his Italian accent making the words sound truly romantic and meaningful. Grace stifled a giggle on seeing Ellis shake his head in mock despair for his friend. Mario then gestured generously with both arms open wide to come on into the restaurant before turning and leading the way for them to follow.

'Sorry about the kiss and all the dramatics,' Ellis whispered to her as they followed Mario along a dark corridor and through an archway that led into the restaurant. It was full of locals all laughing and talking, while children dashed around giggling and teasing each other . . . like a big family gathering. So warm and cosy and welcoming. Then, across a terracotta tiled floor, dotted with more people seated at wrought-iron tables covered with all kinds of delicious-looking foods – plump green olives, bruschetta, mozzarella mingled with beef tomatoes, giant pizzas, pasta, meatballs, and lit by candlelight that made the wine glasses twinkle to create a magical ambience. 'Mario is old-school Italian and hasn't caught up yet with the modern, politically correct way to greet a woman these days.'

'Oh, it's fine,' Grace assured him, 'like you said at the airport . . . when in Rome, and all that,' she said, attempting a dodgy Italian accent as she shrugged dramatically in the same way Mario had, making them both laugh.

'Come, only the best for my special guests.' Mario stopped walking and clicked his fingers. Instantly, a waiter appeared and led them through a small arched doorway and into a private dining room. Grace gasped, for it was truly entrancing. A small enclave, as if chiselled right through the ancient Venetian architecture. The room was made of brick with a ceiling sloping on either side, so low and atmospheric that they both had to duck as they stepped in and walked towards the table set in the middle beside a metal railed opening that looked directly out onto the canal. Tealights flickered on the ground beneath each railing, radiating a rippling golden glow across the water. Grace glided towards the chair that the waiter had slid from underneath the table for her; he flicked open a starched white napkin across her knees as she sat down. Ellis sat down too and, after the waiter and Mario had left, he looked at Grace and said, 'Welcome to Venice, and happy birthday, Grace,' before lifting a bottle of prosecco from an ice bucket beside him and pouring a generous measure into a glass flute that he offered her. He then poured some prosecco for himself.

'Thank you.' Accepting the glass she took a sip and let the bubbles linger on her tongue before swallowing, thinking how wonderful this was and how kind and generous of Ellis to arrange such a treat for her. Grace felt so touched by his gesture that her eyes smarted momentarily with emotion, for it suddenly hit her that life really could be so sweet . . . if she could let it be. But she had been so detached since the split from Matthew, with caring for Cora and turning her back on her dancing career, that she really had lost her way and denied herself the sweetness in life. The emotion she felt right now was sorrow for the part of her that had been sad for far too long. She felt sorry for that woman inside her. Pitied her even. It was a cliché, she knew, but life really was too short for regrets as big as the ones Grace already had. Jamie was right, the old Grace needed to come back, like a butterfly emerging from a cocoon, and as she swallowed another mouthful of prosecco and glanced out across the beautiful Venetian view, she made a mental note to find out about dance classes as soon as she got home. And Grace vowed to find a carer to sit with Cora while she honed her dance skills once more.

She knew that she'd never return to the West End, not at her age when there were younger, more nimble dancers desperate to realise that dream. But feeling energised and alive here in Venice was making her see that it could be possible to inject some fun and passion back into her life once more. Rejuvenation or self-care, they called it. Grace had read about it in a magazine during one of her late-night duty stints, about the importance of taking time out to do the things that made you feel happy and good about yourself. A long hot bubble bath with a good book (chance would be a fine thing). Grace remembered the last time she had tried and Cora had bellowed the very second Grace's big toe had touched the velvety, warm water. But she could book in for that long overdue haircut and try out the salted caramel smoothie. Maybe some clothes shopping, too. A trip to the cinema. A walk in the park. She used to love sitting in the sunshine in the long grass and just thinking; watching the world go by as she tracked the clouds drifting across a turquoise sky.

'And here's to Connie and finding out her truth,'

Ellis added, smiling and tilting his head to one side.

'Yes, to Connie,' Grace said, carefully chinking the side of his glass. 'And to us finding a living relative.'

*

Later, having enjoyed a delicious meal of the finest ravioli stuffed with lobster in a luscious limoncello sauce, followed by the tastiest tiramisu that Grace had ever had the pleasure of eating, they thanked Mario for his hospitality and stepped onto the gondola that he had arranged to take them on to the townhouse.

The Venetian night sky was bright with stars, the breeze warm and the moon was bathing the canal in a silvery beam as Grace sat down on the padded seat next to Ellis in the middle of the magnificent gondola, her suitcase safely stowed at their feet. Looped around her index finger was the ribbon tied to the balloon that was wafting above their heads in the breeze. Ornate lampposts, each with three bell-shaped lights encased in pink glass, gave the view a halcyon feel, making Grace wonder if Connie had also ever been here on a night like tonight.

Perhaps Giovanni had brought her to Mario's Ristorante for pasta and prosecco to celebrate her birthday too. Ellis had explained that Mario's father had first opened the restaurant in 1910, so it was entirely possible. And thrilling for Grace to imagine herself walking – or should that be floating – in Connie's shoes all these decades later. Music drifted in the air, lovers strolled arm in arm along the sides of the canal, laughing and teasing. And it was so calm and peaceful and so very different to London, Grace thought. The gondolier, dressed in traditional dark jeans, striped top and a straw boater, handed them a blanket to slip over their knees and then pushed his oar into the water to steer them majestically on their way.

Soon they were in the Grand Canal and Grace gasped on seeing the famous Rialto Bridge floodlit in twinkly gold lights, people standing on the intricately carved stonework, waving to them as their gondola passed underneath. On they drifted, taking in the atmosphere, the lights, the noises; the sheer ambience was mesmerising, not to mention Ellis's solid thigh, which was pressed against Grace's leg underneath the blanket, making her wonder if she should shift along a bit. But there wasn't really anywhere to go on the narrow gondola and, besides, it felt rather nice. Grace hoped Ellis's girlfriend wouldn't mind her taking just one teeny-tiny moment to imagine being here with a boyfriend of her own. Not Phil. Not Matthew. But someone like Ellis. Charming and kind. And who made her feel like the only woman in the world.

And then she saw it.

Grace stopped daydreaming and gasped as the famous Salute came into view. The two marble domes with delicately intricate detailing was there right in front of her, and from the exact same angle as the first painting she had picked up in Connie's storage unit. And it was breathtaking. And if Ellis's theory was correct and Connie's husband, who they now knew to be Giovanni di Donato, was the artist, then he had most definitely been here. And what if Connie had been sitting beside him as he painted? Whispering words of encouragement, with a flask of hot coffee on standby to sustain the talented artist at work. It thrilled Grace to think so as they drifted on past in silence, soaking up the atmosphere and sheer reverence of the place and all its possibilities . . .

14

VE Day and the oddest thing happened as I joined the conga in the middle of Trafalgar Square with Bunty and Joyce from the factory. It was such a marvellous feeling to dance and celebrate now that Hitler has surrendered and the war is over. A few minutes earlier, and Giovanni had whooped and lifted me high in the air, swinging me round and round before bringing me back down to earth with a long, lingering kiss, full on the lips in the middle of the street, and I've never blushed so much in my entire life. But I really had no need to as Bunty and Joyce were each kissing men in uniform too, and they hadn't even met them until today.

As everyone in the conga laughed and snaked through the crowds, I kicked my legs out side to side, gripping Joyce's waist in front of me, and as I looked out into the throng of people all around me, that's when it happened. I saw my darling Jimmy! Pale and ethereal almost, and with a vacancy in his eyes that I had never seen before. He was standing there and staring directly at me as if he and I were the only people in the world. It was the strangest feeling as my ears blocked out the noise of the crowd and I felt a floating sensation, all dreamy and slow as Jimmy lifted a hand, hesitated, and then turned and walked away. I watched as he faded, just like a ghost drifting back towards heaven.

The sun was dazzling, of course, making my vision filmy, and the streets were so crammed with everyone singing and cheering and waving flags, so I know I was mistaken. It couldn't possibly be Jimmy, as I know that he's gone, but I definitely saw a chap who looked just like him. Black curls the colour of treacle and green eyes, just like our darling Lara. So much so that it near took the wind right out of me and I stopped up short suddenly, almost making the conga line topple over on top of me. Bunty took the brunt of it, with being behind me, and wasn't at all pleased on smudging her newly applied red lipstick on the back of my tea dress, and catching her hair on a button, making her victory roll tumble free all over her face in a terrible mess. She looked such a fright that she then had to hastily redo it all in the Lyons Corner House on the Strand, where Joyce's cousin, Edie, works as a Nippy, and so was able to quickly chivvy her through to the staff room. By the time I had checked on poor Bunty and let Giovanni know where we were headed to, Jimmy's ghost was nowhere to be seen and I missed my chance to go closer to him. I would have done anything to be near him one more time. I couldn't sleep last night for dreaming about Jimmy. We were back on the carousel at the fair on Blackheath, only this time our sweet baby Lara was in Jimmy's arms and his face was a picture as he gazed down at her adoringly. It was around then that I woke up and felt tears on my pillow.

Oh poor Jimmy. I'm so sorry you had to go, my darling, and I know that seeing you was a vision, a mirage of wishful thinking, the celebratory champagne I'd had at the Rainbow Corner club earlier playing games with my head, no doubt. But you gave your life to this dastardly war so it's only fitting that you should be there on the day we celebrated Hitler's demise, if only in my imagination and dreams. You will always be my first love, my darling sweetheart, even though Giovanni is my truelove now. Meeting him has made the dark cloud lift and the light in my life come back on, and I know that he will adore Lara as soon as Mother agrees to let me bring her back to London, and it will be safe for her now so there really is no reason for Mother to object.

I will pretend she is my young sister, if that is what

201

it takes to have her close to me without the taint of illegitimacy. I know that Mother has grown very fond of her, and Lara, likewise. I see the bond between them every time I visit the village of Tindledale, and it breaks my heart to know that Lara views me as a doting sister rather than her proper mother. But in time that will change and Giovanni and I will become a family with Lara at the heart of it, with us, here in London, for Giovanni wishes to love Lara as his own and has no desire to return to America and to his disapproving parents. We have that in common, you see, except his downfall – as far as his family is concerned – is his love for art and not for the law; his lawyer father owns a firm in Manhattan in New York, and always envisaged Giovanni would follow in his footsteps. But Giovanni has no desire to practise law and he really is a very talented artist, for I have seen some of his pencil drawings and they are terrific.

'Bingo!' Grace clapped her hands together and then swivelled the screen of her laptop around so that Ellis, who was sitting opposite her, could take a look at the page of Connie's diary entry dated 1945. 'See this paragraph right here . . .' She tapped the screen after jumping up and dashing round to stand next to him.

They had just got back to the townhouse and were sitting around a red metal table on the small balcony off the sitting room, admiring the view, boats and gondolas drifting along the canal, an elderly Venetian woman pegging her washing out on a little line looped between two flower boxes beneath her windows, a baker further along offloading trays of bread and scrumptious-looking cakes from a boat and into the back of a café. Grace was mesmerised by the ordinary, day-to-day life of the people who lived here, and was grateful that they weren't staying in one of the touristy areas where she might have missed it all. They had also enjoyed lunch in a traditional Venetian *cicchetti* bar, serving wine known as *ombra* with small tapas-style plates of meatballs, fried squid, boiled eggs and sardines, with herby tomato stacked bruschetta and slices of bread with *baccalà*, a creamy cod topping that had tasted delicious. Sitting on high stools at the bar alongside native Italians all chatting enthusiastically and using their hands to articulate, Grace had loved the buzzy, frenetic yet friendly atmosphere. It made her feel alive and like she was properly a part of life once more.

She had also been stunned when she'd first seen inside the Airbnb the previous night. It was actually a Venetian loft, with original wooden beams in the ceilings and Caravaggio-style murals on the walls of every room, and furniture that wouldn't look out of place in a high-end, five-star hotel. It really was spectacular, and she had sent Betty and Larry a text message to say thank you for choosing such a sumptuous place for them to stay. Betty had replied saying that Ellis had chosen it having stayed there before, and so of course Grace had then gone off to bed wondering if his girlfriend had been with him on that occasion. She had found out that her name was Jennifer and she had sounded very sophisticated and efficient when she had called Ellis's mobile when he was in the bathroom last night.

Grace hadn't been sure if she should take the call when the phone had rung, and had still been deliberating when Ellis had yelled for her to get it, if she wouldn't mind. And so the woman on the other end of the line had started the conversation with a very breathy, 'Darling, I'm looking at venues for our engagement party and would love your input . . .' at which point Ellis had appeared and taken over the call.

Grace had heard him say, 'Hi babe,' as he padded off to the privacy of his bedroom and then, 'Just work. I'm helping her out for my aunt and uncle.'

And then, 'Sure, Jennifer, I can't wait either,' before promising to check his emails for details of the venues that she was going to email links to, and that he'd take a look and let her know his favourite one. So not only did Ellis have a girlfriend, but she was soon to be his fiancée, and so any flirty fantasy notions Grace might have inside her head must be banished immediately.

She had taken a deep breath and exhaled, as if to eradicate all but totally professional, work-related, searching-for-a-living-relative-for-Connie-type thoughts from her head, then and forever more. And there would be no more silly pondering on how soon-to-be-engaged Ellis's thigh felt against hers. As Grace Quinn was most definitely not like that. No, she wasn't a Perky Yoga One. And then, as if the universe had been colluding to reinforce this thought, Grace's mobile had rung just as she was about to fall asleep and it had been Phil. And he had been absolutely fuming. Grace had never heard so much emotion from Phil, but then he never had been one for saying how he really felt, until last night . . .

'So you make up some bullshit story about your mum not letting you come on the spa break and then I find out from that gay boy holed up in your house that you've gone off to Italy. Grace, when I said you should get in someone to look after your mum, I meant so that you could come away with me and we could have some sexy time.' Grace had blanched at this point as she hated that phrase. 'Not so you could lie to me and go off with another geezer. And all that crap you came out with about not being able to go out anywhere new . . . well, that was obviously a load of old rubbish too. Because, *Italy*. It's not exactly round the corner. Anyway, you're dumped. Not that you were much cop in the sack anyway. I've had hotter dinners—' At which point she had hung up and thanked her lucky stars. Phil had then sent her a text a few minutes later saying she owed him three hundred and seventy-six pounds for the whole spa weekend since he never would have paid his mate for the booking if he had known she was going to fleece him over it.

'Well done, Grace,' Ellis grinned, leaning forward in his chair and bringing her thoughts back to the moment. 'So we now know that Giovanni is definitely the artist and therefore Connie as his wife was heir to his artwork that was in her possession . . . well, in her storage unit until we had it moved to a secure place. Nice work.' She beamed, and then

quickly adjusted her face so it wasn't quite so jubi-
lant or – dare she think it – flirtatious-looking.
Because that wouldn't do. She'd hate Jennifer to feel
betrayed in any way by another woman; not that
she would know how Grace was behaving, but
that wasn't the point. Grace of all people knew what
betrayal felt like, not that Matthew had been inno-
cent in his affair with the Perky Yoga One, of course
not. But Grace used to wonder, in the early days
after it all happened, just how much of a part the
Perky Yoga One had played in luring Matthew into
thinking 'it just happened'.

'Thanks, Ellis,' she replied, sombrely. 'Another
piece of the puzzle solved. I'll make a note in my
pad.'

'Sure,' Ellis said, turning his head to look up at
her, his eyebrows creased with curiosity. 'Are you
OK, Grace?'

'Yes, thanks, I'm fine. Would you like more coffee?
I could pop out this time to get it,' she said, hurriedly,
suddenly wanting to get away from him. But then
a stab of her old step-counting anxiety reared up
and she regretted the words as soon as they left her
mouth. Thinking about Phil's phone call was making
her feel unnerved. Whilst it was a relief to not have
to pretend their relationship was anything real any

more, his words had still hurt. Since last night, she'd had a little voice of doubt whispering in her ear . . . 'not much cop in the sack' . . . and the inevitable conclusion to that being, *no wonder Matthew cheated on me.* And so she was battling to get back those euphoric feelings of renewal that she had felt on first arriving here in Italy.

'I'm not sure we have time for more coffee,' Ellis said, looking at his watch. 'We need to head to the station soon to catch the train to Santa Margherita.' And Grace could have kissed him in relief. Aghhhh. No. Not a kiss. That's not what she meant. Sorry Jennifer. Certainly not. Maybe just a courteous hug instead, perhaps . . .

15

The train journey from Venice to Santa Margherita gave Grace plenty of time to rinse her head of all the negative thoughts as she gazed through the window at the sheer magnificence of the Italian scenery. Romantically remote farmhouses in lush green fields. Vineyards with ride-on tractors trundling up and down the rows of vines. An ancient little white church with a bell tower flanked by cypress trees, olive groves stretching as far as she could see into a cloudless, sunny blue sky above. Grace had been mesmerised and now, once again, felt light and energised, because Italy was so cathartic and restorative and she just loved the way it made her feel.

Letting out a long sigh of contentment, she reached into her bag to retrieve her laptop. They had changed trains in Milan, but with only an hour or so there, they hadn't had time to look around the city, but just outside the station they had discovered a coffee bar. And Grace had loved people-watching the smart Italian women with their tailored clothes and chic leather handbags and swingy hairstyles and such sophisticated style. Not to mention the breathtakingly beautiful architecture of the actual station building, with its intricately carved stone, reminiscent of Roman baths, and with winged horses standing majestically on the roof. Grace had captured it all in photos on her phone, but she was really here to work. To find out what had become of Connie's relatives, and not daydream in a semi-meditative state as she stared out of the train window.

'What are you doing?' Ellis asked as Grace tilted the laptop screen and fitted in her ear pods, intending on finding some 1940s or 50s music to create a nostalgic mood as she read on in Connie's diaries.

'Um, I thought I should carry on reading, see if I can get a head start on things before we get to Santa Margherita,' she said, keeping her eyes on the screen.

'But why now? Are you crazy to miss this magnificent view?' he laughed, lifting his Ray-Ban sunglasses off, and she could sense him staring right at her. Silence followed. Then, 'Grace, are you sure you're OK? You seem distracted . . .'

She took out her ear pods and looked across to where he was sitting opposite her. He was wearing a navy polo shirt with beige chinos, his dark brown hair a little messy, the tendons in his muscular forearms flexing as he lifted a hand up to push his hair away from his face; despite her earlier resolve, it was impossible not to muse on how handsome he was. And other people saw it too, for Grace had spotted two young Italian women nudge each other and exchange smiles as they had passed through the carriage looking for their seats. One of them had accidentally bumped into Ellis's shoulder as she went by his seat, but it was him who apologised in Italian with, '*mi dispiace tanto*' and had sounded so sexy it had made Grace blush and push her face further towards the window, hoping he wouldn't notice her cheeks which were like a pair of rosy red apples.

'Honestly, I'm fine. I just want to read more about Connie and make sure I don't miss anything – clues and stuff – while I'm here . . .' She let her voice drift away.

'But my colleague in the auction house told me the name of jeweller's shop where I'm guessing Giovanni commissioned Connie's jewels from, and we have the name of the powder pink villa. I reckon we have enough to be going on with when we get there, don't you? Come on, let's enjoy the view while we can.' And he shifted from his seat and came to sit in the one next to her. Folding his arms and nudging her playfully, he glanced sideways at her with a big grin on his face.

Grace opened her mouth and then faltered, unsure if she should do as he was suggesting or stick to her own plan. And why had it got so hot on the train all of a sudden? Had the air con gone off or something, as Grace could now feel the cotton fabric of her sundress sticking to her skin and the backs of her bare legs sweating on the PVC seat. She attempted to shift position and cross her legs, then instantly wished she hadn't when a hideously embarrassing squelching noise practically ricocheted around the whole carriage when the train got a bit of a lick on, causing her thigh to suddenly lift and then unceremoniously thwack back down.

'Oh God, kill me,' she groaned inwardly, or so she thought, but the words must have come out as Ellis laughed and said, 'Now why would you want him to do that?'

'Pardon?' she said, momentarily befuddled.

'Want God to kill you!' Ellis said. 'I hate it when that happens too – my old leather lazy boy sure knows how to near rip the skin off my bare back when I'm crashed in a waist towel after a shower, but you can't blame God. It's not his fault.' And he laughed some more, making Grace smile too as she tried ever so hard to shove the image from her head of Ellis, sprawled half-naked on a leather armchair, with just a fluffy white towel tied around his abdomen.

'Um, well, I guess if you put it like that,' Grace attempted, closing her laptop screen because it would be near on impossible to concentrate on Connie's diary in any case, with him sitting in such close proximity. His citrusy scent was all around her and that solid thigh was brushing against hers again. *Sorry, Jennifer, but I honestly didn't do anything to make him sit next to me, not that it means anything anyway, of course not, and I promise from now on to imagine him covered in disgusting Marmite or something instead of semi-naked in a towel.* Grace turned to face the window, determined to keep her eyes on the view and very definitely away from Ellis, who was about to become engaged to Jennifer.

16

The burnished orangey-red sun was setting on the sea as they arrived in the beautiful bay of Santa Margherita, where the atmosphere was reminiscent of a timeless, old-world ritziness. Grace thought she could just imagine Elizabeth Taylor strolling along in a cream sheath dress and oversized shades, surrounded by paparazzi as she made her way back to a yacht moored in the harbour. The promenade was lined with palm trees and green slatted benches to sit on and admire the view. Elderly women clad in black serge dresses meandered along by a row of smart blue and white striped beach huts, with pots of pink and purple bougainvillea hooked onto the sides. Families with young children rambled over the pebbles on the beach and Grace sighed in contentment and appreciation to be in yet another wonderful part of beautiful Italy.

After checking in to the boutique hotel and

admiring their adjoining rooms on the fourth floor with balconies, giving a splendid view of the coast-line, they decided to take a walk to see if they could find Connie's powder pink villa right away. Or at least get an idea of where it was so they could make a head start in the morning.

While Ellis had dealt with some work calls, Grace had spoken to an older guy on the desk in the hotel lobby; he had heard of the villa, explaining it was *molto grande* and set up high on the cliff top with lots of sunroofs and arched verandas, whose shape he had described with his hands, gesticulating animatedly. Grace had thought he was making a rainbow shape at first, only cottoning on when he had pulled out a mobile and shown her a picture of a villa with something similar. Interestingly, he had told her that the powder pink villa was where the artist had lived and that everyone locally knew of him but had rarely seen him. *Un recluso*, appar- ently. Until he died over twenty years ago! At which point Grace's heart had sunk, this news making it harder to continue to harbour any hope of finding him as a living relative. And poor Connie, losing her truelove all over again. He was also able to give Grace a location for the powder pink villa . . . sort of – that it was beside an orange grove, at the end of a path, with the nearest proper road being called Via Arancia, which translated literally as Orange Road, she later discovered, on relaying the information to Ellis.

'I think it's all the way up there,' Ellis said to Grace, looking at the maps app on his phone before pointing over her left shoulder and up a hillside far into the distance. The hotel where they were staying was near the seafront and so they could see that Connie's villa would take some time to get to, and it would be dark soon. So instead, they crossed the road and headed towards a central piazza with a fountain in the middle and lots of narrow, cobbled lanes leading off it, which were lined with candlelit restaurants and cafés with sun-bleached striped canopies, in search of something to eat.

After choosing a fish restaurant and being seated at a lovely table under a yellow canopy with a perfect view of the fountain in the piazza where they could people-watch and soak up the evening's atmosphere, they shared an enormous salt-baked sea bass with lemon and herbs, a Caprese salad and garlicky tomato bruschetta. Grace was enjoying a glass of white wine that the waiter had recommended from a local vineyard, when her mobile rang. On pulling the phone from her handbag and glancing at the screen to see that it was Bernie, her heart sank, and so she put the phone back in her bag and tried to ignore it. Her sister would only be calling to complain about something again, and she didn't want anything to spoil so much as a second of the magical time she was having here in Italy.

Fortunately, the phone stopped ringing, and Grace took another mouthful of the crisp, yet fruity-flavoured wine and sat back in her seat feeling contented and relaxed. She was over her earlier embarrassment on the train, and now settled back into the easy and amicable yet professional conversations that she had enjoyed with Ellis in the café at home.

'Everything OK?' Ellis asked, lifting the empty wine bottle and motioning to the waiter to bring them another one, please.

'Yes. It's my sister . . .' Grace told him, trying to sound breezy.

'Take the call if you like, I don't mind,' he smiled.

'Oh no, it's fine. I'll talk to her later,' she said vaguely, helping herself to an olive from the bowl on the table.

'Don't you want to talk to her now?' he asked.

'Um, not really,' she said, discarding the olive stone onto the side of her plate.

'Why not?' he asked, taking an olive too.

'Oh . . .' Grace paused, forgetting how direct he could be, but wondering what to tell him without having to explain it all and likely ruin the evening's lovely ambience. She didn't want anything to change the atmosphere, for she was feeling so relaxed, it was as if she had escaped to some place where nothing bad could ever happen. A bubble that she didn't want to burst by talking about her real life. Not yet. She knew she would have to return to reality at the end of her time in Italy but, for now, she wanted to savour every second. 'Well, it'll be a tense conversation and I don't want it to spoil the mood.'

'Why is that?'

'You really don't want to know,' she tried, but Ellis was having none of it.

'Yes I do . . . and it might help to offload,' he said, lifting one eyebrow.

'OK,' Grace sighed. 'She'll be calling to tell me off again,' she settled on, hoping he wouldn't pursue it, but of course he did.

'Ah, does she make a habit of doing that?' His forehead creased in concern.

'Oh, yes.' And Grace was just about to explain a bit more, if only to end the conversation and move it on to something else, when the phone rang again.

'Guess you should answer, it might be important. It could be something to do with your mother . . .' he said, and Grace stopped short as she hadn't realised that he knew anything about Cora. She hadn't talked about her in any of their previous conversations in the café, but there was no time to ask him how he'd heard about her as the phone stopped ringing, only to start up again almost immediately. Reluctantly, Grace pulled the phone from her bag.

'Hi Bernie, how are you?' she answered, the wine having relaxed her enough to attempt a more laid-back approach for a change.

'Where on earth are you?' Bernie started, skipping any pleasantries.

'Italy. But I'm guessing you know that already or you wouldn't be asking,' Grace said, her buoyant mood deflating immediately.

'Charming! And there's no need to be flippant, Grace. It's really not on, you know,' Bernie huffed.

'What do you mean? Being flippant, or me having some time off?' Grace asked, glancing away from Ellis who was sorting out the second bottle of wine with the waiter, then topping up her glass and pouring some for himself.

'You know what I mean. You swan off to Italy without so much as a courtesy call to let any of us know. Sinead and Mikey had no idea either. And Mum has been calling me, practically in tears. She's devastated that you've gone off and left her with the neighbour. In fact, I couldn't believe my own ears when she told me you had disappeared. What on earth possessed you to do such a thing?'

'Stop it!' Grace said, before gulping down a big mouthful of wine.'

'I beg your par—'

'Why must you always exaggerate so much?' Grace was almost certain that their mother wasn't devastated at all. Most likely, she couldn't wait to see the back of Grace for all the complaining she did about everything Grace did for her. That was another thing that Grace had gained clarity of thought over since being away from her normal life: that her mother was an ungrateful, selfish cow (there, she had said the 'c' word again, if only in her head, Jamie would be pleased), who enjoyed tormenting the only one of her grown-up children who could be bothered to care for her.

'Well, if you're going to be like that,' Bernie huffed.

'Like what?' But Grace didn't wait for an answer, instead she took a deep breath and decided to stop this conversation before it turned into a row and then ruined her evening, and so changed tack with,

'Look, Bernie. Mum is absolutely fine. I haven't just left her with a random neighbour as you're implying. I left her with Jamie, who we have all known for absolutely ever. He is very experienced and he's actually a real nurse, remember, and Mum likes him, much more than she likes me, so I have no idea why she would be crying on the phone to you.'

'What is that supposed to mean? What are you saying? That I'm lying?' Bernie said, indignant.

'No, that's not what I'm saying.' Grace mouthed, 'sorry' to Ellis, and he shook his head and smiled in solidarity before picking up his own phone and busying himself with looking at the screen. 'Bernie, I'm saying that I will call Jamie later and make sure that Mum is OK.'

'Well, if you had made an effort to call her before now, then you would know that she isn't. She said that you left two days ago and you haven't even phoned her once. You can't just not bother with her, you know.'

'That's rich coming from you . . .' Grace said, the words spilling out of her mouth before she had a chance to properly think through the consequences. She had wanted to avoid a full-blown argument, if only for her own self-preservation, and now she'd gone and lit the touch paper by confronting Bernie with her 'lack of bother' for their mother.

'How dare you! I love my mother more than anyone. She means the world to me,' Bernie exploded so passionately that, if Grace hadn't known better, she might be convinced that her sister truly meant every single word. 'And don't you think I wished that I had time to look after her like you do, but I don't, Grace. I'm a very, very busy person with a responsible job an—'

'Sorry, Bernie. But I have to go.' And Grace did what she wished she'd had the courage to do at least a year ago, and pressed to end the conversation with her sister, Bernadette, because there was no point in trying to make her see how far removed from the reality of the situation she was. Bernie was perpetually busy, and blinkered, and convinced that her life was a trillion times more stressful, or indeed important, than anyone else's, and that's just the way she was. Grace doubted if Bernie would ever change; she had been like it as a child, always trying to curry favour with their mother, to be her favourite, even if it meant telling tales or defending Cora's criticism of her siblings. But it didn't mean Grace had to put up with it any more. So, after dropping her phone back inside her bag, she drained the last of her wine and vowed to enjoy the rest of the evening, in fact all of the time she had left here in Italy. She would call home later. But for now she was going to work on the assumption that Jamie would, as he had promised to, let her know right away if Cora really was upset by her absence.

'Top-up?' Ellis said, lifting the bottle of wine.

'Oh, yes please,' she said, gratefully, pushing her glass towards the centre of the table.

'I see what you mean, Bernie sounded very fierce,' Ellis said, softly.

'Could you hear?'

'Sure, it was hard not to with her yelling at you like that. And sorry for probing you like I did before . . . guess you should have ignored the call after all. You look totally ashen.'

'Sorry,' Grace instinctively said, her kneejerk reaction to perceived criticism born from learning early on with caring for her mother that it was the best way for an easier life.

'Hey, don't apologise. I shouldn't have been a jerk and interfered. It was none of my business.' And he shook his head apologetically.

'You did me a favour, I think . . .' Grace said, tentatively.

'I did?' he asked, looking baffled.

'Yes, standing up to Bernie isn't what I would normally do, but I actually feel better for doing so,' she said, nodding her head in confirmation.

'Then that's a good thing. Want to talk about it? I promise not to interfere again,' he said, pouring her an extra generous measure of wine.

'I shouldn't really, it will only ruin a perfectly lovely meal.' She busied herself with taking a piece of rustic bread from the basket and biting into it.

'You wouldn't be doing that. But I knew something was up, you've been . . .' he paused, clearly searching for the right word, before settling on, 'different, for the whole day.'

'Oh, that's not the reas—' she muttered through a mouthful of the bread before washing it down with a big gulp of wine, but he quickly cut in.

'Well, I'm a good listener, if you change your mind.' And he momentarily touched his fingertips to the top of her bare arm, quickly moving his hand away seconds later, but not before Grace had felt a tingle that swirled right through her, almost making her gasp out loud. Inhaling through her nostrils, then letting out a long puff of air, she finished the wine, and then, after studying his face momentarily, their eyes meeting in a silent exchange, she told him all about it. Told him what her life was really like caring for a challenging parent and trying to navigate her way around Cora's needs, plus dealing with her three oblivious siblings.

Ten minutes later, and Ellis was shaking his head in bewilderment. 'Grace, I had no idea. I mean, I know that you're a carer for your bedbound mother,' he started, and then when she didn't say anything, he expanded with, 'Aunty Betty mentioned it.' She glanced downwards at the table as he added, 'But only in passing, and certainly not in any kind of judgemental way, I promise you, Grace.'

'Why do you say that?' she asked, picking at the cuticle on her left thumb.

'Well, the way you shy away from talking about it, for starters, and the losing eye contact thing you do . . . that's a dead giveaway that you feel embarrassed, or ashamed, perhaps. That others are judging you. Why is that, Grace?' And he stared directly into her eyes.

Grace blinked and went to look away again, but swiftly brought her eyes back to meet his, determined not to prove him right about the eye contact thing. Yes, she knew she did it, but gosh, must he be so direct? Was it an American thing? Or maybe she just wasn't used to people, men like Matthew and Phil, actually being interested in how she felt.

Jamie of course did, but then they'd been friends for absolutely ages and so that was different somehow. And Grace hadn't ever properly confided in Matthew, or Phil, about how she really felt about being Cora's carer, so it was her own fault really . . .

'Oh, um, err . . . I'm not really sure,' she managed, taken aback.

'Come on, Grace. What's so wrong with being a carer? Other than it being damn hard work, I imagine.'

'Yes. Yes, it is.'

'Then hats off to you, it's an admirable thing to do.' And he nodded his head and laid his hands palms up on the table as if to underpin his statement.

'I've never really looked at it like that,' Grace said, letting her gaze fall now on the candle between them on the table. Ellis was looking at it too and so she figured he couldn't really pass comment about the eye contact thing.

'Why the heck not?' he asked, his New Yorker accent seeming stronger all of a sudden.

'Because . . . I don't know, it's not exactly something everyone needs to know about and, like you said, it's damn hard work,' she ventured, unsure from being put on the spot, but it was an answer at least.

'Oh, I see. So it's modesty. You're doing a good thing, but must keep quiet about it in case people think you're humble-bragging.'

'Well, not exactly. I can't just leave my mother on her own . . . someone has to look after her.'

'Then tell me, because I honestly think you should be proud of yourself. What you do is amazing. I don't think I could do it and I hope I'm never put in a position where I have to find out. But why don't you talk openly about it? I imagine your mother appreciates you caring for her very much.'

Silence followed as Ellis waited for Grace to talk to him some more.

'I might keep quiet about it because . . .' She let her voice fade away.

'Go on,' he prompted.

'Well, it might be because my mother can be very difficult and very unappreciative.' There, she had actually said it out loud.

'Grace, I'm sorry to hear that. In what way is she difficult?' He raised his eyebrows.

'Yes, I know it must be very hard for her with nothing to do except lie in bed all day watching TV, but she can be very ungrateful,' Grace said quietly. 'And unkind. Hurtful even,' she added when Ellis didn't say anything. He just listened, his eyes softening when she glanced up from the candle to look at him, wondering if she was saying too much, but he seemed interested. Really interested. And so she added in almost a whisper, 'The stuff she says to me makes me feel utterly rubbish about myself. She knows all the buttons to push to make me doubt my capabilities, appearance, morals . . . everything. And it makes me feel ashamed.'

'Oh Grace, that's terrible, and it would be wrong of me to criticise your mother, so I won't. But I will say that you must try not to let her manipulation and controlling behaviour define you. I imagine she is jealous of you and that's her problem.'

'But she's my mother. I can't just abandon her.'

'Sure, I get that. But it doesn't mean she has the right to deliberately hurt you. You are more than that, Grace. From where I'm sitting I see someone wonderful. You're kind and compassionate – just look at how much you care about finding out the truth for Connie. And you are smart too.' Grace felt her cheeks blushing. 'Don't ever doubt that. And you're beautiful – the way your gorgeous green eyes light up when you smile. And your red curls—' And for some unfathomable reason that Grace couldn't explain, she interrupted him by blurting out, 'What colour hair does Jennifer have?' which momentarily seemed to throw him off kilter as his mouth opened and then closed before his forehead furrowed, he opened his mouth again and said, 'Jennifer? Um, blonde. But it changes all the time. It could be pink the next time I see her.'

She nodded and pushed her chair back. 'Err, I need the bathroom. Sorry. Be right back.' And she dashed off inside the restaurant.

In the safety of the bathroom, she stared at her face in the mirror, wondering why on earth she would say such a ridiculous thing. Ellis was mostly likely sitting there now thinking she was some kind of fruit loop to come out with such a random question about hair colour. But she couldn't work out where she was with him.

Is he flirting?

Or just being kind, trying to give me a boost?

If he's flirting then he has no place to be and I should tell him so.

But I like it.

Splashing her face with water, she took a deep breath and willed herself to get a grip, telling herself he was just being friendly and kind. Of course he was.

After smoothing her sundress down and tidying her hair, she returned to the table where Ellis stood up and pulled her chair out.

'Are you OK?'

'Yes, I'm fine, thanks,' Grace said, busying herself with sorting out the napkin which had dropped onto the floor in her haste to get away.

'I didn't mean to overwhelm you with compliments, and you don't need my seal of approval at all, definitely not in a patronising, arrogant way . . . I hope it didn't seem like that.' Grace quickly shook her head. 'I just wish you could see your qualities for yourself.'

'Thank you,' she smiled, swirling the last of her wine around the bottom of the glass. 'Honestly, it's OK, I appreciate you being kind.' Ellis studied her for a moment, as if trying to work out whether to say something else, before seemingly deciding not to, then nodding and settling on, 'Cool. And I say, more power to you for coming away to Italy. You sure need the break by the sounds of it and, from what you've told me about Jamie, I reckon he will take great care of your mother,' Ellis said.

'I'm sure he will. But I wish Bernie and the others could see it like that.'

'I imagine Bernie probably does . . . deep down.'

'Really? Why do you think that?' she said, curious to hear his reasoning and feeling more relaxed now that he wasn't paying her loads of compliments.

'Because she knows that you do it all for your mother, and that she isn't taking a fair share. And she feels extra guilty knowing that a neighbour is now taking care of Cora. That's why she takes it out on you. Tries to make out you're the inadequate one. They call it deflection.'

'Do they?' Grace marvelled, for she had never seen it this way. Only ever feeling as if she just wasn't doing the caring for Cora well enough. But if what Ellis was saying was true, then it would make sense that Bernie, Sinead and Mikey were so keen to pack their mother off to a home or pay for her to be cared for by strangers. They would be doing their bit, albeit financially, but they wouldn't feel guilty about leaving it all to her.

'Yes, those psychotherapist types,' Ellis grinned, and nodded as if attempting to convince himself that he really did know what he was talking about.

'Ah, those types,' Grace teased, making Ellis laugh by cupping her chin as if pondering deeply, the wine having made her a bit tipsy. But it was nice to be able to chat about being a carer, without the judgement that she had envisaged, which she had now come to realise was mostly in her head. The shame of how her mother made her feel, with the abusive comments and stuff, now eased slightly, and she felt stronger for sharing it with Ellis. Maybe she'd even look into care-home options when she got home . . . or at least start discussing it with Cora so they could come up with a longer-term plan for her care that worked for all of them.

Grace was determined to build on her new-found feelings of confidence and become more independent. She might even find a flat to rent. Now felt like the right time to do that; as much as she did love her mother, Grace couldn't continue living the way she had been for the last year or so. Ellis was right, she was worth more than that. More than the daily taunts and jibes that Cora meted out.

'Come on, you. How about we get out of here and find a gelato place,' Ellis said, bringing her back to the moment. He pushed his chair back and stood up, then, after pulling his wallet out, he left more than enough euros on the table to cover the bill.

'OK, I'd like that. But please let me pay for dinner,' she said, going to hand the notes back to him. 'You've paid for practically all the meals so far.'

'No way. It's my way of thanking you for being such great company this evening,' he said, chivalrously. And, after helping her with pushing her chair back across the bumpy cobbles, he gently took her arm and looped it through his before leading them off towards the seafront.

*

Later, after strolling along the promenade, the lights from the boats twinkling in the warm, starry night sky, her arm still looped through his because Grace had convinced herself that he was just being friendly, in a brotherly sort of way. Or was she still secretly liking the way he was with her? Being so close to him. And so had thrown caution to the wind about Jennifer ever finding out? They had enjoyed deliciously creamy salted-caramel gelato in buttery waffle cones from a little café crammed full of locals – children too, even though it was late in the evening by the time they discovered it. And Grace had thought how marvellous it was that whole families were spending time together, social-ising and laughing and chatting like they actually loved and cared about each other. Unlike her own family, which always seemed to be at loggerheads. But Cora had a lot to answer for with it being that way, as she had often set out to cause division between them all as children, often pitching Sinead,

Bernie, Mikey and Grace against each other instead of fostering unity.

Grace and Ellis had eventually got back to the hotel, having laughed and teased each other all the way, trying each other's gelato and rating it on a scale of one to ten, where he had asked if she wanted to share a nightcap in the hotel's small bar. The way he had looked at her, brushing a stray strand of hair back over her shoulder had implied the possibility of the nightcap turning into something much more, and so Grace had politely declined. Ellis hadn't pressured her, instead giving her kiss on the cheek and wishing her goodnight.

In her bedroom, Grace flopped on the bed and called Jamie, forgetting how late it was. He answered with, 'What time do you call this, lady?' in a low voice, presumably so as not to disturb Cora.

'Oh, I'm so sorry, did I wake you up?'

'Yes you did, but don't worry about that. Are you having a fabulous time?' And then not waiting for an answer he continued with, 'Don't tell me you're calling to check on your mother because I can tell you that she is absolutely golden. In fact, she is currently snoring away, perfectly contentedly. I can hear her from across the landing.'

'Really?' Grace said, imagining Jamie in the spare

bedroom trying to block out Cora's thunderous snores.

'Yes, really.'

'Sorry, I know how loud she can be.'

'Don't you dare apologise,' he chastised halfheartedly. 'And her ladyship hasn't once called out in the night since I've been on duty, so you might want to have a chat to her about it when you get home. All that wanting the lamp switched on and needing the loo and stuff is a ruse, I reckon. Designed to get you at it . . . to make a fuss of her.'

Grace fell silent for a moment, taking in what Jamie was telling her. So Bernie really had been fibbing in that case. Grace knew it, but part of her couldn't believe it for sure, until now.

'But why would she do that?'

'I don't know, and I'm not about to waste time wondering what goes on in her head. And nor should you, sweetheart. Not when you are in *bella Italia*.'

'Hmm. Has Bernie been in touch?' Grace ventured.

'Oh, yes, that madam called the house phone and then had the temerity to tell me off when I answered . . . for "letting you run off to Italy at the drop of a hat".' And Grace could just see him doing quote signs in the air with his fingers before rolling his eyes.

'I'm sorry, Jamie,' she groaned inwardly.

'Oh purlease, honey, stop apologising. I soon put her right. Bernadette Quinn doesn't rattle my cage. And she should know that from the time she tried to lock me in the shed when we were kids.'

'Ah, yes I remember that. Her face was a picture when you found that loose panel and escaped, only to tip a bucket of freezing cold water all over her new Sarah Jessica Parker-style perm, complete with the oversized pink bow on top,' she laughed.

'Yes, hilarious – howled for hours she did!' he replied, laughing too at their shared memory.

'And sorry about Phil turning up . . . he phoned me, and—'

'Ugh,' Jamie responded dramatically. 'What did you ever see in that caveman? He said you were dumped so I'm presuming it's OK to slag him off now?' He paused and Grace could hear him drawing breath as he checked.

'Ah, yes. Sorry if he was rude to you,' she swiftly confirmed.

'Grace, the guy could barely string a sentence together properly, and as for his silly alpha-male posturing when he managed to galvanise his two brain cells into action and work out that I'm gay . . . well, it serves him right that he tripped over his own feet when he stormed off down the street. Face-planted the pavement, he did. Trust me, he won't be knocking on your door any time soon.'

'Why, what did you say to him?' Grace resisted the urge to giggle.

'Only that he should think himself lucky you were on the rebound after Matthew, as he was punching so high it's a wonder he didn't get altitude sickness. Honestly, Grace, he really is a bit bottom of the barrel, to be fair. Anyway, enough about Bernie and that dollop, Phil: tell me about Italy. And Ellis. What's he like? He's American isn't he? Has he made a move on you yet?'

'Shhhussshh,' Grace instinctively said, conscious that Ellis was on the other side of the adjoining wall. 'That's the other reason I'm calling you.'

'Oooh! Have you snogged him then?' Jamie asked, his voice full of glee.

'Nooo. Of course I haven't,' Grace admonished.

'Well, you could do worse. I heard he's a bit of a catch, to put it in Betty's words.'

'What do you mean? When did you and Betty talk about Ellis?'

'That time I was waiting for you, before we went over to Connie's flat. Between me and you, I got the impression that she's hoping cupid might make a little appearance while you two are in *bella Italia*,' he said with a flourish.

'Don't be daft,' she reacted.

'Well, Betty said you and he would make such a lovely couple.'

'But he has a girlfriend,' she told him, wondering why Betty would say such a thing, or perhaps Jamie was embellishing the conversation with Betty; it wouldn't be the first time he'd tried to engineer a hook-up. When she had first split up with Matthew, Jamie had tried to set up a blind date for her with one of the doctors at the hospital where he worked . . . and it had all been very awkward.

'Really? Oh that's a shame, Betty never mentioned it,' Jamie said, sounding deflated. 'Or maybe Betty doesn't like the girlfriend? Yes, that could be it . . . perhaps the whole family hates her and this trip to Italy is a big plan to sideline her in favour of you. Oh Grace, wouldn't that be amazing? You could live in LA or wherever it is he comes from. Of course, I'd have to join you, what with being your best friend and all,' he laughed, seemingly having it all worked out.

'New York. He lives in New York,' Grace interjected, and then promptly followed up with, 'but don't get carried away. He's getting engaged. And anyway, there's absolutely nothing going on between Ellis and me.'

'Are you sure?'

'Yes I'm sure. But . . .' Grace stopped talking.

'I knew it. Something has happened hasn't it?'

'No. Well, yes, he's been a bit flirty . . . I think.'

'What do you mean "you think"? Either he is or he isn't, what's he done?' And Grace told him about what happened at the airport and on the train and then tonight, how attentive he was, the compliments and then the arm looping thing and touching her hair. Silence followed. Then, 'He fancies the pants off you! A man doesn't say or do stuff like that unless he wants you. And that's the top and bottom of it!' Jamie declared.

'Must you be so dramatic?' she whispered. 'What if I'm just being desperate?'

'What do you mean, desperate?' he puffed, as if the very notion was preposterous.

'You know, imagining it all. It's been a while. Maybe I'm out of touch and he's just being friendly, a shoulder to cry on as it were . . .'

'Oh, Grace, please tell me you didn't cry on him? I want you to be having the time of your life, not feeling sad.'

'No, not literally crying, as in crying actual tears.

I just talked about Cora, what it's really like looking after her. You know, how cruel she can be. And how indifferent the others are about it all.'

'Ah, well that's OK. Not that it's OK what Cora says, and I will have a word with her before you get back. But it's OK that you feel relaxed enough with Ellis to talk to him. I'm liking the sound of him already.'

'But what if I'm letting my neediness and loneliness or whatever you want to call it get in the way of proper, rational thought. It could just be wishful thinking, that someone like Ellis would fancy me. It's not like real life here. It's a bit like being in a dream, in fact . . .'

'OK, Grace, listen to me. Firstly you are not desperate. You are bloody gorgeous. You are bright, caring and kind,' he said, echoing Ellis's words from earlier in the restaurant. 'Plus, you can knit the longest scarves in the entire universe.'

'Oi, I thought you liked my scarves,' she laughed.

'I do, but they are a bit long, to be fair.'

'OK. Maybe I do get carried away, but there isn't much else to do when you're sitting up all night on watch duty with a bedbound mother.'

'Well, you'll be able to knock that on the head

when you get home and get a proper night's sleep, as madam does not need her lamp turning on every five minutes! Anyway, getting back to the flirtation theory: he looped your arm through his, remember, you didn't run after him all whiny-like and pleading, "Please Ellis, please, please, please flirt with me because I'm just *sooo needy*" . . .'

'Ha-ha, you know what I mean, Jamie.'

'No, I don't. Tell me,' he said, annoyingly.

'Well, it's been a while, since, well, since I first dated Matthew, so what if I'm reading it all wrong and Ellis isn't being flirty at all? Just friendly. I know how casual it can all be these days, what with "swiping right" to hook up for sex.'

'Oh, don't be daft, Grace. You don't just stop knowing if someone is flirting with you. Trust me, he is flirting.'

'But he has a girlfriend, remember!' Grace whisper-yelled right into the phone.

'And? You don't know her. And she's not there. So what happens in Italy stays in Italy.'

'Stop it. I couldn't do that to another woman. It's not right. You're terrible.'

'Am I? Or are you just virtue-signalling?'

'Virtue-what?' she asked, baffled.

'Oh never mind,' Jamie said, letting out a long puff of air. 'Grace, you don't know Jennifer, you don't owe her anything.'

'Oh, come on, what about the girl code? You know how destroyed I was when I caught Matthew—'

'Forget about Matthew. And forget about that awful one with the horse teeth—'

'Horse teeth?' Grace quickly interjected.

'Yes, that yoga one with the great big galloping horse teeth. Honestly, Grace, I don't know why you have her on a pedestal the way you do – she really isn't much of a looker. Not that it's all about looks, but you know what I mean. You are a million times more beautiful than she is. Inside and out.' Silence followed. 'And no, I'm not just saying that because you're my best friend. I'm saying it because it's true. And can I tell you something else too while I'm at it?'

'Why not? Seeing as you're on a roll,' she quipped, bracing herself for what was about to come.

'Good. Can you tell that I'm feeling brave with you hundreds of miles away and not next door like you usually are?' And he paused to take a deep breath before launching back in with, 'If you stopped using what happened to detach yourself from life – yes, it was disgusting and shitty and heartbreaking what Matthew did – but nobody died and now you have to let it go. Move on already, Grace.'

'You know, I had already come to that conclusion,' she jumped in.

'Excellent. So we are on the same page. You can do this, Grace. You can get your life back and move on. You always could. Look at you now. In gorgeous Italy. And you travelled there all by yourself by putting one foot in front of the other without counting a single step, I trust?'

'That's right.'

'Well, there you go. You are strong, Grace. Now, get your backside out there, darling, and live your best life!'

'And that told me,' Grace thought as she ended the call . . .

17

The next day, Grace felt remarkably renewed and full of vigour after possibly the best night's sleep ever. And it was absolute bliss not having to get up in the night to see to Cora every twenty minutes. Long may it continue when she returned home. Having had the foresight to pack her trainers, Grace had actually gone for a run, something she hadn't felt like doing, or indeed had the energy for, in ages. She had run all along the Santa Margherita promenade as the sun had been peeping over the tips of the lush green, pine-tree-clad cliffs, and it had been amazing, making her feel joyous and euphoric and like absolutely everything was possible. She knew it sounded cheesy, but she really did feel brand new, and that she could be whoever she wanted to be here in Italy where nobody, apart from Ellis, knew her or anything about her. If there was a way to bottle the feeling so she could keep hold of it when she got back to London, then she was determined to find the recipe for what felt like a magic potion.

After the run she had gone back to the hotel to shower and meet Ellis, and so it was now almost midday by the time they had hiked all the way up the tiny, winding mountain roads to reach Via Arancia. They had thought it would be a nice way to see more of Santa Margherita and of course the breathtaking view of the Riviera, away from the promenade and the tourists, but they hadn't anticipated quite how far it would be. And Grace now wished that she had eaten more for breakfast. Even though it was delicious – hot coffee with a big bag of *cornetti* which they had torn apart and eaten slathered with deliciously salty butter and locally made peach jam that she had bought to share with Ellis from a little bakery she'd discovered near the harbour. They had sat on the balcony of their adjoining bedrooms and gazed wistfully at the tranquil vista, content in each other's company. Ellis had asked if she was OK after their heart-to-heart last night and she had told him yes, and that he had helped her far more than he would ever know.

'Look, there's a single-track road over there,' Ellis

said, pointing behind a tree to an opening. They could see a small field with what looked like an abandoned white stone hut in one corner surrounded by long grass.

'Shall we take a look?' Grace asked, flapping the hem of her T-shirt around in a desperate attempt to create a breeze, for it was roasting hot up in the mountains, especially in the clearing without the shade from the pine trees.

'Sure,' Ellis said, walking on, and then, 'Grace, come and take a look at this,' he added, excitedly, over his shoulder, 'I think I can see the powder pink villa up ahead.'

They walked on side by side for a little while longer until they came to another clearing with another abandoned white stone hut in a field, this time with goats mooching around in the grass, the brass bells on collars around their necks jingling merrily.

And then it appeared in full splendour.

The powder pink villa where Connie had actually lived.

It had to be. And it was absolutely glorious.

Between the pine trees on the far side of the field, Grace could see a magnificent three-storey villa accessed by a long path and surrounded by citrus trees. The orange and lemon scents were intoxicating in the heat. Chalky pale pink render with stunning archways led on to terracotta-tiled verandas swathed in pink bougainvillea.

'Wow. Who lives in a place like this now?' Grace pondered, imagining a movie star, or a singer perhaps, for it was truly impressive and would most likely take a whole team of people to maintain it. She wondered if they would mind them taking a look inside, as she'd really love to see where Connie had actually lived and where she might have written the diaries that Grace was still reading through.

Lifting a hand to shield her eyes from the dazzling sun, Grace gazed at the breathtaking view all around her: sea water glittering below, a majestic cruise liner on the horizon, a cloudless blue sky above. Rows of higgledy-piggledy sun-bleached painted pink, white, blue and green houses hugging the mountainsides, their shutters thrown open wide. And people on scooters zipping along the narrow, bendy roads. She could hear cicadas singing in the trees and in the moment it felt, and looked to Grace, like a perfect paradise.

Closing her eyes momentarily, she drew in a big lungful of the deliciously fragranced citrusy and pine-laden air and focused on taking a snapshot of the scene to have permanently etched in her mind's eye. And to think that Connie would have seen this exact view too. In fact, she most likely stood in the very spot that Grace was in now, as they were on the only road that led right up to the powder pink villa.

'Come on, let's go and find out,' Ellis said, spontaneously grabbing her hand and practically running her all the way to the gates at the entrance to the long path. On a pillar to the right-hand side was an intercom pad. He pressed the buzzer. No answer. Grace gave it another press, but still no answer.

'What now?' she said, her heart sinking with disappointment as she looked again at the gate. It was securely locked and padlocked. As she was pondering all the options, a black cat with white splodges on its face came sauntering towards them.

'We climb over?' Ellis suggested, pulling his wallet and mobile phone from his pockets and handing them to her. 'In case they fall out,' he shrugged by way of explanation. 'I'll go first and then you can come over and join me.'

'What?' Grace exclaimed, aghast. 'You're not serious, are you? We can't just break in to Connie's house. We don't even know for certain it's the right villa – I can't see the Casa di Donato name plaque anywhere, can you?' she said, stalling for time as she racked her brain to try and come up with a less risky option.

'No, but it has to be. The guy in the hotel told you so; he even said Mr Donato lived here. Come on, it'll be fine. There's nobody in there, you can see the shutters are all down on the windows. Maybe it's a holiday home now . . .'

'But it's still wrong. What if there's security inside? You know, guard dogs and such like. And look up there.' She pointed to a CCTV camera at the top of the pillar. But before she could stop him, Ellis had stuck his foot on a groove in the ironwork of the gate and managed to pull himself up high enough to swing his other leg up and over the top. Within seconds he was jumping down onto the grass on the other side of the gate with a boyish grin on his face, his dark brown hair flopping into his eyes, and Grace couldn't help but see a glimpse of a much younger man, the boy he'd once been, and it was appealing to see this fun, effervescent side of him. Even if he was scaring the hell out of her with his risk-taking. The cat, keen to see who the intruder was, came running towards Ellis, before brushing up against the side of his leg, then did a little spin as if trying to catch its tail like an excited dog.

'See, the cat is pleased to see me. He doesn't mind us being here at all,' Ellis said, crouching down to stroke the cat's head. 'Ah, look, she's called Gypsy,' he added, taking a look at her pink velvet collar. 'Come on,' he encouraged, pushing his hand through the railings. 'Put my phone and wallet through and then pass me your bag. I can probably cup both hands together around one of the railings if you want a leg up.'

'I can't climb over!' Grace said, horrified, scanning the wrought-iron gate that was at least ten foot high as she tried to ignore the rivulet of sweat that was snaking a path all the way down her back. She felt panicky all of a sudden, even though she was absolutely desperate to see inside Connie's gorgeous villa. But what if they got caught? What if the police arrived and they were carted off to an Italian jail? She knew Jamie had said for to live her best life, be more adventurous and all that, but getting herself arrested in a foreign country was surely a step too far. It was insane.

'Why don't we just come back later and see if there is somebody in then?' she proposed. 'Or we could look for other houses nearby . . . stick to the plan to talk to the neighbours. That's what we said.'

'But there aren't any neighbours, Grace. We've

trekked for half a day and Connie's villa is the only one for miles around. Giovanni di Donato certainly was a recluse! We don't have to go inside . . . I'm not suggesting we actually break in,' he grinned mischievously, scooping Gypsy up into his arms.

'Well, that's good,' she replied, looking all around in a desperate attempt to see if anyone was coming to catch them. The CCTV camera could be linked to the nearest police station for all they knew, and the *carabinieri* could be on their way. *Oh God. Why does he have to be so presumptuous and forward?*

Grace was racking her brains trying to decide what to do, looking at Ellis's pleading, puppy-like toffee-brown eyes and adorable but wholly inappropriate grin, when she heard a sound on the path behind her. Footsteps. Running. A man's voice yelling something in Italian, and then:

'Hey. What's going on?' the voice added in perfect English with a hint of an Italian accent. Grace swivelled around to see a tall, dark and extremely good-looking man running towards her with an attractive woman wearing a floaty kaftan over a leopard-print swimsuit dashing along after him.

'Tom. Be careful,' the woman yelled, pushing her shoulder-length brunette bobbed hair behind her ears. 'They might be armed.'

'Georgie, stay back. I'll deal with this,' the guy said urgently, pushing the sleeves of his crisp white shirt up, as if contemplating a dual or something. With his black curly hair, model looks and passionate aura, Grace thought he looked like a young Gregory Peck, or Elvis or Cary Grant, or a combination of all the sexy Hollywood heartthrobs that she enjoyed admiring in her favourite films.

'But he's got hold of Gypsy,' the woman stated, striding right up to the gate and elbowing Tom out of the way, then turning to Ellis she pushed up her shades, looked him directly in the eyes and said, 'Do you speak English?'

'Sure do, ma'am,' Ellis said casually, giving Gypsy another stroke and making Grace gulp. People were passionate about pets and so she wished Ellis would just put the cat back down on the ground, because who knew what this woman was going to do if he didn't. She looked fierce, with her hands planted firmly on her hips, blue eyes blazing and her nostrils flaring, and Grace secretly felt a little bit in awe of her fearless boldness.

'Good. Then step away from my cat right away, or I'll . . .' She paused as if deciding on the appropriate repercussion for Ellis if he didn't do as she'd instructed, 'I'll get over that gate and take her right off you and then you will be extremely sorry. What are you, American?' she demanded in a deadly voice.

'Yep,' Ellis replied, his face a mixture of apprehension and amusement.

'Well, I can tell you that I have stood up to far bigger Americans than you before,' she started, pointing a pretty sparkly gold-painted fingertip in Ellis's direction. Grace surreptitiously inspected her own raggedy nails and made a mental note to venture to a salon some time soon as part of her rejuvenation plan. 'Oh yes, a ginormous pretend cowboy at JFK airport! And he had a clenched fist this close to my face too!' And she lifted a balled hand up to her own face to demonstrate the proximity. 'After I messed up all his travel documents.'

'Georgie, I don't think we nee—' the guy called Tom started, but the woman carried on with,

'And a Russian businessman. I escaped from his car after he tried to seduce me with some massaging seat contraption and, you know, it turned out that he was an illegal arms supplier to the Bratva – that's the Russian mafia in case you didn't know. So, come on . . . step away from my cat. Pass her through the railings right now.' And the woman pushed her arms out towards Ellis.

Grace held her breath, hoping Ellis would oblige as she could see out of the corner of her eye that the gorgeous-looking guy was shaking his head, but she couldn't be sure if he was bemused by the way the woman was handling things, or if he was sizing Ellis up to give him a punch in the face if needs be.

'Ellis, please. Hand the cat over,' Grace said, then turned to the woman and added, 'I'm really sorry, we didn't mean any harm. We came here hoping to find someone who might have known, um . . . err, a friend of ours. She used to live here in this villa—'

'It's true,' Ellis chipped in, 'and then we spotted Gypsy,' he gave the cat a farewell stroke before handing her over, 'with her little paw caught in a rut in the path – she's fine,' he hastily added, on seeing the woman's face crease in concern. 'But I thought it best to hop over the gate and help her, just in case,' he finished, not daring to meet Grace's gaze as she lifted her eyebrows in shock at his blatant untruth.

'Then, we must thank you for helping,' the man stepped forward and put out his hand, which Ellis shook politely. 'My wife adores Gypsy and when we saw you on the security camera with her in your arms . . . well, you can imagine how it looked.'

'Yes, I can. I'm so sorry,' Ellis said, having got himself back over the gate and onto the path in record time.

'I thought you were trying to steal her,' the woman called Georgie grinned, and then quickly followed with, 'sorry if I got a bit carried away with telling you about my previous encounters and all that. Anyway . . .' she turned to Grace, 'tell me more about your friend, what's her name? We might be able to help you out.'

'Oh, that would be great,' Grace said, surreptitiously wiping the sweat from her top lip.

'But it must have been a long time ago that your friend lived in the pink villa because my grandmother bought it back in the Nineties, more than twenty years ago,' Tom said.

'Ah,' Grace started, taking in this new information and wondering if it was then that Connie had returned to London to live in the flat in Blackheath. And if so, why? It must have been around the time when Giovanni died, but why didn't she stay here in their beautiful home with such a glorious view?

'Her name was Connie, or Constance di Donato. She lived here with her husband, Giovanni – he was an artist, and a recluse – he died over twenty years ago, we've been told,' Grace explained to them, rummaging in her handbag for the paper fan that she had bought last night from a little shop near the promenade.

'And we've since found out that he's an eminent artist. You see, I work for Sackville and Bush auctioneers in New York and we've auctioned some of his work,' Ellis said, 'and Grace.' He paused. 'Sorry, we didn't introduce ourselves properly, I'm Ellis and this is Grace . . .' He gestured to her. Tom and Georgie quickly shook hands with her and confirmed their names before Grace took over and explained more about Connie, and that they were trying to track down a living relative to inherit her estate and the contents of the wonderfully presented storage unit.

'Wow!' Georgie said. 'It's a proper mystery. How exciting.' And then turning to Tom she asked, 'Would your Nonna Maria be able to help? Maybe she knew Grace and Ellis's friend, or might remember something to help them find a relative.'

'I'm sure she will if she can. But she's very old and her memory is affected by the dementia,' Tom told them, and then explained, 'Maria is my grandmother, on my mother's side. I'm happy to ask her. Let's swap numbers and I can call you later,' and he put a hand in his jeans pocket to presumably pull out a mobile to type the number into, but it wasn't there. 'Do you have your phone with you, Georgie?' he asked, patting his back pockets to be sure.

'No, I've left it by the pool – it was all such a rush,' she said, giving Gypsy a kiss on the top of her head.

'And mine is flat!' Ellis said, sighing as he inspected the screen of his phone.

'I have mine,' Grace said, starting to rummage in her bag. 'Or we could come back another time if that's easier for you,' Grace offered, desperate to get in the shade now, figuring it must be at least 40 degrees and the fair, freckly skin on her arms was starting to burn, and she really wished she hadn't worn jeans and trainers for the hike up here. Georgie had the right idea in sparkly flip-flops, a swimsuit and kaftan, and Grace made a mental note to see if she could find something similar when they went to the shops in Portofino tomorrow.

'Look, instead of trying to do all this out here when it's absolutely roasting,' Georgie started, grinning at Grace, who smiled in agreement, 'why don't you come in with us now and we can exchange numbers in the shade of the terrace? And you're welcome to join us for a cold glass of homemade lemonade, if you have time?' She grinned kindly at Grace who could have given her a massive hug and a kiss right there, such was her relief at the thought of escaping the scorching sun.

'Are you sure?' Ellis asked, sheepishly, 'I mean, we were trespassing . . .'

'Err, you were,' Georgie teased, laughing, 'but technically, Grace wasn't. And so come along, darling, let's get out of this heat.' And she gently tucked Gypsy under one arm and looped her other through Grace's arm and led her towards a side gate as if they were best friends who had known each other for ever.

'You're *both* very welcome,' Tom smiled to Ellis. 'Come on,' and as they followed behind, Grace could hear Tom telling Ellis about an old school pal who had gone to work at Sackville and Bush auctioneers years ago and wondered if Ellis might know him, and soon they were chatting away as if they were old friends too.

*

Later, having swapped numbers, Grace was sitting on the edge of a magnificent infinity pool sipping delicious ice-cold lemonade as she dipped her toes in the refreshingly cool water. It turned out that Georgie and Tom and some of their friends were staying in the annexe in the grounds of the main powder pink villa, which was why the shutters were still closed up at the front. Apparently, Tom's Nonna Maria was reluctant to let them have free run of the pink villa as a pool party some years ago had got out of hand, with someone spilling red wine all over an exquisite oriental rug in the library that had come with the villa when they had purchased it.

Grace wondered if Connie had originally chosen the rug. She also felt disappointed that they weren't going to see inside the home that Connie and Giovanni had lived in, but it was wonderful to be in the garden, admiring the lush palm trees that were so tall they must have been just the same when Connie lived here.

Grace could imagine Connie pottering around the garden with a basket looped over her arm in which to gather sun-ripened figs from a huge tree situated in the sunniest spot. Or sitting on one of the many verandas, enjoying a cocktail as she gazed down at the blissful view and inhaled the delicious scent of oranges and lemons from the array of fruit trees. The scent of frangipani too lingered in the warm breeze. Grace glanced towards the far edge of the pool that – with its infinity effect giving on to the ocean beyond – made her feel as though she was on the top of the world.

Closing her eyes, she drifted the tips of her fingers in the cool water and imagined she was back in the 1950s with a handsome truelove mixing her a martini, just as Connie would have been. She then imagined Connie, Giovanni and little Lara here all together, blissfully happy away from the critical eye of Connie's controlling mother.

Then her thoughts floated on to the current day and she inwardly pinched herself at the surreal nature of the moment. The thrill of acting spontaneously, even if she had panicked when Ellis had climbed over the fence. With hindsight, she was pleased that he had, for otherwise she wouldn't be sitting by Connie's pool right now and enjoying the magnificent scenery all around her. And for one bizarrely strange moment she wondered if this was what Matthew and the Perky Yoga One's lives were like. Sunbathing by infinity pools in paradisiacal places.

Hmm, maybe it had been at the start, but then she remembered the last time she had looked at Matthew's Facebook page. It had been on that evening when she'd been at a low ebb after Cora had created such an almighty fuss about the spa trip. On Facebook, Matthew had been bemoaning the lack of sleep that came with having toddler twins, and how he was having to 'swerve the rugby boys' weekend away this year because of FAMILY COMMITMENTS' followed by the rolling eyes emoji, but he 'wouldn't have it any other way' . . . so perhaps not.

Maybe the grass wasn't greener on the other side after all . . . and she had spent all those lonely evenings stalking her ex-fiancé to see what she had perceived as being perfection, a gloriously happy life, when in reality it was all just an airbrushed façade. She could see it now. Or perhaps it was because right now, right here, she felt happy in herself and so the need to live vicariously, and with a degree of self-loathing and inadequacy, had vanished. She was content.

18

The next day, and Grace was feeling very fragile as she climbed inside the taxi that had arrived to take them to Portofino to visit the jeweller's. One look at Ellis and she could see that he felt the same way too, with his Ray-Ban shades firmly in place and a pale tinge to his usually tanned face. His dark brown curls were much messier than usual too.

They had ended up staying at the powder pink villa until late in the evening, having watched the stunning sunset over the Italian Riviera and eating al fresco on the veranda. An exquisite feast prepared by a local chef of ham and mozzarella Stromboli followed by scallop and pesto linguine, then marinated cherries with mascarpone and amaretto biscuits. Many bottles of locally sourced prosecco accompanied the meal, finished off with grappa shots so strong that Grace had gasped and pressed a hand to her chest on trying one. Ellis had been spared the grappa experience as his mobile had rung, having recharged on Tom's charger, and it had actually been Jennifer calling to talk to him. Grace had heard him say something to her about it being late here in Italy and that he'd catch up with her properly in the morning, but she must have been insistent as Ellis had wandered off to the far side of the pool for some privacy.

And then later, even through her own merry state, Grace remembered him being unusually monosyllabic in the taxi back to the hotel. Or maybe it was the hare-brained way the driver had chatted on in Italian without drawing breath and gesticulating animatedly as he tore around the hairpin bends in the road, boldly close to the cliff's edge. Grace recalled gripping the door handle so tightly that her knuckles had still been aching when she'd climbed into bed what felt like just a few hours ago. She pulled her own shades on and sipped some more water from a bottle in her hand.

'Sorry I'm late,' she said, seeing that it was almost ten past eleven on the clock on the dashboard and they had agreed to meet outside the hotel at 11 a.m. 'It took me longer than usual to galvanise myself into action.'

'No worries, Grace,' Ellis said, more formally than

usual, continuing to look out of the window and away from her. She pulled the seatbelt over her shoulder and wondered what was up with him. She hadn't seen him hungover before so maybe this was just his way, detached and quiet.

'Are you OK?' she checked.

'Sure. You?' he replied, folding his arms.

'Yes, just about. I'm not used to late nights or grappa shots, come to think of it. But I had a great time. Did you?' she tried again.

'Yes. A great time.' He didn't expand any more than that and stayed staring out of the window. Grace, not wanting anything to spoil their last whole day here, decided not to question him further, and so instead settled back in the worn leather seat and focused on admiring the view as the driver set off. She was grateful to be on the sea-view side of the car and stared, mesmerised, at the magnificence of the rugged, rocky shoreline as the taxi zipped along the costal road, imagining herself to be Audrey Hepburn in the Galaxy chocolate advert with 'Moon River' playing in the background. With the timeless, pastel-coloured houses coming into view and the lack of the commercial petrol stations, Costa coffee outlets and suchlike that were on every corner in

London, Grace was able to imagine being back in the Fifties and to experience the view just as Connie had done when she had travelled in the open-top car to Portofino and then on to San Fruttuoso, which she wrote so beautifully about in her diary.

On arriving in Portofino, Grace stepped out of the taxi and was delighted when the driver told them they weren't far from the main piazzetta square, just a short walk away in fact, and where the bustle of the shops and cafés were beside the water's edge.

'Shall we head to the harbour first?' Grace said, keen to see if she could find the spot where Connie had been standing in the photo that had fallen out of the back of her diary. The one where she couldn't be sure if Connie was feeling sad or shy.

Grace had scanned it and was now searching on her mobile to find it. 'Here it is.' She turned her screen towards Ellis.

'Cool. Let's do that and I can take a picture of you in the same spot,' he smiled, and Grace's spirits lifted on seeing that he seemed to have perked up. He had most likely just been feeling as fragile as she had in the taxi. She couldn't expect him to be upbeat for every second of the time they were here together. They were just two . . . She paused her thoughts to wonder what exactly they were, before settling on 'friends', then swiftly changing it to 'colleagues', after all, who had kind of been put together.

Moments later, and Grace was sure that she had found the same place where the black-and-white photo had been taken by the water's edge. To her left she could see the rows of tall, narrow houses, only in real life they were warm, earthy tones of sun-faded orange and yellow, pink and white. Colourful bunting buffeted between lampposts, giving the place a special carnival atmosphere, even though it was an ordinary day for the people lucky enough to live here. The cafés and shops below, with their awnings extended and paper lanterns swaying in the warm breeze, were exactly the same all these years later. And the domed building on the cliffside, which she now knew from Google was called Divo Martino church, was in the same spot, she could see, as she lifted her phone and placed the picture of the photo up in the air beside it. So it had to be where Connie had stood. And it was glorious and marvellous and thrilling to have time-travelled almost, back to when Connie, a woman in her twenties, had been here too. But the moment was tinged with sadness because Grace couldn't help wondering how Connie had gone from being here, surrounded by such beauty, to a sparse flat in London.

'It's awesome to think that Connie and Giovanni were right here,' Ellis said, lifting his shades to get a better look at the screen of Grace's phone. 'I reckon Connie was just about there . . .' He pointed to a spot in front of them.

'I think so too,' Grace beamed, her heart lifting on taking it all in, and determined to savour the experience of being here instead of dwelling on Connie's eventual fate.

'OK. Strike a pose and I'll take a picture,' he said, taking her phone from her hands. Grace had just tidied her hair and straightened her sundress when an older man wearing a black cap came along and said something in Italian to Ellis, motioning with his hands for Ellis to move next to her, presumably so he could be in the picture too. Ellis responded in Italian but the man was insistent, saying,

'Show her you love her,' in heavily accented English, and literally took Ellis by the arm and placed him next to Grace. 'Bellissime,' he declared, touching his fingertips to his lips in a kiss before majestically lifting the now open hand up to the air. Only, he still wasn't satisfied, and motioned for Ellis to place his arm around Grace.

'Do you mind? If only to make an old man happy,' Ellis whispered out of the side of his mouth, treating her to a big burst of his citrusy scent as he moved in close.

'Of course not,' Grace replied, through a smile, and as Ellis put his arm around her and gently cupped her shoulder, she secretly allowed herself a moment to believe she was here with him as more than a colleague, or indeed a friend, because her whole body was tingling from the close proximity of his touch. It was unlike anything she had ever felt before, yet it made no sense, as her head knew that he was with Jennifer, but her body clearly hadn't cottoned on. And she most definitely wasn't mistaken in sensing that he felt it too, as he was drawing her in even closer now as she instinctively lifted her arm and let it move around his firm back. She could feel his taut abdominal muscles under her fingertips as they curled around his body.

After a scrumptious seafood-topped pizza and a restorative glass of red wine in one of the harbour cafés, they had found the jeweller's and pressed the buzzer to be allowed in.

'They must have some very expensive diamonds in here,' Grace said, as an extremely glamorous Italian woman with long, glossy black hair and wearing a beautifully cut cream trouser suit came sashaying towards the door.

'*Ciao, per favore entra,*' she smiled, standing aside to let them in. They stepped inside and she closed and locked the door behind them.

And then it hit Grace.

The perfume.

The woman was wearing Van Cleef and Arpels, one of the perfumes from that day when Grace had been shopping in Selfridges with Matthew, the day he'd proposed to her over lunch. She stopped walking.

'Are you OK?' Ellis asked softly, placing his hand on her arm. 'You look dazed.'

Grace took a moment, as if to check her feelings, and then on realising that she felt absolutely OK, she nodded and grinned.

'Yes, I am, thanks. Just a few seconds of déjà vu,' she told him, swiftly adding, 'but I'm over it now.' And she really was. As if by magic in the moment, she felt nothing. Maybe a fondness for the memory of that day, but not the aching, crippling yearning that she had felt for months on end whenever she had taunted herself in the early hours of the morning by deliberately letting her mind go back there. She smiled and pushed her hair back over her shoulders and followed the woman towards the glass counter that was crammed full of beautifully dazzling diamonds.

After explaining in Italian the reason for their visit today, Ellis pulled out his wallet, removed one of his business cards and placed it on the counter.

'*Un momento*,' she said, picking up the card and disappearing behind a red velvet curtain.

Moments later, an older man appeared and gestured for them to come through to a small room behind the velvet curtain and then asked them to take a seat at the table in the centre of the room.

Grace glanced at Ellis to gauge his reaction, and on seeing that he appeared quite relaxed, she went along with it too.

'Thank you for coming to visit us,' the man said in heavily accented English after they had all introduced themselves, Marco being the son of the original jeweller who had opened the shop back in 1923. 'Your colleague explained in the telephone call from America that you wish to talk about a number of commissions from a long time ago.'

'Yes, that's right,' Ellis confirmed, and pulled out his phone with all the pictures of Connie's jewellery on. 'Fortunately, Grace found the collection in an abandoned storage unit in London.' Marco shook his head and sighed before taking the phone and swiping through the pictures.

'It is very sad to see these pieces hidden away like this. Such beauty and craftsmanship. I remember my father making this ring, here. I was just a child when it was made, it would have been in the Fifties some time,' and he tapped the screen and turned it to show Grace and then Ellis, 'with the finest diamonds sourced from a dealer in Naples. Giovanni was very discerning and it was our honour to serve him right up until he died.'

Grace's heart was crushed on having this news

271

confirmed. She knew it was the most likely outcome, but still . . . it felt like a blow. An avenue closed.

'May I ask when he died?' Ellis said solemnly, glancing in her direction.

'Ah, it was a long time ago. Some time in the Nineties. Sorry, I don't remember exactly when. But his wife, Connie, she very sad when they took his body away.'

'Took him away?'

'Yes, he go back to America on an aeroplane. But she say he love Italia. His family, his brothers they no listen to her and bury him there.'

'Oh no, that's so sad,' Grace said, thinking how awful it must have been for Connie to have her husband taken away from her and buried thousands of miles away. Her heart must have been broken all over again to not even have his grave to visit. It would have been the same with Jimmy. Nowhere for Connie to go to talk to her trueloves, to mourn their loss.

'It very sad,' Marco said quietly. 'This brooch here was the last piece we made for him.' And he tapped the screen.

'I remember seeing it in the jewellery box,' Grace murmured, wondering why Connie hadn't kept it with her, if only as a keepsake to remind her of

Giovanni. Why had she stored it away? It's as if she'd packed up her whole life when he died. Sold the villa – hadn't Tom said his grandmother had bought the pink villa in the Nineties? Grace guessed that this must have been after Giovanni died. Maybe Connie just couldn't bear the thought of living in it without him. And Grace swallowed hard as she tried to stifle the surge of emotion within her, her own heart aching for the sadness and loss that Connie, the woman she shared a birthday with, had endured in her lifetime.

'Where is the collection now?' Marco asked, scrolling some more.

'In the safe at Cohen's,' she assured him, then added, 'That's the storage company where I work.'

'Good, because the whole collection, it worth lots of money. Near a million pounds,' Marco told them, and Grace caught her breath as she instinctively went into her handbag to find her phone.

'I had better call Larry and make doubly sure he is locking the safe at all times. You know how he is for leaving it open when he's topping up the petty cash tin,' she breathed, panic swirling within her in case something happened to Connie's jewels.

'Ha, yes I do. But let's break the news to him when we leave here,' Ellis suggested, calmly. 'Uncle Larry is bound to hyperventilate again as soon as he knows the jewels are worth a million pounds.'

'I'm guessing then when your friend phoned Larry, he didn't give him an exact figure . . . as in pounds – a million of them, to be precise,' Grace pointed out.

'Obviously not.' Ellis pulled a face. 'But that's my fault as I asked him not to panic Uncle Larry . . . I'll call the London bank where the paintings are stored and make arrangements for the jewels to be taken there too. That way Uncle Larry will only have a few hours or so of being responsible for the jewels before the couriers arrive to collect them.'

'Good idea,' said Grace, her mind still boggling. A million pounds. That was even more than the paintings were worth. Maybe they should call Betty first and let her explain gently to Larry. But then the jewels had been perfectly secure in unit 28 for all these years so no need to panic them just yet, another half an hour or so would be fine. But then, what on earth was Connie thinking, leaving them in the unit with just an ordinary padlock on the door? And without a will to pass them on to anyone? And yet again, as she had done a hundred times or so since opening unit 28, Grace tried to work it all out. Why would Connie do such a thing? Why did she return to London? And why didn't she sell some of her vast material wealth to make her end of life a little more comfortable? Would she really have had no idea of the value of all the items in unit 28? Surely, she must have done, if she had been with Giovanni to choose the jewels. Or maybe not. Maybe she genuinely had no idea . . . Grace wasn't sure, but she was going to have a very good go at finding out. There had to be more to it. And there had to be a living relative somewhere . . .

She turned her attention back to Marco, who was still scrolling through the pictures and making comments about each of the items that he remembered. When he paused, she asked,

'Marco, can you tell me about Connie, please? Do you remember her? Did she ever accompany Giovanni when he came to buy the jewels for Connie?'

'Oh, yes. I remember her well because she was the English lady. So very glamorous and so beautiful,' he said. 'Fresh white skin and dots, how do you say in English? Brown dots on her arms? Like you have.' He pointed at Grace.

'Freckles?' she smiled, intrigued on hearing this snippet of personal detail about Connie.

'Yes, like an English rose, is how you say, yes?'

275

Marco checked, and Grace nodded. 'And so happy. Always smiling when she came to the shop. But then every lady is happy when they come here with their husband to buy a new ring. Or a necklace or a brooch, yes?' he laughed. 'But she tell him off too. She say he must not spoil her. Connie was a very gracious lady.' So Grace had her answer . . . Connie definitely knew the value of the jewels in the leather case that she had carefully placed on the vintage dressing table.

'Do you remember Connie's daughter too, by any chance?' Grace ventured, remembering the words in the diary on VE Day. Connie's plan was to be reunited with Lara as soon as she and Giovanni were married, so if that had happened then surely she would have lived with them here in Italy. Grace figured Connie and Giovanni might have brought Lara to the shop too, perhaps to choose a birthday present, something special when she turned sixteen or twenty-one.

'Her daughter?' Marco repeated, looking uncertain as his forehead creased. 'No, I never see them with a girl.' Silence followed as he seemed deep in thought for a while before adding, 'Please, hold on,' and handed Ellis's phone back to him, stood up and said, 'I'll be back.'

A few seconds later, and Marco returned with a thick, dusty old ledger and started riffling through the pages.

'I never see a daughter here in Italy but they did buy a necklace for a child. I remember, because my father . . . he never make one like it before,' he said, enthusiastically, his Italian accent getting stronger.

'Really?' Grace held her breath as she leaned forward to the ledger as if this somehow brought her closer to Connie and to finding out the truth.

'Ah, yes. I have it here,' he tapped the page. 'A white gold Star of David, diamond tips on each of the star's six points,' he read aloud.

'I remember it!' Grace said, excitedly. 'Yes, I saw a necklace with a Star of David pendant in the leather jewellery box. Is there a picture of it on your phone, Ellis?'

They all looked at the phone as Ellis checked.

'Yes, here we go.' And he placed the phone on the table so they could all see the screen.

'Yes, that's the one,' Marco confirmed. 'See here, it matches the description. It was commissioned in 1952.'

'So it was the same year as the black-and-white picture was taken of Connie by the harbour,' Grace pointed out to Ellis, 'and if Lara was born in 1940, then she would have turned twelve in 1952.'

'Yes, the necklace was a gift to celebrate a girl's bat mitzvah,' Marco said. 'I remember it very well as my father had to work fast through the night to finish making the pendant so Connie and Giovanni could take it with them on the boat to America.'

'*America?*' Grace was flabbergasted. She swivelled in her seat to look at Ellis.

'Why would they go to America in 1952?' he asked, creasing his forehead and shaking his head.

'Because Giovanni was American? A GI, remember? American Italian,' she said quickly, her mind racing with trying to work it all out. 'To visit his family there . . . maybe. It's the most obvious reason.'

'True. But back then it would have been considered a very long way to sail for just a family visit. My guess is that the journey would have had to have been for a very important reason. And why the rush to have the necklace ready to take with them? If the necklace was indeed for Lara, and the timings work for it to be her bat mitzvah, traditionally held for Jewish girls when they reach the age of twelve; but surely Lara would have been living here with them in Italy? And if she wasn't, then what was she doing in America without Connie, her mother? How did she get there? And why? And . . .' Ellis paused, holding eye contact with Grace, who couldn't wait to hear if he was thinking the same as her, and so blurted out,

'What if she's still there?' in unison with him.

20

After leaving the jeweller's and wandering around picturesque Portofino, exploring the narrow cobbled streets crammed with stylish boutiques, Grace had bought gifts for Larry, Betty and Jamie, before they had climbed the steep path up to Castello Brown on the hill. From there they had meandered along the botanical footpath, sheltered from the sun by trellises covered in delicately scented pink roses, while Grace wondered if Connie had ever walked this path too. Then, remembering the dried pink rose petals inside the envelope in the hatbox with *Glorious day, Portofino – 1955* written on the outside, Grace was certain Connie had. So she carefully picked up some petals from the ground to have as a keepsake of a wonderful experience too. Inhaling the scent and hoping to remember it always before it faded just like Connie's petals had.

Walking on, they were surrounded by olive trees,

giving glimpses of the gorgeous gardens belonging to the villas nestled high in the hills. They had sat in stunned silence on reaching the lighthouse, and savoured the view stretching along the breadth of the Italian Riviera – from Punta Manara near Sestri Levante to Capo Noli beyond Genoa – as a man on the next table had pointed out to them while they enjoyed tall glasses of San Pellegrino on the terrace café under the shade of the olive trees.

Now, heading back to the main square, Ellis's mobile rang.

'Hi Tom,' he answered, and then after a quick 'yes, that's great, thanks, we'll see you there in ten' conversation, he ended the call and turned to Grace. 'Tom and Georgie are bringing Nonna Maria to the gelato café in the piazzetta. Apparently, the peach ice cream is her favourite and she remembers Connie and Giovanni very well. Connie was her friend and that's the reason she bought the pink villa. Even though her memory is fading, she was able to tell him all about Connie in very vivid detail right back to when she first arrived in Santa Margherita.'

'Oh, that's fantastic,' Grace said, excitement bubbling inside her. At last, she was going to find out about the real Connie from someone who actually knew her.

*

Nonna Maria didn't look like a traditional Italian granny. And certainly not like the image Grace had held in her head since first hearing about her. Dressed head to toe in expensive-looking designer clothes, topped off with a jaunty Gucci logo silk scarf at her neck, lacquered jet-black big hair and enormous Versace shades, Nonna Maria was the epitome of glamorous chic from a golden era. She had an ageless face, which had clearly had many aesthetic treatments, giving her a near flawless complexion and tautness befitting a much younger woman. On the seat beside her was a soft tan leather tote nestling next to a white bichon frise sitting on a little fluffy cushion.

'Hi Grace, Ellis,' Georgie said, standing up to give them each a kiss on the cheek when they arrived.

'Good to see you again,' Tom smiled as he introduced them, in Italian, to Nonna Maria and then asked in English if they'd like some gelato. 'It really is the best you'll ever taste,' he said persuasively, handing them each a menu.

'Get the peach cup. Two scoops; they make it from peaches picked on the mountainside,' Nonna Maria instructed in English, with a very breathy but regal-sounding Italian accent, as she reached a bony, diamond-jewelled hand out to clasp Grace's forearm.

'Oh, um . . . yes please. I'll go for the peach cup in that case.' She grinned up at Tom as she settled into a seat, not daring to disagree with the formidable-looking Nonna Maria.

'Same for me too, please,' Ellis nodded, taking the chair beside her.

'I'll organise the ice cream and leave you all to chat,' Georgie offered, then dashed off inside the café.

'So you want to know about Connie?' Nonna Maria said, getting straight to the point.

'Yes please,' Grace replied, finding her phone inside her bag so she could make some notes.

'Put that away,' Nonna Maria ordered with such directness it made Grace's face flush; she did as she was told to right away. Out of the corner of her eye, she saw Ellis, who was sitting on her left, surreptitiously slip his phone back inside his pocket to avoid a telling off too. 'You young people with your phones stuck in your hands. No wonder the passion has gone from your lives. No wonder the beauty . . . you don't see it. Pah,' and Nonna Maria batted her hand in the air before giving her dog a reassuring pat on the head. 'And no wonder you ruin my special rugs with your bacchanalian parties.' And she gave Tom a withering look. 'My dear friend, Connie's rug, I should add. She chose it from a shop in Rome. Handmade. And your friends . . . they come and vandalise it.' And Grace held her breath, poised to hear more about Connie.

'Nonna, it was an accident,' Tom soothed, pulling up a chair close to his grandmother. 'And we've been over this many times – plus the rug is spotless now that it has been expertly cleaned.'

'Nothing is ever an accident,' she said slowly, lifting a shot glass to her crimson-coated lips containing a liquid (which looked very much like the grappa that Grace had struggled with at the pool party) and chugged it in one without so much as a flinch. Grace widened her eyes in awe. Nonna Maria was certainly some woman, and Grace hoped she had even half her panache when she reached old age.

'Nonna, please tell us about Connie,' Tom said to move Maria on from her angst over the rug.

'Who?' And she gave them all a blank stare. Grace smiled to stifle a sigh of disappointment.

'Your friend,' Tom prompted. 'Connie and her husband, Giovanni.'

'I have a picture, if that would help. But it's on my phone.' And Grace tentatively put a hand back inside her bag in the hope that Nonna Maria would agree to seeing it to help her fading memory return.

'Let me look.' Nonna Maria seemed to have no issue with the phone now. 'Ah, darling Connie. That's my friend. The English lady. Everyone knew her when she came to live in Santa Margherita. And they all want to be her friend. The new bride with a dashing American husband. A golden couple. The best socialites. You know . . .' she paused to clasp Grace's arm again, 'they threw the best parties on board Gio's yacht. Cocktails and caviar. And dancing. He was a marvellous raconteur and Connie with her fine English manners and gentle warmth . . . well, we all glowed in their company. Superb.'

'Ooh, how wonderful that you were at the parties. I've read about them in Connie's diary,' Grace told her.

'Does she mention me?' Nonna Maria swiftly asked, 'they used to call me, Cristal.'

'Yes, she did!' Grace suddenly remembered. 'She wrote about her new friend . . . a beautiful, vivacious Italian woman called Cristal.'

'Ah, that's Connie, always with a compliment. But where did she go?' Nonna Maria said vaguely, gently tracing an index finger over the screen. Silence followed. Grace wasn't sure if this meant that Nonna Maria didn't know her friend had died. She could feel them all looking at her.

'I'm very sorry . . . she . . .' Grace started, but faltered on seeing Tom quickly shake his head.

'Nonna, you told me she went to London, remember?' Tom intervened, and Grace inwardly sighed with relief, for it was true: Connie had gone to London . . . when she'd left Italy. Maybe Nonna Maria didn't need to know that her friend had since moved on to a permanent place of rest.

'Ah, yes. When Gio died,' Nonna Maria sighed. 'Such a handsome, charismatic man, so young at heart and so full of life. Practically a boy, but the heart, it stopped beating. Just like that!' she tutted, clicking her fingers dramatically. 'But he adored Connie . . . until those bastards took him from her.'

'What do you mean, Nonna? Who took him?' Tom prompted tactfully, as Nonna Maria pulled a packet of long, thin cigarettes from her bag and lit one up. After tilting her head, she puffed a regal smoke ring up into the air, turned to Grace and told her.

'When Gio died, his relatives couldn't wait to drag his body back to the family plot in their private cemetery in America. Connie had no say in the matter and I tried to get her to fight but she was far too broken with the grief. They had worn her down. They never liked her.' Nonna Maria pulled a face of disgust.

'Why was that?' Ellis said.

'Where is your ice cream?' Nonna Maria replied, tapping the table in front of Grace. 'Get the girl her ice cream,' she added, just as Georgie returned carrying two cups and spoons.

'Sorry about the wait.' Georgie grinned amiably, before sitting down next to Nonna Maria. 'It's crammed in there, but so worth it . . . wait till you try this gelato.' And she placed a cup in front of Grace that contained a gloriously peach-fragranced swirl of creamy loveliness.

'Thank you,' Grace said, unable to resist scooping a spoonful into her mouth right away. The taste was sensational, of fresh, juicy peaches with a hint of warm cinnamon and vanilla, reminiscent of a peach cobbler with custard. Grace could see why it was Nonna Maria's favourite. Hers too now.

'You're a good girl, *tesoro mio*,' Nonna Maria said to Georgie, 'and you are my favourite,' before shooting another look in Tom's direction. He just shrugged and smiled, as if he was used to being continually chastised by his grandmother and took it all in his stride. 'Take your pick of my rugs when I die! And don't let the vultures beat you to it.' And then Grace realised that Nonna Maria was actually tipsy; she was slurring her words and almost toppling over in her seat . . . and she didn't give a damn.

'Oh, Nonna, come on, less of that talk. I don't want your rugs, not when I'd rather have you.' And Georgie patted Nonna Maria's arm affectionately.

'Nonna, you were talking about Gio.' Tom surreptitiously smiled at Grace as if to telepathically tell her they'd be here all day at this rate . . .

'Yes. They took him away from Connie. To punish her.'

'Why?' Tom said.

'Because Connie was a Jew and they were Catholics. But worse than that . . . she was the mother of a bastard child born out of wedlock. When Gio fell in love with Connie, his father, of the wealthy Donato dynasty, was running for office, to be a US senator, and the scandal of his son marrying a Jew with an illegitimate child would ruin his chances. This was the Forties. Everything was different then,' she clarified, shaking her head. 'Not like today when a woman can go to a clinic to pick a father for her baby and we are all happy for her.

A baby is always a gift!' she declared passionately, before leaving them all to ponder on this thought while she took a long drag of her cigarette and exhaled another smoke ring away from the table and up into the air above her head. 'That's why they come here, to Italia. Gio was banished with his new bride. And because he was an artist. Not a lawyer like his father wanted him to be. The pink villa was the sweetener, somewhere to hide them away like a dirty family secret.'

'Sweetener?' Grace ventured, feeling intimidated, but in awe too of Nonna Maria.

'A wedding present, his father said, but I knew it was a bribe. Connie adored the pink villa and made it into an exquisite home, landscaping the gardens and filling the villa with the finest furnishings, full of beauty, style and class, much like the lady herself. That's why I bought it when they forced her to sell it – something in the deeds, they said, a stipulation, that the family home was only hers to live in while she was married to a Donato. Nonsense! But like I said, Connie had no fight left in her by then. Or money to pay lawyers to fight the wealthy Donato family. She had no money or assets of her own, just the gifts from Gio. She lived on in the villa for a while but it was never the same . . . not without her darling Gio, and with only the memories of happier times to haunt her.'

Grace sat silently for a moment, trying to imagine the unbearable pain and hurt this must have caused Connie, to not only be cast aside by her own parents at such a young age, but then by her husband's parents too. Banished in shame to a village called Tindledale when she was only seventeen years old, pregnant and alone and grieving for Jimmy, and then later banished to Italy so as not to shame the US senator of the wealthy Donato dynasty.

'Oh poor Connie,' Grace said quietly. 'The more I find out about her life, the more my heart breaks for her. It was all so unfair.'

'But you must not upset yourself, young lady. Connie wasn't one for pity,' Nonna Maria said. 'No, she was stoic and always conducted herself with class and decorum. Not like us Italians with our fiery passion,' and she did a deep, throaty laugh.

'Did you know anything about Connie's parents, or her child, Lara?' Grace ventured, desperate to know anything at all more about Connie's family, as it seemed they were running out of options to find a living relative, but Nonna Maria responded blankly.

'Who?' she said, the light seeming to have faded in her eyes.

'Connie's baby, she was called Lara,' Ellis tried, but it didn't help.

'She was taken too. Everyone Connie loved was taken from her,' was all Nonna Maria added.

'Who took her, Nonna?' Tom tried as well, but she carried on talking about Connie and Gio, leaving Grace to wonder if this meant that Lara never did come to Italy with Connie. Or did Nonna Maria mean that Lara had died too? But it still didn't explain why Connie went to America with the necklace for a child and then presumably brought it back, only for it to be found in the jewellery box decades later? And from what Nonna Maria had managed to tell them about Giovanni's family, it seemed highly unlikely that Connie would have been visiting them, let alone taking a Star of David necklace for another young girl's bat mitzvah, when his family were Catholics and so opposed to Connie. So it must have been for Lara: who else could have it been for?

'I don't know,' Nonna Maria said, bringing Grace back to the moment. 'Connie didn't have a baby when she came to Italia.' Ah, so Grace's suspicion was correct . . . Connie wasn't allowed to bring her child. But how could her parents have prevented it? Connie would have been an adult by then. A married woman, too. Unless . . . and an awful, devastating chill ran right through Grace as she considered another possibility . . . did Lara die in the war? Is that why she didn't come to Italy? Did Connie take her back to London before the war ended, when she was still a young child? Is that what Nonna Maria meant?

But this couldn't be right, as Connie had been full of joy on VE Day at the end of the war, dancing and planning her future with Giovanni . . . and Lara. They were to be a family, together. So what had changed all that? Grace just couldn't work it all out and vowed to speed-read through the rest of the papers from Connie's unit that she had stored on her laptop. She had read most of the diary pages and ad hoc notes, but they had tailed off in the early Fifties, with just the odd words here and there on each page from then on – *Glorious day. Sad. The warm sun lifts my spirit. Marvellous trip out. Party on the yacht*, that kind of thing. Very bland compared to Connie's emotionally descriptive earlier entries, and no mention of Lara, which in itself was very ominous . . . but people didn't just disappear, Lara had to be somewhere, and Grace wasn't about to give up now. Giovanni's family behaving the way they had towards Connie just made Grace more determined to put right the wrongs that had been meted out to her.

21

Back at the hotel, and Grace opened her laptop as Ellis talked to Larry to explain that Connie's jewels would be collected tonight, having made all the necessary arrangements with the bank. They were sitting at the table on the little balcony over-looking the seafront, the warm, evening sun bathing the palm trees in a glittery, golden sheen.

'I'll get some wine and snacks,' Ellis said, having finished the call, but before Grace could respond, he had jumped up from the table and darted back through the green shuttered doors to his bedroom. She wondered what the rush was . . . it was as if he couldn't wait to get away from her. And he had been very quiet on the bus back from Portofino, staring blankly out of the window for the twenty-minute journey along the rugged costal road to right outside the hotel. Then striding ahead, barely waiting for her to catch up as he entered the lift.

Why was he being so distant? They had stood in the lift together and Ellis had barely said two words to her – mostly 'sure', 'great' and 'yes' or 'no' to her chitchat about how nice, if bittersweet, it had been to get an insight into Connie's life from people who actually knew her when she was young and vibrant. And how they had promised to keep in touch with Georgie and Tom, who were also returning to England soon. She could hear Ellis talking on the phone again now, the sound of his voice drifting through the partially open balcony door to his bedroom.

'Jennifer, hey, babe, I'll be back tomorrow . . . yes, I can't wait to see you too.' And, unashamedly, Grace leaned across in her seat towards his bedroom door in a bid to hear more. But Ellis must have moved away from the door or indeed gone to get wine and snacks now, as all she could hear was the sound of the cicadas in the foliage below the balcony, mingled with the waves rippling over the pebbles from the beach across the road.

Grace returned her attention to the keyboard on her laptop and opened a folder titled 'Connie's Contents'. Scrolling through, she discounted all the diary pages that she had already read and moved on to the miscellaneous letters and papers folder to see if there was anything more left to read that she might have missed. *Ah, here we go . . .* She clicked on a photo and saw that it was dated March 1946, so after the war had ended and after Connie and Giovanni had married. The writing in the photo was like a diary entry but had rip marks down one side of the paper, as if it had been torn from the actual diary for that year. She slipped off her sandals, tucked her legs up underneath her and started reading.

Today is the day I will become a mother. A proper mother to my darling daughter, Lara. Giovanni is driving me to Tindledale to bring her home to London and then on to Italy with us when we sail next week. It's all arranged with Mother and Father after I wrote to them soon after my last visit to see Lara, setting out my wishes to have her with me all the time. I've missed her so much these last two months without a visit, but it couldn't be helped as Mother wrote back explaining that Lara was terribly unwell with measles and so it would be prudent of me not to visit in my condition. With the pregnancy so recently confirmed by the doctor in Harley Street, Giovanni agreed too that it would be wise to wait until Lara's health is restored.

Ah, Grace felt her heart lift on knowing that Connie was pregnant for a second time, but then immediately wondered where that child was now. She found a pad and made some notes.

Another child.

Born some time in late 1946.

Grace read on, keen to see if she could find a name for the second child. But then, hold on, her heart sank all over again, for surely Nonna Maria would have mentioned Connie having a child born in Italy soon after she arrived here. Instead she had specifically said, 'Connie didn't have a baby when she came to Italia' and 'a baby is always a gift'; that's what Nonna Maria had said, and so Grace felt almost certain that the pregnancy hadn't succeeded. It seemed most likely, as there was no mention of another child in any of the diaries. *Oh Connie, how did you endure such heartbreak after all that you had already been through?*

Grace read on.

I feel so happy and cannot wait to wrap my arms around my daughter and tell her she is coming home with her mummy. When I think of this moment soon to come, my heart fills with an abundance of love, for she is such a sunny, cheerful

little girl and one that her daddy would have been
so very proud of.

Grace smiled to herself, revelling in Connie's joy. But as she read on, Grace felt her body go numb, a feeling of fear trickling from the back of her neck, snaking a path around her shoulders and down her arms before settling in her throat as she held her breath . . .

She's gone. I can barely bring myself to write the words. Mother and Father have taken her from me. My darling, sweet girl, Lara, with her twinkling eyes and treacle-coloured curls has gone. When we got to the cottage there was no answer to my knock on the door; the house was shut up and so Giovanni went to the manor house across two fields at the other end of the country estate to find Father's friend. Lord Montague does important work for the Home Office and was rather terse when he arrived back at the cottage with Giovanni. But on seeing my distress, which was so terribly hard to hold in, he agreed to open the cottage door so that I could look inside for myself.

I tore through every room, checking inside cupboards, looking underneath and behind all the furniture like a wild woman, I even opened the door of the grandfather clock in the hallway, lifted lids off chinaware on the mantelpiece and thank heavens I did or I wouldn't have found Lara's tiny silver baby bangle. But I knew. As I frantically searched, I knew that it was pointless. Mother had taken my baby. The baby she never wanted me to have. The baby that she had brought up in the countryside and passed off as her own, as I later discovered from Lord Montague when he referred to my sister, little Lara. All that was left of my sweet, dear girl was the silver bangle, the pink teddy from her daddy, Jimmy, and the matinee set that I knitted for her, both forgotten in the airing cupboard on the landing. Of course, Lara is too big for baby clothes now, but I really can't help feeling it a cruel act by Mother and Father to leave behind the only things she has from her proper parents, Jimmy and me.

Hugging the little jacket, hat and bootees to my chest, I can still smell her beautiful baby scent and will treasure this for ever until I see my cherished Lara again. Dear Giovanni managed to persuade Lord Montague to spill the beans during a man-to-man discussion, on the proviso that I waited in the car, him not wanting to distress me further, and so I did, clutching the pink teddy that Jimmy had won at the fair.

Lord Montague told Giovanni that Mother and

Father have gone to take care of Aunt Rachael in Manhattan. America. They said it was their duty to assist Aunt Rachael as her health is ailing and the children of their society friends in Germany and Poland are relying on her to help them secure safe passage to America and so cannot be expected to endure further suffering, for they are orphans now. Persecuted by Hitler for being Jewish, they have already experienced unimaginable pain and horror in the death camps the Allies have liberated them from.

Lord Montague assured Giovanni that he had arranged everything so Mother, Father and Lara had all the necessary papers to sail in comfort aboard the Queen Mary from Southampton in February. Whilst I cannot begrudge Mother and Father going to the aid of Aunt Rachael and all those who have suffered and now have nothing, they have still stolen my dear daughter from me. For she has been gone already for a whole month, likely never having had the measles, and so on hearing this news I cried openly, howled even, without giving a damn if my distress unnerved Lord Montague.

Grace could bear it no longer and so closed her laptop and stifled a gasp. Pressing her hand over her mouth, overwhelmed at the surge of emotion she felt on reading of Connie's pain, she let tears trickle down her face and spill onto the table in front of her. How could they? How could Connie's parents be so cruel as to take her child away? The betrayal enraged Grace. The matter-of-fact way this pompous-sounding Lord Montague had ripped Connie's heart in two by telling her what he had done. For he did do it. He sent Lara away, whether it was unwittingly or not, he still did it. And so yet again, Connie was let down . . . no, much more than that, she was deceived by her spiteful, unfeeling parents who clearly had absolutely no regard for their daughter's feelings or wishes. Let alone those of her child, their grandchild.

How did this separation affect Lara? Did they even care? And did she even know that Connie was coming for her, to love and cherish her at the start of what could have been a wonderful life in Italy, surrounded by love and people who knew how to have fun and to laugh . . . not be stuck with a pair of puritanical control freaks thousands of miles away. For it wouldn't have been like it was now, with flights to America whenever the fancy took you. No, Connie would have been bereft, knowing that it might be years before she could see her only child again. And indeed it was so, because Grace was now convinced that Connie and Giovanni had gone to America to visit Lara, to give her the necklace for her bat mitzvah on her twelfth birthday. So if Lara was born in 1940 and was six years old in 1946, then it would have been another six years before Connie would see her. That's if she was even allowed to see Lara, but what if she wasn't? What if Connie's hateful parents had prevented her, and that's why she returned with the Star of David necklace and hid it away in her jewellery box . . . ?

'Why would you do it? Why would you be so cruel?' Grace whispered to herself as she made her way towards the edge of the balcony. With her elbows perched on the rail she let her body rest forward, cupping her face in her hands, her shoulders taut with sympathy as she imagined Connie's distress. Then, glancing up, she gazed at the turquoise sky and whispered a silent 'sorry' to Connie, before wiping her eyes and resolving to find Lara . . . no matter what it took. And then at least she could try to reverse some of the damage that Connie's parents had inflicted upon her. Grace would show Lara the diaries, the letters, the love her mother had for her, and pass on Connie's carefully stored possessions too, which she was now convinced were all waiting there for Lara to inherit. Connie had gathered everything she had of any value and kept it safe for her daughter to find. All that was left now was for Grace to find Lara. And then she said a silent prayer . . . *please let Lara still be alive.*

22

Grace swivelled around to see Ellis approaching from his bedroom, carrying a bottle of wine and a brown paper bag. 'Hey, what's up?' He dumped everything on the table and went to her. Through the tears which still filled her eyes, she could feel his arms folding around her and pulling her in close, instinctively comforting her. 'What's happened? Is it your mother? Has she done something to you?' he asked, the concern clearly palpable in his voice.

But Grace couldn't speak. She couldn't tell him because his kindness made her cry even more and she instinctively dipped her head into his chest. And they stood together in silence for what felt like forever. Until Ellis moved his hands on to Grace's shoulders and stood back just enough to see her face. After tilting her chin up so as to look straight into her eyes, he spoke in a soft voice, his toffee-coloured eyes searching hers, pleading to know why she was so distressed.

'Grace, darling, please tell me why you are crying?' he asked, gently dabbing his thumb on her cheek in an attempt to stem the tears. She opened her mouth, hesitated as another sob caught in her throat and then, as if on autopilot and in slow motion, her lips moved towards his. And he responded, sending a spark of pleasure to the very core of her, taking some of the anguish away. She could feel his fingertips stroking the side of her face, his other hand tangled in her copper curls. His tongue entwined with hers making her tingle all over with longing for him.

After what felt like an eternity of bliss mingled with a feeling of heartache for Grace, they pulled apart and Ellis rested his forehead on hers. More silence followed, except for the sound of the cicadas singing in time to the beat of her heart. The still-warm evening sun furled around her bare legs and arms, making the moment feel even more intense and sensual.

'Oh, Grace,' he said softly, just holding her until the tears stopped flowing. But then when they had, he lifted his hands away from her body and gently uttered, 'We can't do this . . .'

And suddenly Grace felt a surge of panic.

So intense.

She backed off and turned on her heel.

He reached out a hand to stop her.

She pushed it away and ran as fast as she could from the balcony and into her bedroom. Once there she ran into the en-suite bathroom and, after closing the door, she made sure it was locked. With both hands on the edge of the washbasin, she leaned forward and then glanced up at her reflection in the mirror as if searching her own face for the answer.

What had she done?

She pressed the tips of her fingernails hard into the skin on the palms of her hands as if to bring herself to her senses.

How could she?

But in the moment she had realised. She was falling in love with Ellis, wasn't she? She knew it for sure now. Maybe a teeny-tiny bit. As if the small amount that she could admit to somehow exonerated her. Because she couldn't bring herself to even consider if it was any more than that; her Catholic upbringing just wouldn't allow it. For she felt shameful even having such feelings or even thinking such thoughts – or were those Cora's critical words whizzing around inside her head? Tart. Home-wrecker. Slapper. That's what her mother would say. And, worse than that, she had kissed him. Initiated it. Kissed a man she had no right to kiss. What on earth was she thinking? She was no better than the Perky Yoga One. She let the thought linger for a while. And then something else came to her . . . Ellis did kiss her right back. Of that she was sure. So did that make him no better than Matthew? She certainly hadn't forced him to. He could have moved away from her. Made an excuse. Something. Or just downright rejected her and asked what the hell she thought she was doing. He was the one with the girlfriend, after all.

But deep down, Grace knew she was just procrastinating and there was no denying it. For it was true. She was falling for Ellis. Like properly falling for him. And she had been since the first moment she set eyes on him in the office back at Cohen's Convenient Storage Company. But how could she be? *He has a girlfriend and you're a fool. Don't be that woman, Grace. You are not a Perky Yoga One. So don't go there. Don't be the one who will get hurt all over again.*

Maybe she should go home now; surely there was a flight tonight? She should get far away from Ellis before she was tempted to kiss him again. They had enough to go on now to try to trace Lara, if she was still alive. Ships sailing to America had passenger lists, didn't they? Maggie would know for sure. Yes, good idea. Grace made a mental note to call Maggie first thing in the morning and ask how she could go about finding the names of all who had sailed on the *Queen Mary* from England to America in 1946. The heir-hunter people in America would find Lara, for sure. There was enough money at stake to make it worth their while. Aunt Rachael! Another clue right there. She had helped the Jewish people build new lives in America. Someone was bound to know of her, where she had lived in Manhattan. Grace could feel her body trembling as she raced through all the possible options. All they needed was a tangible clue, a pointer in the right direction, an address to get started with and then Ellis could find Lara when he returned to New York.

To his girlfriend.

Jennifer. Even her name had Hollywood star quality all over it. Just like Jennifer Aniston. Grace had met her once. Well, not met her, *exactly*, but she had been in the bathroom of a restaurant with Jennifer Aniston one time. It was years ago, when Grace and Jamie had been to see a West End show in London. *Chicago*. And after the show, they had gone for something to eat and Jennifer had been right there when Grace went to the loo. Looking gorgeous and golden, tiny and twinkling . . . there was just something quite magical about her. Proper star quality emanated from her. Jennifer had looked just like she did in the movies. Even washing her hands with an assistant standing close by, Jennifer had been gracious and said hello and smiled on catching Grace's eye in the mirror. Grace had tried to talk but had managed only to let her mouth sag open momentarily before hurriedly reuniting her jaw with the rest of her face as Jennifer had glided away. And that's exactly how Grace imagined Ellis's Jennifer to be like. Wondrous and beautiful. Not ordinary, with a sunburnt nose and a serious inferiority complex . . . that, let's face it, was not attractive at all.

So Grace turned on the tap and after cupping her hands together she made a little bowl of cold water to splash on her face and bring herself to her senses. This was the second time she had run out on Ellis and it was getting ridiculous. Especially after all the pep talks she had given herself about being so over Matthew. So over the anxiety and the step-counting. And she was. She really felt that she was. She felt different. Lighter and much more like her old self, the person she had been before Matthew . . . so why was she panicking now? Maybe Ellis did fancy her.

Or did he respond to her kiss because he was feeling sorry for her? Or did he respond because he could, and get away with it, just like Matthew had for all those months before she had found out about his dalliance? Maybe she should ask Ellis about Jennifer. Ask what he was playing at when he was about to get engaged. Yes, that's what she should do. But it wasn't as easy as all that.

A knock on the door.

Grace turned and with the sound of her own heartbeat drumming in her ears, she managed a wobbly, 'Yes?'

'Grace, are you OK?' Ellis asked softly.

Silence followed.

'Um . . .' she faltered, wondering what to say.

'Grace, please come out. I can't talk to you through a door.'

After counting to ten in her head, Grace rubbed her palms across her face to remove any last trace of tears, took a massive breath hoping to invoke a sense of calm and tentatively unlocked the bathroom door.

'I'm sorry,' she said quickly, keeping her head down so as to avoid his gaze.

'What for?' he asked, concerned.

'You know . . .' she started, flapping a hand

around and shrivelling a little inside. Surely he wasn't going to make her spell it out. 'For . . . well . . . what just happened,' she finished quickly. Oh God, she wanted to run right back into the bathroom. Instead she swallowed and got a grip. 'For kissing you. I'm very sorry and it will never, ever happen again. You have my word. And please tell Jennifer I was completely out of order. A moment of madness. That's all. She has absolutely nothing to worry about.' And she glanced up to see Ellis with his eyebrows dipped. 'Actually, on second thoughts, don't say anything to her. She doesn't need to know that an over-emotional English woman snogged her fiancé-to-be on a hotel balcony and liked it, a lot! No, it will only spoil the engagement for her.'

'*What?*' Ellis shook his head. 'What are you going on about? What I do is my own business. If I want to kiss a woman then I will. And I will like it. A *lot* too, if I want to,' he countered, his eyebrows dipping in the middle even more.

'But you can't say that,' she said.

'Why not?'

'Well, what about Jennifer for starters? Your girl-friend. Or have you forgotten about her?' Grace became conscious of her voice being far too loud and her left index finger whirling right in front of his face. She jerked her arm back down by her side and huffed out a long breath before folding her arms instead like a petulant teenager.

'Whoa.' Ellis held up his palms in defence. 'Hang on a minute. Let's just rewind things here.' He stared at her and Grace wasn't sure if he was cross, confused or amused as he shook his head as if to gain some clarity. 'What's going on here?'

'Why don't you tell me?' she said, sounding far more accusatory than she had intended.

'Jennifer isn't my girlfriend!'

'What?'

'Is that what you think? Is that why you ran off after kissing me?' He had his hands on his hips now.

'Well, yes . . . sort of.' Grace fidgeted, bobbing from one foot to the other wishing he wouldn't be so damn matter-of-fact about it all. Couldn't he see she was cringing on the inside? And what did he mean, Jennifer wasn't his girlfriend? She had heard her with her own ears on the phone, talking about the engagement.

'Sort of?' he laughed. 'What do you mean, sort of?'

'Well, technically you were the one who said to stop. Said we can't do this . . .' Grace said, trying to get her head around this revelation and wondering if he was telling her the truth. Maybe not. Maybe he was lying. Trying to wriggle his way out of what just happened between them. Well, she wasn't going to be duped . . .

'I only said we can't do this because you were crying, Grace. It wasn't right . . . I didn't want to take advantage when you were clearly vulnerable at that moment. I'm sorry if I made you feel rejected, but I didn't know why you were crying . . .'

'I was upset about Connie . . . you know her parents took Lara to America and didn't even tell her? I found a photo of a few stray pages and it was all there in black and white. Connie was so happy when she went to the village, Tindledale, expecting to collect Lara and bring her here to Italy, but the cottage was empty. Imagine that . . . your child, the person you love more than anything, just gone. Taken away from you. All the dreams and the future life you imagined together just snatched away . . . It's cruel and it's—'

'Life is cruel,' he said. 'But you know, I reckon Connie's parents thought they were doing the right thing. Protecting Connie and Lara. It was a long time ago and like Nonna Maria said, times were different then. There was a lot of stigma attached to illegitimate children and the mothers of illegitimate children in those days. It's wonderful that you feel so impassioned by Connie's story . . . well, it's not wonderful that it's upsetting you this much, that's not good at all, so maybe take a step back now? For your own sanity.' He nodded, his eyes full of concern.

'I know . . . I've got too close,' she agreed.

'Why is that? Have you had someone taken from you too? Is that it? Is that why Connie's story upset you like this?' he asked, straight to the point as always.

'Um . . . yes,' she said, 'my ex-boyfriend . . . he cheated on me, but it was ages ago now,' and she looked away. 'It sounds so trivial by comparison . . . I mean, it's not the same as a child being take away or your truelove dying as Connie's Jimmy did . . . those things are life-altering and devastating and people never get over them. And people cheat all the time, it's not like I'm the only one it's happen—'

'Oh, Grace, please don't be so hard on yourself,' he jumped in. 'There's no measure or rule book for grief, and that's what it is when you lose someone, whether it's a relationship break-up or a death . . . it's just a different type of grief. And it comes and goes. You can be over it one day and then weeks, sometimes months later, or even years later, it can reappear to wallop you right in the face when you least expect it.'

'Thank you,' she smiled, letting her head dip down to one side. 'You're so kind. And not at all like any man I've known before . . . except for Jamie, of course, he's kind too,' and she grinned. 'But he's gay.' And she pulled a face and shrugged.

'Well, for what it's worth, I think the man who cheated on you lost out, big time.' Then, gently unfolding her arms, he took her hands in his. 'And just so you know, Jennifer is my flatmate. And best friend. She's not my girlfriend . . . I did have one of those, but she cheated on me too.' He gave her a wry smile.

Silence followed as his words sunk in.

'Oh.' She willed her cheeks not to go bright red like a pair of plum tomatoes – and that's what she felt like right now . . . a prize plum. How could she have got it so wrong and jumped to conclusions? She had put two and two together and come up with a trillion pieces that didn't fit together after all. 'And I'm sorry you've been through the cheating thing too.'

'Don't be. I'm over it . . . well, for today at least.' And they both laughed. 'So, tell me why you thought I was getting engaged?'

'When I answered your phone that time . . . Jennifer thought I was you and mentioned it, about the picking a venue—'

'Ah, yes, well she *was* getting engaged, and she wanted my help to pick a venue . . . That is until her *girlfriend* got cold feet and called the whole thing off. As you can imagine, she's devastated. And I've been trying to support her from over here.'

'Ellis, I'm so sorry . . . that's awful,' Grace said. 'And I don't need to imagine . . . I was engaged too, once upon a time . . . until I found him in bed with another woman.'

'You actually walked in on him?' Ellis said, shaking his head and covering his face with hands.

'Yes.'

'I did wonder if you'd had your heart broken. I thought it might explain why you were being so cool with me during our time here.'

'Cool?' Grace echoed, wondering how he could think that. Yes, she had been cautious, but then he had a girlfriend, or so she had thought.

'Yes, cool. You must have known that I was attracted to you, Grace?' he said softly, making her pulse quicken all over again as he pulled her in close. 'That I fancy the arse off you?' He stepped back until they were standing facing each other but not touching. 'That's what you say in London, don't you?' And he smiled, making her smile too with his attempt at Britishness again, his American accent making it sound funny.

'Um, err . . . yes we do, but I, no, err . . .' she floundered, inwardly cursing herself for sounding like such a babbling, blithering buffoon and not the nonchalant, sophisticated siren she yearned to be inside her own head. Like one of her screen idols – Audrey, or Marilyn, or even Elizabeth Taylor; she never would have bleated on like this with Richard Burton when they fell in love on the set during the filming of *Cleopatra*. 'No, I didn't realise exactly.'

'Well, please do realise, *exactly*. Grace Quinn, I'm crazy about you.' And it made her blush because nobody had ever said stuff like this to her before, not even Matthew. Come to think of it, Matthew hadn't ever really been one for any kind of talk of feelings and suchlike. Grand gestures, yes, he had been very good at that . . . like when he proposed, doing the whole down-on-one-knee thing in the busy restaurant. And he had basked in the congratulations he had received afterwards when complete strangers came over to shake his hand and the women cooed, telling him how they wished they had a guy as romantic as he was. It was funny how things turned out, Grace thought.

'But tell me something.' Ellis continued, 'why did you think I had a girlfriend? Apart from the phone call, of course, which to be fair wasn't exactly conclusive proof – as you now know,' he said, playfully tilting his head to one side.

'Because you said so . . . in the café, remember? You told Cheryl, the waitress, that your girlfriend was the jealous type,' she said, letting her voice fade away as it seemed so irrelevant now.

'That was only to let her down gently. I couldn't let her come to America and look for a hook-up. She's just a kid, in college, I guess. It wouldn't have been right to lead her on.' He let go of her hands and raked his fingers through his hair. 'Oh Grace, what must you have thought of me? I put it out there so blatantly how I felt about you. I flirted with you. At the airport, the kiss and the embrace . . .' He let go of her hands and shoved his own hands inside his jeans pockets. 'I was so happy to see you. I had missed you. I realised it in Berlin, when I couldn't stop thinking about you. And then on the train, in the restaurant – I even told you were beautiful – now that's a come-on if ever there was one, in the piazzetta by the water when the old guy even helped me out . . .' He shook his head. 'Jesus, you must have thought I was such a jerk carrying on like that when I was supposed to have a girlfriend. Why didn't you say something, ask me outright . . . if you fancied me too?' He paused and crouched down slightly until his eyes were level with hers. 'You do, don't you?'

'Yes, of course I do,' she told him, the relief of being able to tell him making her feel a little lightheaded.

'Phew.' He stood back up to his full height and started pacing around the room before stopping and walking to stand in front of her again. 'You know, we could have got this straight days ago and had so much more fun in this incredibly romantic country . . .' He grinned, cheekily, and she glanced sideways, not even wanting to contemplate what might have been, '. . . if you had just told me you felt the same way too.'

'It wasn't that easy,' she said, solemnly, and then, lightening up, she added, 'I could hardly say, "Hey, Ellis, I fancy the arse off you and I know you have a girlfriend so why are you flirting with me?" I just figured that I had got it all wrong. That I was reading something into it. Like a fantasy, I suppose . . .' She looked away, feeling a bit foolish now.

'But why would assume you had it wrong? Like I said before in the restaurant, you're beautiful and kind and compassionate. I don't say that lightly, or to every woman I have dinner with, you know . . . And hot, too. Grace, you are *really* hot.' He nodded slowly, staring right at her.

'Stop it,' she smiled bashfully.

'Why, when it's the truth? Oh Grace, you are adorable,' he laughed, before she could respond and then swiftly added, 'in a genuine, down-to-earth, cute, hot, gorgeous, sexy AF way,' and he pulled her in close again. 'Now, did you mean it when you said it would never, ever happen again? The kissing thing? Because that's not going to work, Grace.' And he tilted his head to one side and pulled a sad, puppy-dog-eyes face. She looked at him. 'Because, you see, I kind of liked it. A lot. Not the tears, I hated seeing you crying,' he said, kindly. 'That's not what I meant. But I hope you will kiss me again . . . is what I mean . . . if you'd like to.'

'Oh,' she squeaked, rooted to the spot and then, 'well, um, yes, I think I would like to.' And laughed before kissing the side of his neck.

'Ever since the first moment I saw you, Grace, I wanted to kiss you. Hold you. Hell, I wanted to make love to you. These days here in Italy with you have been agony and ecstasy all at the same time.' And he passionately kissed her another time, his lips warm on hers, his arms wrapped around her body, which felt as if fireworks had just exploded somewhere deep within her. Grace melted into his embrace and then, after gently pulling back from him, she looked him right in the eyes as she slipped the straps of her sundress from her shoulders, letting it float to the floor. As she stepped out of the puddle of fabric at her feet, he pulled his T-shirt off over his head, treating her to another burst of his citrus scent and a preview of his muscular chest and well-defined six-pack. After he had unbuttoned his jeans and pushed them off too, Grace slipped her hand inside his and led him over to the bed for a blissful last night in beautiful, romantic Italy.

23

Back home, and Grace floated into work with an enormous smile on her face. Her bottom had barely touched the seat of her office chair when a woman walked into the reception area with the biggest bunch of delicately scented pink roses that Grace had ever seen. After thanking the florist for the delivery and opening the little envelope attached to a bendy stick in the bouquet, her smile widened even further.

To Grace,
   Pink roses to remind you of the botanical footpath in Portofino and so you have a little piece of Italy to ease your return to work.
   With love
   Ellis xxx

Ah, she hadn't even realised that he had seen her save the pink rose petals on the footpath up to the lighthouse. How thoughtful and kind. Pressing her nose into the roses, she breathed in the sweet, evocative scent and then carefully placed the bouquet on her desk before sending him a text to say thank you, and with three kisses too. A reply came back almost immediately.

You're welcome. See you soon, I hope. I'm missing your gorgeous face too much xxx

Grace pressed the phone to her chest, vowing to make it happen as soon as she could. They had kissed and caressed in bed in the early hours of their last day together, a warm breeze fluttering over their naked, entwined bodies as they had talked about what next. Both keen to be together but each knowing that it wasn't as easy as all that with them living in different countries. So for now they would have to make do with text messages and FaceTiming, which they had been doing ever since they parted at the airport to board their separate flights home.

'Ooh, what lovely flowers. Who are they from?' It was Betty coming through the door with a twinkly look in her eyes.

'Err . . . they are from Ellis,' Grace beamed, showing her the card, but then wondering how Betty was going to react to knowing her nephew was missing her employee's 'gorgeous face'.

'Well I never!' Betty marvelled, her own face breaking into a big smile. 'I take it you two hit it off over in Italy, then?'

'Um, you could say that . . . I think I might have fallen for him, like properly fallen for him,' she replied, then instantly wondered if she had said too much as Betty clasped her hands together and gasped, momentarily holding her gaze, before flinging her arms around her and giving her a massive bear hug. After letting Grace go, Betty bellowed, 'Did you hear that, Larry? Grace and Ellis are a couple. Who would have thought it, our lovely Grace and our marvellous nephew – a match made in heaven, I say, and I bet Ruth . . . that's Ellis's mum by the way . . .' Betty paused and patted Grace's arm to explain, '. . . is over the moon. Ruth has been despairing of him for years of ever finding a properly nice partner such as you. Ruth is a typical fussing Jewish mother and she won't settle for just any girl for her only son. But she needn't worry now that Ellis has met a gem. In fact, I think I should call her right away and celebrate the wonderful news with her—'

'Steady on, love, it's early days . . .' Larry popped his head round the door. 'You and our Ruth will have them married off within the week at this rate.' And he winked at Grace, making her blush. 'It's not like it was back in our day, dear . . . let them settle into each other first.'

'Oh, I know you are right,' Betty rubbed her husband's arm before giving him a kiss on the cheek. 'But it is very exciting. I said to Ruth on the phone that Italy was just the thing for the youngsters to have a nice time togeth—'

'Come on, now, anyone would think you and Ruth had planned the whole thing . . . you're like a pair of silly old romantics,' Larry laughed before going off to greet someone who had arrived in the reception area. Grace, on spotting a coy smile on Betty's face as she bustled off into the little kitchenette area, was very happy if she had indeed 'planned the whole thing'.

'Less of the *old*, thank you!' Betty called out over her shoulder, pretending to chastise Larry, and Grace grinned; she wished she was still in Italy with Ellis, but being here at work wasn't so bad . . . Larry and Betty were kind and loving and it made Grace feel content and at home.

'Let's get those gorgeous flowers in some water,' Betty said, opening a cupboard presumably to look for a vase. Grace went to help Betty as she was groaning now as she tried to bend into the cupboard under the sink to reach the vase.

'Someone here to see you, Grace.' Larry reappeared, gesturing to the customer waiting area. 'I've asked him to take a seat.'

'Him?' Grace said, handing the vase to Betty and wondering who it could be. Jamie was at work – she knew that for sure as she had spoken to him earlier. Not Phil, surely? Although she wouldn't put it past him to turn up here expecting another hand-out for the spa trip that never was.

'Yes, an older gentleman,' Larry said, discreetly lowering his voice, as Grace walked past him. 'Very dapper, too. Want me to come with you and see what he wants?' And without waiting for an answer, Larry followed her out to see who it was.

'Mr Conway!' Grace stepped forward to shake his hand. 'What are you doing here?' she added, surprised to see him. 'How are you?' Then, remembering her manners, Grace introduced him to Larry. 'This is the gentleman who now lives in Connie's flat in Blackheath.'

'That's right,' Mr Conway said, getting up from the leather bucket chair to shake Larry's hand, then turning to Grace he added, 'I'm very well, thank you. In fact, I'm here to show you something if you have some time to spare. Sorry to arrive without warning but we thought it best to show you right away . . .' And he looked towards the door as if he was expecting someone else to join them. 'Shan't be a jiffy,' and he whizzed back out of the door, only to return a few seconds later with Lady Bee in tow, who had told him to go ahead and check if they had the right place before they turned up unannounced.

After another set of introductions, Larry invited them all to come into the office and make themselves comfortable on the sofas.

'So what is this all about?' Larry asked.

'Ooh, we have guests.' Betty appeared. 'I'm putting the kettle on – would anyone like tea or coffee?' The perfect hostess as always. Grace jumped up to give her a hand.

'Don't be daft, dear, I can manage, and you'll want to be there to hear what's going on,' Betty said in a hushed voice to Grace as she followed her back to the little kitchenette area and flicked the kettle on.

'If you're sure?' she said, keenly.

'Of course, I am. Here, you can take the babka tin and offer it around. Freshly baked this morning, thankfully.' She handed the cake tin to Grace before doing a shooing motion with her hand on the side of Grace's arm.

'It's a good job Mr Conway remembered where you said that you worked, my dear,' Lady Bee started. 'Or we would never have managed to get this to you.' And she fished inside her handbag and pulled out a faded blue Basildon Bond envelope and handed it to Grace.

'Oh, thank you. What is it?' she said, turning the envelope over. And then her heart almost stopped as she gasped on seeing cursive letters in black ink from a fountain pen. But then she sagged on realising that this wasn't Connie's handwriting . . . yes it was old-fashioned and very similar to Connie's, but Grace had read enough of Connie's diaries and letters to know that it wasn't exactly the same. So whose writing was it then?

'It could be a missing piece of the jigsaw,' Lady Bee said, covertly. 'Mr Conway will explain,' and she gestured grandly for him to speak, making Grace smile and wonder if she was indeed connected to the royal family or something, for she had a very imperious air about her.

'Yes, I do believe it is,' he said, unbuttoning his blazer so as to get a little more comfortable on the sofa as he leant forward to tell Grace. 'I'm in the process of having the flat renovated, sprucing it up with new carpet and a lick of paint, plus replacing the old kitchen units, and my decorator found some post that must have slipped down behind an old kitchen cupboard. And I do hope you'll forgive me for reading the contents . . .' He coughed politely and straightened his cravat. 'On first glance, I thought it might have been an airmail letter that I had missed from my daughter who lives in New Zealand.'

'Of course,' Grace said, keen to read the contents herself.

'The letters inside are quite revealing and I remembered that you were trying to find a relative to inherit from your friend, Connie.'

'Yes, that's right,' Grace said, hopefully. She could feel Larry beside her shifting in his seat in anticipation too.

'Why don't you take a look,' Mr Conway said, indicating the envelope.

And so Grace did. Carefully lifting out and unfolding a bundle of letters written on sheets of thin, pale blue airmail paper.

To Constance,

I feel it prudent to return the postcard you sent to Lara for it will only confuse her when she is so settled here in her new home. It really does not become you well to insist on disregarding what is best for her and putting your own needs before those of a child. Father and I trust that you will refrain from such emotional outpourings in future, if not for Lara's sake, then for those of your new husband's family, for I am quite certain that Senator Donato would not take kindly to you jeopardising his political career if he were to know of your meddling. I urge you to do the right thing and allow Lara to live a respectable life that is free from your continuous letters and cards which will only be returned to you or destroyed from now on.

With fondness,
Mother

Grace clutched a hand to her throat, thinking what an awful, cold, mean, heartlessly ruthless woman Connie's mother was. How could she threaten her own daughter in this way and deny her any contact, not even a letter or a card . . . it was just horrible.

'There's more,' prompted Mr Conway, as Grace carefully folded the acerbic letter and put it back inside the envelope. She read the next one, this time in Connie's handwriting, assuming it had been written several years later, for the Star of David necklace was mentioned in the first paragraph.

A Postcard from Italy

My darling Lara,

I am so looking forward to seeing you to celebrate your twelfth birthday next month and fastening a very special necklace around your pretty, grown-up girl's neck. I continue to hold you in my heart and look forward to our reunion soon. Your stepfather and I are very much looking forward to bringing you back home with us to Italy . . .

Grace turned the page to read on but there were no more words, just the faint outline of many dried-out splashes of water – tears perhaps – that had made the ink smudge and fade until the words were illegible, apart from one sentence written in Connie's mother's handwriting . . . *if you insist on visiting then you must not scare Lara with your whimsical notions of taking her far away from all that she holds dear . . .*

'I'm assuming this letter was also returned to Connie by her mother . . . who clearly wasn't going to entertain Connie taking Lara back to Italy,' Mr Conway suggested.

'A cruel woman, if ever there was one,' Lady Bee gave her opinion. 'Mr Conway has already read aloud the contents to me,' she went on to explain before accepting a piece of babka cake and popping it on a napkin that Betty handed to her. 'Mmm, this is delicious,' she then added, after taking a small bite and dabbing the napkin to the corner of her lips.

'Yes, Connie's awful mother nearly ruined her life. If she hadn't met Giovanni and found some happiness . . .' Grace said, shaking her head. 'But I don't understand how this helps us find a living relative . . .'

'There's this too,' Lady Bee said, handing Grace another envelope, a thick cream embossed one this time, with weightier paper inside.

Grace pulled out the letter and inhaled, drawing in a faint but familiar scent . . . Van Cleef and Arpels. It must be Connie's perfume, she knew it! Grace inhaled again, holding the sheets to her nose, as if drawing Connie towards her, wanting to hug and comfort the scared, lonely young lady who was all alone, heartbroken and pregnant after one moment of loving indiscretion that changed the course of her life for ever . . . and then banished and broken on her return to England as an older woman without Giovanni, and with such deep and pensive eyes . . . haunted almost, is what Larry had said. Grace read the letter aloud so that Larry could hear Connie's words too.

To my darling Lara,

Before my time draws to a close I wish for you to know the truth of your heritage. But first, I must apologise if this news comes as the shock I anticipate it may do, for I am quite certain that you have grown up believing me to be your sister.

Dearest Lara, the truth is that I am your mother. Your devoted mother who has loved you from the moment you were born, and such a beautiful baby you were, with curls as black as treacle and eyes like emeralds and just the same as your father's, my first truelove, Jimmy Blake, who was from Franklin Street, Deptford in London. He was a hero taken from us in the war before you were even born, my love. But he would have loved you so much, of that I am most certain.

I have let you down so terribly and am full of regret for not standing up to my mother and insisting that you be with me, as any young girl should be with her mummy. I did try, sweetheart, but on visiting you to celebrate your bat mitzvah I saw for myself how very happy you were in America with your school chums and Lady, the sweet little cocker-spaniel puppy that you had wanted for such a long time. Mother said it would have been cruel to uproot you from all that you knew, to have to leave Lady behind, and it broke my heart to agree with her. However, I hope for your sake that she was right and that you have been happy and enjoyed a settled, respectable life that I could never have given you. For I am ashamed to this day to tell you that I was unmarried when you were born and it would have been so truly unfair of me to place that burden on your young shoulders too, which would have been an inevitable consequence if I had put my own desire first and insisted on you coming back to Italy with me.

So it brings me to tell you that everything I have of sentimental meaning and monetary value is waiting for you, my darling, for it is all that I can give you, in addition to my love which you have always had. The jewellery and the paintings may be of considerable value and I hope my diaries and letters give you some comfort in knowing that you were loved so very much, for it is time now for you to know the truth of your heritage and inherit what is rightfully yours. I leave it all to you, my darling daughter Lara.

Your devoted mother,

Connie xx

And there beneath Connie's name was a PS giving the address of Cohen's Convenient Storage Company. Connie had even thought to write her unit number, 28, and an additional PPS urging Lara to *ask for*

Larry Cohen as he has taken good care of everything for all these years . . .

Grace caught a sob of emotion in her throat. And with trembling hands she dipped her nose to the paper another time before carefully placing it back inside the envelope.

Silence followed and they all sat motionless momentarily.

'Oh Connie,' Grace uttered to herself. Larry placed a comforting hand on her shoulder.

'No wonder she looked so haunted,' Larry lamented, shaking his head.

'That poor, poor woman, and what was her mother thinking, punishing her and Lara like that? I know times were different back then, but for good-ness' sakes . . . to keep a mother and child apart just to keep up appearances is despicable . . .' It was Betty; she had been standing behind the sofa and heard the contents of the letter too.

'Don't be upsetting yourself, love. We must look on the bright side now that we have this informa-tion,' Larry said, getting up to give Betty a hug.

'How is this a bright side? It's so sad,' Betty said, patting Larry's arm.

'Because we now know that Connie stored the contents of unit 28 for her daughter, Lara, to inherit,'

Larry said, 'and Ellis told us that something in writing from Connie to this effect would be very helpful in proving this. Plus Connie specifically mentions the paintings and jewellery, so there's no doubt now that they were indeed Connie's to bequeath and that Lara is the heir.'

'True,' Grace spoke this time, and stood up too. 'Thank you so much for bringing the letters to us,' she said, looking first at Lady Bee and then at Mr Conway. It felt good to know that they knew for sure now that Connie had carefully stored all her beautiful, treasured possessions for her only child, Lara, but there was something missing. 'It's just such a pity that we still don't have an address for Lara. When you handed me the bundle I was hopeful, but this is Connie's address here on the airmail envelope so I'm assuming her mother just returned any letters that Connie sent to Lara. And this envelope has only Lara's name on it . . . I wonder why Connie never posted it?' Grace thought aloud as she tapped the front of the cream envelope.

'Ah! Yes, I didn't think of that,' Larry sighed, and Betty gave him a look.

'Maybe Connie died before she could post it,' Lady Bee said in a stoic, matter-of-fact manner. 'She had a fall in the street, remember, and the woman who works in the post office in Blackheath Village did tell me later that Connie had only been in there a few days before asking how much the postage was to send a letter to America. She remembered because she said that dear old Connie was confused and unsure about where exactly in America she wanted to send the letter, managing only to say Manhattan as she fumbled in her purse before saying that she would have to come back later as she had left the letter in the kitchen at home.'

'Oh no,' Grace gasped, on realising that even right up to the very end Connie had been caring for Lara, wanting to do the best for her . . . it was just such a pity the same kindness and consideration had never been shown to Connie, firstly by her own mother and then by the universe, fate or whatever, towards the end. Because, if Lara had somehow received the letter, then maybe she would have come to England . . . maybe she would have been with her mother when she died. Then maybe Connie wouldn't have been all alone and would have got her happy ending after all.

'There is one other thing,' Mr Conway said, standing up and rummaging inside his blazer. 'The decorator chap found this too, just a moment before we left to come here this morning.' He glanced at

Lady Bee who leaned forward to see what it was. 'Ah, here it is . . . not sure it will be of much use, though, as it's dated November 1946.'

And he handed a postcard to Grace.

A picture of the breathtakingly beautiful Italian Riviera on the front and Connie's handwriting on the back next to an address in Manhattan. Grace felt her pulse quicken as she held her breath.

'I need to call Ellis,' she said, her fingers shaking as she fished inside her jeans pocket to pull out her mobile.

He answered right away.

'Hello, Grace . . . this is a nice surprise, or am I dreaming?' he laughed, sounding sleepy, for it must be early morning in New York, she thought on glancing at the clock on the wall and swiftly counting back the hours in her head. But this was too important, as time could be running out for them to find Connie's daughter.

'No, you're not dreaming . . . it's really me, and I have some news.'

'You do?'

'Yes, that's right. I know where you need to go to start the search for Lara. I have an address right here . . . on a postcard from Italy.'

EPILOGUE

Santa Margherita, Italy . . . Three months later

Grace buckled her seatbelt and gazed out of the aeroplane window, barely able to quell the swirl of delight that was building within her. Not long now and she would be back in beautiful Italy with her boyfriend, Ellis, for a wonderful weekend together. Pushing her sunglasses up – she had treated herself to a pair of tortoiseshell Versace ones, just like Nonna Maria's – not real, expensive ones, but near enough. Grace's shades were fake and therefore a fraction of the price, from a stall in Greenwich Market. One of the places she liked to wander around on a Saturday afternoon on her way back from an art gallery in London or a dance class at the famous Pineapple Studio. Yes, she loved going out on her own now. She loved the freedom of it. The feeling of doing exactly as she pleased and whenever she liked. Because it had turned out that Cora wasn't as immobile as she had led Grace and her three siblings to believe.

While Grace had been away, her brother Mikey, outraged and egged on by a still fuming Bernie, because Grace had had the temerity to leave Cora and go to Italy, had installed a secret camera in her bedroom. Mikey had never liked Jamie, his macho ego uncomfortable around 'gayness', as Mikey ignorantly called it, and so the camera was installed with the intention of spying on Jamie. Or, to put in Mikey's words, 'to make sure the staff aren't slapping the old dears around like you see on those undercover documentary programmes on the telly' as he had said that time before in the phone conversation when Grace had called him asking him for help caring for their mother.

But an altogether different scene had met their eyes on watching the film back. Jamie had told Grace all about it when she had first arrived home the day after Ellis had made love to her all night long.

'There I was, dashing around, making her ladyship a mug of warm milk with a pinch of nutmeg sprinkled on the top, just the way she likes it, when your Mikey, Sinead and Bernie burst through the back door into the kitchen and near scared the life out of me,' Jamie had said, clutching a hand to his chest at this point. 'Then the next thing I know, there's this almighty palaver with Mikey running up the stairs and yelling for Cora to *get up*. To get her, and I quote, "lazy, selfish, conniving backside out of the bed *at once*". Well, obviously I elbowed my way round them and into Cora's bedroom with the intention of putting a stop to it all, thinking Mikey had seriously lost the plot, figuring all that financial wheeling and dealing he does had addled his brain. And I know your mother can be extremely difficult and controlling but . . . well, she was in my care and Mikey was absolutely livid. Who knew what he was capable of? But there he was, ripping a camera and a bundle of wires from the top of the wardrobe while Bernie was shoving an iPhone screen into my face! "Watch this!" Bernie had instructed, you know, in that bossy way she has. And so I did. Bold as brass your mother was, Grace, mooching around her bedroom without a care in the world. The camera had caught Cora practically springing out of bed every time I left the room. And to think they installed a camera to catch *me* out. Flaming cheek. *But* . . . and if that wasn't bad enough . . . the proverbial cherry on the top of the very mucky cake that Cora had cooked up, was a film clip of her wiggling her ample hips and doing a shoulder-shimmy in time to the *Countdown* theme tune!'

At this point Grace's eyes had almost popped right out of her head, barely able to believe what she was hearing, before she had then confronted her mother too, demanding a full explanation, and remembering that time when she had wondered how things had moved themselves around in Cora's bedroom. Well, now she knew! Cora had been playing her daughter for all that time.

After Grace had watched the film too, Cora had broken down; it had been awful seeing her hard, bitter façade crumble so pathetically as she had admitted that she was scared of her own increasing frailty and what would become of her as she got even older. But rather than be angry, Grace had felt an over-whelming rush of relief, as the revelation had set her free. She was no longer tied to caring for her mother, who no wonder had refused to consider a care home, for she would have been found out to be a fraud right away. So Grace had listened as her mother explained that she knew all her children hated her, but she was lonely, and that, 'I suppose I wanted you to stay with me when you came back home', to which Grace had told her mother that she would have done so anyway if she had just been honest.

But that was in the past now. A week later, Cora had had a modest win on her scratchcard and so given Grace the money to enrol on a part-time performing arts teacher-training course to make up for having used her as an unpaid carer for all that time. And after many evenings of chatting things through, Grace had come to understand that her mother was scared and lonely, and so they had organised some things to do together, too, and had already enjoyed cinema visits and trips to the garden centre café. Cora had also taken it upon herself to join a slimming club in a bid to lose some of her bulk and had already teamed up with a couple of other ladies her age and now that she had the mobility scooter, she regularly went to the bingo with them.

Grace smiled to herself as the lush mountainous terrain came in to view. The pine trees and sunshine glittering over the Ligurian Sea as the aeroplane landed at Genoa Airport. She couldn't wait to see Ellis, who was arriving from New York a few hours after her and coming straight to the powder pink villa to meet her there. Having kept in touch with Tom and Georgie, they had squared it with Nonna Maria for them all to be allowed to stay in the villa for the weekend. And Grace couldn't wait to see inside the home where Connie had lived and had been so happy with Giovanni.

Stepping out of the taxi that Grace had hopped into at the airport, not fancying another long, hot walk up the windy mountain road to the powder pink villa, with a suitcase in tow, she was happy to see that Georgie and Tom were already here.

'Hi Grace,' Georgie smiled, looking radiant in a white floaty sundress as she walked towards her with Gypsy tucked under her arm.

'How was your journey?' Tom said, kissing her on each cheek and then taking her suitcase from the boot of the taxi and wheeling it off towards the metal gates at the entrance to the villa.

'Hi Georgie, it's so good to be back here in Italy,' Grace said, giving her a hug. 'And the journey was fine, thanks, Tom,' she added, walking alongside Georgie as they followed Tom down the long driveway and up three stone steps to the door of the villa that was framed by an array of exotic vermilion red begonias.

'You can take it from here,' Tom said, opening the door and placing Grace's suitcase inside.

'Aren't you coming in too?' she asked, baffled that they were leaving her on her own when she had only just arrived.

'Oh, we have some things to do in Portofino,' Georgie said vaguely, fiddling with Gypsy's little collar before kissing the cat on the head.

'Yes, that's right,' Tom chipped in, putting his arm around Georgie. 'But you'll be fine. Ellis will be here before you know it and so why don't you go and have a look around and make yourself comfortable. There are drinks in the bar off the dining hall and snacks in the kitchen if you're hungry.' And then, before she could ask more, they had both practically scarpered back down the driveway and disappeared out of sight. How odd, Grace thought, but in her anticipation to see where Connie had lived, she let it go from her mind.

Inside, and Grace was completely overcome as she imagined Connie closing the huge oak door behind her and walking across the marble tiled floor and into the vast sitting room which had two sparkling chandeliers and an array of sumptuous patterned silk sofas dotted around. Magnificent floor-to-ceiling windows looked out onto a wrap-around veranda that gave a panoramic view of the dazzling Italian Riviera. Then, leading off the sitting room, was a dining hall with a long table that could seat twenty people, at least, comfortably. An opulent mural covered the whole of one wall – beautiful

Renaissance women draped in fabric and lounging around a table laden with food – grapes, cheeses, bread and flagons of wine. Grace stepped closer and saw Giovanni's initials in the bottom right-hand corner. She crouched down to gently touch an index finger there, knowing that Connie would have done exactly the same for sure.

Standing up, Grace closed her eyes for a few seconds and imagined Connie and Giovanni, in happier times, Frank Sinatra music playing, or Dean Martin, or Pavarotti perhaps, as they entertained their friends in here with fabulous feasts followed by cocktails on the veranda, for there was another veranda just through the opened wooden doors. She could hear voices floating in from outside and went to investigate. Maybe Georgie and Tom were still in the grounds.

As Grace walked down the path, tilting her face up to the gloriously warm sun, inhaling the scent of frangipani, the sound of birdsong all around, she could hear a man's voice. Ellis. And her heart lifted in anticipation of seeing him. But what was he doing here already? And she could hear female voices too. Three of them, if she wasn't mistaken . . . laughing and then shushing covertly as if they were embroiled in some kind of conspiracy. She kept on walking and, as she reached the little rose garden in the far corner, with the pine-tree-clad cliffs for a backdrop, Grace could see Ellis. Her pulse quickened as she ran towards him, keen to give him a big hug as she had missed him so much. They had spoken every day since they were last here in Italy together, but it just wasn't the same, and as she reached him and he wrapped his arms around her and pulled her in close, she could feel tears of happiness bubbling up inside her.

'Hey, darling,' he said softly, as he pulled back to see her face. 'This is supposed to be a surprise, a happy one I had hoped . . . please don't cry.'

'And it is,' she laughed, wiping her eyes, 'I'm just a bit overwhelmed, I guess. I thought you weren't arriving until later. I'm so pleased to see you . . .'

'And me you. Let's have a proper reunion later when it's just us,' he grinned, giving her a kiss on the lips.

'I can't wait,' she grinned right back.

'But first . . . come on, there's someone else here who can't wait to see you.'

'Who?' she asked, intrigued as she glanced over his shoulder.

But Ellis didn't say . . . instead he took Grace by the hand and led her over to where three women were sitting in the shade underneath a pergola, a flurry of yellow butterflies floating around the nearby honeysuckle.

'Grace,' he said, stepping forward towards the oldest of the three women who was standing up now, the two younger women on either side of her. 'This is Lara.'

'*Lara?*' Grace couldn't believe it and her mouth dropped open and her eyes nearly popped right out of their sockets.

A short silence followed as she stood, dumbfounded.

Then after quickly recovering herself, she swallowed and blinked and took another look at the woman, as if checking for real that she was actually here. Grace saw the impish green eyes, like emeralds . . . just as Connie had described. Her hair was still curly, but a silvery grey now with age. And there it was too, a look of Connie, when she was standing by the boats in the picture taken in Portofino back in 1952. Grace could actually see Connie, Lara's mother, looking back at her. And she caught her breath.

'But how? How did you find her?' She swivelled her head to look at Ellis and then back to the woman standing before her. 'And why did you keep her a secret until now?' she said, half laughing and half chastising as she batted his arm with her hand.

'Your boyfriend knocked on my front door,' Lara said, in a refined New York accent, smiling as she took both of Grace's hands in hers. 'And I can't thank you enough for giving him my address.'

'Your address?' Grace echoed, laughing harder as she tried to figure it all out.

'That's right. The one on the postcard from Italy,' Ellis grinned.

'You still live in Aunt Rachael's house in Manhattan?' Grace asked, still stunned. The address on the postcard was where she had asked Ellis to start the search, imagining someone there might, by some miraculous chance, have known where the previous occupants had moved to, or a neighbour perhaps might know of Aunt Rachael and her relatives from England and what had happened to them . . . if the young girl who had moved to America all those years ago was even still alive? But what were the chances of Ellis actually finding Connie's daughter, Lara, living right there . . . in plain sight for all this time? It was truly remarkable.

'Well, it's my house now,' Lara said. 'My Aunt Rachael died when I was a child and left the brownstone to my parents and—' She paused, abruptly.

'Oh dear, please excuse me,' she then added, and turned away as she tried to correct herself, 'the house was left to my, um . . . grandparents, I guess, and then in turn to me. I'm so sorry, I promised myself I wouldn't do this. Not here in this wonderful place . . .' she finished, fishing in her bag before pulling out a hanky and dabbing her eyes.

'It's OK, Mom.' One of the other women moved forward to put her arm around Lara as she steered her towards a white wicker sofa, then introduced herself to Grace. 'I'm Patty, Lara's daughter, and this is Ellen, my sister,' she said, and Ellen gave Grace a hug, and then after settling their mum in the seat, Patty explained, 'It's been quite overwhelming for her; you see Mom didn't know . . .'

And so as they sat in Connie's picturesque garden, drinking ice-cold lemonade, Lara's daughters told Grace what had happened all those years ago. It turned out that Lara had indeed grown up believing that Connie was her older sister, and with only a faded memory of seeing her occasionally during the war in England, so she had no real recollection of her. Although Lara did remember her bat mitzvah party ending abruptly when Connie turned up in the middle of it and a very strained atmosphere ensued. Lara remembered being told to take her beloved dog, Lady, out into the garden and to stay there with Aunt Rachael and all their friends. It stuck in her mind as she had been allowed to eat chocolate cake before tea and that was never normally allowed. Lara didn't recall ever seeing Connie again after that day, and her instinct, at even such a young age, had told her not to ask about Connie or indeed mention her name ever again . . . and so through the mists of time her 'sister' had faded from her thoughts completely.

'And so thank you for not giving up the search, Grace,' Patty said, finishing the last of the lemonade in her glass. 'It means the world to Mom to be here and to see where her actual mother, Connie, lived. Ellis has been so kind in helping us sort out all the travel arrangements; he even drove us to JFK airport yesterday—'

'Yesterday?' Grace smiled, shaking her head. 'Is that when you got here? I thought he was coming today.'

'Yes, that's right. Don't be hard on him, he wanted to surprise you and we thought it would be nice for Mom to meet you here first before we travel on to London.'

'Wow. Does this mean you are coming to Cohen's? That's the storage place where Connie's belongings are,' Grace asked, hopefully, for she wanted so much for Lara to see exactly how Connie had carefully stored all that she owned for her.

'Yes, that's right, we need to take care of some legalities around the paintings and pieces of jewellery. And then we are hoping you can take us to where Connie ended her days. We would also like to find out where she is buried, so we can pay our respects . . . And to Franklin Street in Deptford to see where Mom's father, Jimmy, lived. Mom really wants to visit Blackheath park too, and the heath where Connie met him at the funfair. Ellis has talked us through the whole love story she wrote about in her diaries. About how Connie and Jimmy met and fell in love, and how she never forgot him. Her first truelove. It's so incredibly emotional and bittersweet.'

The conversation flowed for a few hours more until Ellis's mobile rang and he stood up.

'Awesome. I'm coming now,' he said, before slotting his phone back inside his pocket and going to walk away.

'Hey, where are you off to?' Grace asked.

'Come with me,' he said, slipping a hand around hers. 'There's someone else who wants to meet you too . . .'

When they got to the gate, there was a silver

mini-coach parked up and a group of people milling around chatting to Georgie and Tom.

'What's going on?' Grace said, lifting her shades to get a better look at the group. There were two older men, in their sixties perhaps, and two women of about the same age. A younger couple and three small children too, who were dashing around excitedly, teasing each other by seeing who could flip the other one's sunhat off first. 'Are they more of Lara's family?' she added, grinning at Ellis.

But before he could answer, one of the men came over to them.

'Hello, you must be Grace,' he said in English with a London accent, taking her hand and shaking it enthusiastically.

'Um, yes, that's right,' she said, intrigued. He wasn't American, so these people couldn't be part of Lara's family from New York. So who were they?

'It's a pleasure to meet you, Grace. I'm Terry, and this rowdy bunch here is my wife, June,' and one of the women waved over enthusiastically. Grace waved back, bemused. 'And that fella over there is my brother, James, and his wife, Audrey, and then you've got my son, Dougie, and my daughter-in-law, Steph, and their three kiddiewinks, Ben, Bobby and little Kitty.'

'Nice to meet you all,' Grace said, and then in a daze added, 'Did you say Kitty?' What a coincidence, as Grace remembered mention of a woman called Kitty in one of Connie's earlier diaries; she was her best friend and had been with Connie at the funfair when she met Jimmy.

'Yep, that's right. Named after her great-granny she is, God rest her soul.' And he crossed himself before looking skywards. 'But come on, you had better come with me and meet the old fella himself.' And Terry led her round to the other side of the mini-coach where a very frail and elderly gentleman was being helped into a wheelchair.

Stanley!

The man in the wheelchair must be Jimmy's friend. Stanley had been at the funfair too. Grace couldn't believe it. How wonderful. Terry had just said the little girl was named after her great-granny so it all made sense. Stanley was Kitty's sweetheart and so they must have gone on to get married. And so Grace smiled as her heart soared on realising that this gentleman would have actually known Connie, his wife Kitty's best friend all those years ago. He would be able to tell Lara about her mother when she was young and carefree and happy at the funfair, and then when she was courting Jimmy before he went away to fight, and before he ultimately lost his life for his country. It was incredible after all this time. And then Grace wondered how on earth Ellis had managed to find Stanley? And, more importantly, did Lara know that her father's best friend was going to be here in Italy at Connie's home? Or was this a wonderful surprise for her too?

Grace glanced at Ellis and squeezed his hand before stepping forward.

'I'm so pleased and honoured to meet you, Stanley.'

Silence followed.

'Stanley?' the old man repeated, a look of confusion spreading across his papery face, and Grace's heart sank for him on realising that he must have dementia if he didn't know his own name. With a rush of compassion, she bobbed down in front of him and held out her hands which he took in his.

Another silence followed.

Grace could sense Terry moving alongside her and then kneeling down too.

Then, after handing the elderly gentleman a sprig of wild flowers tied in a jaunty yellow ribbon, she turned to look at Grace and said,

'This isn't Stanley. This is my dad, Jimmy!'

Grace gasped.

She stood up and turned to Ellis who, after giving her a kiss on the cheek, gently guided her forward again before stepping back to allow her to take it all in.

Grace could not believe it.

Connie's first truelove. Jimmy. The man she had never stopped loving. The father of Connie's darling baby girl, Lara.

Was it really him?

She crouched down again in front of the man's wheelchair and looked again into his eyes. And then she knew. The impish green eyes. The same green eyes as his daughter, Lara, who was waiting in the garden to meet him for the very first time, she presumed.

'Jimmy, it's . . .' Grace gulped back a tear and felt her face move into a massive smile instead. 'It's such an honour to meet you.'

'And you, my love,' he said in a raspy voice, patting the top of her hand. 'Thank you. Your fella here,' he broke off to nod in Ellis's direction, 'went through it all with me on the phone. He told me how you kept going to find out the truth for our Connie.' He stopped talking, seemingly overcome with emotion as he pulled a hanky from his breast pocket and gave his nose a quick stoic blow, before putting it away again and lifting the flowers up. 'These are for her, my first truelove, Connie,' he said. 'You see, I never got to give her the last lot. Her parents wouldn't have it.' And he shook his head, a smile mingled with sorrow set on his face.

'I know,' Grace said softly, helping to tuck the blanket, which Terry had passed across, around Jimmy's knees. 'But I can't wait to hear all about it from you.' And she stood up and looked at Terry. 'Thank you so much for bringing him here.'

'It's my pleasure, Grace. We can't thank you enough for this. Dad never stopped loving Connie, you know,' he said, quietly, as he moved around to take charge of the wheelchair.

'I can hear you, son,' Jimmy chortled. 'I might be getting on, but I've still got my faculties intact.' He looked up at Grace and then added, 'But he's right, you know. I never stopped loving our Connie.'

'Right, are you ready then, Dad?' Terry asked, smiling and shaking his head. 'To go and meet your daughter?' And he wheeled Jimmy off towards the powder pink villa.

Grace listened to Ellis as they walked up the path, holding back a bit to allow the family to go first.

'Are you sure you're not mad at me?' he asked, for the third time. 'It was a huge gamble, not telling you about Lara and Jimmy right away, but I wanted to take the chance . . . to do a wonderful thing for you, Grace.'

'Of course not, and it is a wonderful thing. I'm so overjoyed that Connie's daughter can meet her father. It's the next best thing to Lara being reunited with Connie. And here in the very place where Connie was actually happy,' Grace said, shaking her head in bewilderment as she went over everything he had told her: how Connie's parents had lied in telling her Jimmy had been killed in the war, presumably to put pressure on her to give Lara up for adoption. But Jimmy hadn't died; he was missing for a while, presumed dead, until he made it back home having survived in a POW camp. He was in very bad health on his return and spent the last part of the war in a sanatorium, believing Connie had forgotten all about him as she hadn't replied to any of the letters he had sent when he'd first enlisted. And this broke Grace's heart all over again, to know that Connie's parents must have deliberately withheld Jimmy's letters from Connie. Then, when Jimmy saw Connie in the crowd on VE Day, saw how radiant and clearly blissfully happy in love she was with the GI, with a diamond ring on her finger, he knew that he had to let her go. But, even though he later went on to marry her best friend, Kitty, after her Stanley didn't make it back home from the war, Jimmy never let Connie go from his heart completely.

'And I still can't believe Maggie kept all this from me,' Grace sighed, incredulous. 'I only spoke to her yesterday and she never said a word . . . Did Larry and Betty know too that Maggie had managed to find out all this about Jimmy?'

'Yes, but only for a short while, I promise. It all happened so quickly, Grace, and we all wanted to surprise you . . . to do something really special for you, and well . . . you do agree that this is much more meaningful than me just phoning you from New York to say that I had found Lara, and then Maggie calling in to Cohen's to tell you that she had discovered Jimmy was still alive?'

'Hmm, I suppose so,' she teased, 'but I can see that I'm going to have to keep a close eye on you from now on, because we have spoken on the phone at least a trillion times in the last few weeks and I never once suspected you were planning such a momentous surprise as this.'

'And it killed me, it really did, Grace, but I promise it was done with the best intentions.'

They reached the path that led down to where

Lara and her daughters were now embracing Jimmy and all his family. Grace stopped walking.

'Do you mind if we join them later . . . there's something I want to do first.'

'Sure,' Ellis said. 'Would you like me to come with you?'

'Could you come and find me in a few minutes?' she smiled, letting go of his hand.

Grace made her way into the villa and went upstairs to the place in the photo where Connie had been standing in the doorway of the veranda with Giovanni's Venice Salute painting on the wall behind her. She stood in the exact same spot and thought of Connie, telling her:

They are here for you, dear Connie. Your first true-love, Jimmy, and your darling Lara, together at last, here in Italy, the place where you found happiness. They've come back to you and will remember you for always. And I will too.

Grace walked out onto the veranda, the scent of lemon from the fruit trees filling the warm air all around her as she gazed across the breathtakingly beautiful Italian Riviera. She stood silently and thought of everything that had happened over the last few months. How her life had changed beyond recognition and how Connie, even after her death, had played a part in that. For if she hadn't chosen Cohen's Convenient Storage Company to look after her precious belongings, then Grace might never have discovered them and ultimately never have met her own truelove. For that's what Ellis was. Grace had known it right from the moment when she first met him. But hadn't allowed herself to even dream of a different life with him at that time. How things change . . . And talking of whom, she felt his hands gently touch her shoulders. Ellis was there now, standing behind her and wrapping her in a hug as he placed his arms around hers. She leant back into him, resting her head on his chest, savouring the moment here with him in this glorious place.

'Are you OK?' he asked softly, his lips warm on the side of her neck.

'Mmmm,' she murmured, nodding her head. 'I was thinking about Connie and how her legacy has changed my life.'

'How come?'

'Well, I wouldn't have met you if it wasn't for her.'

'True. And I have her to thank for that too. I can't imagine my life without you in it, Grace,' he told her.

'It's the same for me,' she said, drawing his arms tighter around her as she snuggled further into his chest, wishing they didn't live so very far apart. She couldn't bear the thought of parting from him again at the airport in a few days' time. Maybe she could move to America? But what about her mother? There was a time when Grace would have jumped at the chance to escape the burden of caring for Cora, but it was different now. She actually enjoyed spending time with her, and the others were visiting more often too . . . Bernie had even been talking of booking a spa day for her and her mother . . . Grace had overheard her on the phone to the hotel when she had last come to see Cora. And Grace would miss her best friend, Jamie, terribly, unless he came to America too, as he had joked about on the phone that time.

Grace and Ellis stood together for a while, just enjoying and relishing each other's company as they soaked up the romantic atmosphere there on the hilltop, until eventually Ellis gently turned her around until she was facing him.

'Grace, I have another surprise,' he said, kissing the side of her neck again.

'Oh?' she smiled, her eyelids fluttering as he traced a path up her neck to her mouth with his lips.

'Are you sure you can handle another surprise?'

'Um, I think so,' she grinned. 'It depends what it is?'

'Well, what would you say if I told you I wanted to be able to see you, and hold you, laugh with you, watch a movie, hang out, shop for groceries, make love to you . . . like all the time?' He pulled a silly face.

'All the time?' She lifted one eyebrow, teasingly.

'Yes,' he nodded and smiled suggestively and then promptly clarified, 'in the evenings, of course . . . and weekends too. When you're not busy doing other stuff, like working, or doing all the other things you enjoy . . . oh jeez, this is coming out all wrong. I'm making myself sound like a crazy, possessive jerk. I mean, I'd like to be with you more, not that I want you to only see me and have no life away from me.'

'It's OK, I know what you mean,' she laughed gently.

'Phew. That's a relief.'

'Oh, why is that?'

'Because . . . I've been offered a job at Sotheby's . . .'

'In London?' she murmured, excitement bubbling inside her, but caution too – she didn't want to get her hopes up, in case he wasn't saying what she truly hoped he might be.

'Yes . . . if you'll have me?' he asked, his toffee-brown eyes searching hers. And, as it sank in, she nodded, slowly at first, until she could bear it no longer and threw her arms around his neck and squeezed him tight.

'Yes please, I'd love to have you,' she gasped, letting him go momentarily so she could look at his gorgeous face again. He smiled, resting his forehead gently on hers, his fingers caressing the tops of her arms.

'Grace Quinn, I love you.'

And as she moved her lips onto his, Grace knew that she absolutely loved him too . . .

BETTY'S TRULY SCRUMPTIOUS BABKA CAKE

Makes 1 loaf

<u>Ingredients</u>
For the dough
100mls milk
350g strong white bread flour
50g caster sugar
7g sachet fast-action dried yeast
1 large egg, lightly beaten
100g butter, softened and chopped into small pieces, plus extra to grease

For the filling
75g unsalted butter
75g dark chocolate
150g caster sugar
25g cocoa powder

1tsp ground cinnamon

For the syrup
75g caster sugar

Method

1. Heat milk in a small saucepan until just warm. In a large bowl (or in a stand mixer fitted with a dough hook) mix flour, sugar, yeast and a pinch of salt. Add the milk, egg and butter, and mix to bring together into a dough, adding another 1tbsp milk if looking a little dry. Shape into a ball, then knead by hand for about 15min (or about 6min in a stand mixer) until you have a soft dough that springs back when pressed. Return to the cleaned-out bowl and cover with oiled Clingfilm. Leave to prove for 2hr until about doubled in size (or leave at room temperature for 1hr, then transfer to the fridge overnight and complete recipe the following day).

2. If dough was kept in the fridge overnight, set aside at room temperature while you make the filling. Grease a 900g (2lb) loaf tin with butter and line base and sides with baking parchment, leaving an overhang to help get bread out of the tin later.

3. To make the filling, melt the butter in a small saucepan. Remove from the heat, stir in the chocolate, sugar, cocoa powder and cinnamon. Set aside to cool briefly.

4. Place dough on to a lightly floured surface and roll into a rectangle about 50 x 30.5cm. Spread the filling over the dough, covering it completely. Roll up tightly from one of the longer sides into a sausage shape. Carefully lift dough on to a piece of baking parchment and chill in the fridge for 15min to make it easier to cut.

5. When chilled, cut the dough in half lengthways so you have two long pieces with the inside exposed. Turn each piece so filling faces upwards. Starting from one end, lift one piece across the other, twisting together but keeping the filling exposed, to make one long twisted braid. Push ends of the twist together to make the length shorter, then squeeze the dough into the loaf tin (it will seem too big but it will fit!) Loosely cover with oiled Clingfilm and leave to prove in a warm place for 1½-2hr or until doubled in size.

6. Preheat oven to 180°C (160°C fan) mark 4. Bake loaf for about 50min-1hr until deep golden, loosely covering with foil towards the end of cooking time if it is getting too dark. When the

babka is almost cooked, make the syrup. In a small pan, gently heat sugar and 75ml water and stir until dissolved. Bring to the boil, then remove from the heat. Remove loaf from oven, brush sugar syrup all over the top to soak in. Leave to cool completely in the tin before serving.

ACKNOWLEDGMENTS

Love and thanks to my kind friend and brilliant editor, Kate Bradley, for always knowing what I mean to write and for showing me the light at the end of a sometimes very long tunnel. Thanks too to Kimberley Young, Emilie Chambeyron, Katy Blott and the rest of the hardworking team at HarperCollins. Special thanks to my amazingly patient agent, Tim Bates, for continuing to help me keep calm and carry on. A special mention to my copy editor, Penny Isaac, for tweaking all my mistakes right from the start. Emily Deane for sharing her legal expertise regarding inheritance laws in the UK, any errors within the novel are totally down to me. Claire, Lucie and Charlotte for sharing a picture of their gorgeous cat, Gypsy, who became the inspiration for the cat called Gypsy in this novel. Thanks to my girls, Tara, Sarah and Ingela for changing my life with their friendship, warmth and unwavering love and support, plus prosecco and passing on a passion for slow cooking. My dear best friend, Caroline Smailes, for always being there and for always getting it. Thanks always to my husband, Paul Brown, aka Cheeks, for knowing exactly when to bring tea and treats to my writing room, and an extra special thank you to my darling girl, QT, the bravest, kindest young girl - you continue to amaze me with your perseverance every single day, my love. As always, I couldn't write at all without my beloved Northern Soul music to evoke the right emotions, so thank you for helping me to keep the faith and keep on keeping on.

Lastly, and by no means least, a huge thank you to all of you, my wonderful readers. You're all magnificent and your kindness and continued cheerleading spurs me on every day – writing books can get lonely sometimes, but having you all there is like a family — our special community — and that is very precious to me indeed. I couldn't do any of this without you. You mean the world to me and make it all worthwhile. Thank you so very much for loving my books as much as I love writing them for you.

Luck and love
Alex xxx

READ ON FOR A Q&A WITH ALEX...

What inspired you to write *A Postcard from Italy*?

I've always wanted to write a book set in Italy, ever since my husband and I went on a cruise soon after we got married fifteen years ago. Our ship stopped at Santa Margherita for the day and so after exploring that part of the beautiful Italian Riviera for the first time, we hopped on a bus and went along the coastal road to Portofino, just as Grace and Ellis do. I was so enthralled by the beautiful, unspoilt scenery combined with the timelessness glamour and so the memory of that day has stayed with me ever since.

What appealed to you about the dual narrative? You did something similar in *The Secret of Orchard Cottage*?

The present colliding with the past is very appealing to me - a modern-day woman discovering how a woman in the past lived her life, with all the similarities in experiences and emotions, even in very different social eras is quite incredible. I like being able to commemorate women and men from years gone by, to celebrate them and acknowledge the contribution and sacrifices they made so that we can live more freely today. I think I'll always be in awe of women like Winnie in *The Secret of Orchard Cottage* and Connie and Jimmy in *A Postcard from Italy*.

The Second World War period seems to hold a fascination for you...
It sure does. I love all things vintage, such as the décor, furniture, clothes, make up and perfume during that period from the 1930's through to the end of the 1950's, but more importantly I'm in awe of how ordinary people lived and in some cases, did extraordinary things during wartime. I have fond memories of my nan, Edie, telling me about her experience working as a Nippy in the Lyons Corner House on the Strand in London and so it was wonderful to be able to immortalise her in *A Postcard from Italy* with a mention on VE Day when

she takes Connie's friend, Bunty, through to the staff room to fix her victory roll after it becomes dishevelled in the celebratory conga. It is these little anecdotes that appeal to me, and the nostalgia of a different time where people seemed kinder and more inclined to come together to help one another; or maybe this is just fanciful thinking. Either way, it appeals to me to keep alive the memory of those extraordinary times during WW2 and then the enormous social change that happened in the aftermath of war and beyond.

The idea of finding treasure in an unexpected place is so compelling, have you ever done that yourself, like Grace does at Cohen's?
Yes, many times. I love rummaging through old second-hand shops and have found many interesting items. My most treasured find is an exquisitely, glamorous swing coat and whenever I wear it I wonder what kind of woman it belonged to in the 1950's, what was her life like, her dreams and aspirations.

The depictions of Italy are wonderful, it feels like the perfect escape, why do you think Italy is such a good location?
Because Italy really does have it all. It's such a beautiful

country steeped in history with glorious weather and passionate people. The sense of timeless romance is appealing too, as is the sumptuous cuisine, breathtaking landscape and architecture.

A Postcard from Italy is going to be right at the top of people's reading wishlist, but which of your books gets the most fan mail?

Oh, definitely *Cupcakes at Carrington's*, my very first book and the start of the series set in Carrington's Department store and then *The Great Christmas Knit Off*, the first of my books set in the fictional village of Tindledale. It's always an honour to hear from readers, when they take the time to tell me how they loved being swept away into a different, but relatable word that often makes them laugh or cry and sometimes even helps them through a difficult period in their life.

How do you decide what to write about?

I really don't know for sure. But thankfully, I always have a new story percolating away inside my head and the ideas come from all kinds of things – it could be hearing something on the news, reading an interesting article in a magazine or simply being nosey and earwigging other people's conversations in a coffee shop. I'm a very nosey author. But the stories always start with a character, usually the main character and once I know their name I can spend months, sometimes years, thinking about them and wondering how their story will unfold on the page. Then, when I'm ready to start writing a new book my editor and I get together and brainstorm the storyline for the character and work out who she needs around her and it goes from there . . . a new book begins, which is always exciting.

***A Postcard from Italy* is the perfect holiday read, what do you think makes the perfect holiday, apart from a good book?**
Spending time with loved ones. We all work so hard these days and so to have precious time away with family or friends to chat, laugh, explore new places or just relax contentedly in each other's company always feels like such a lovely treat. Of course, delicious food and a jug of sangria on a balmy evening watching a glorious sunset sure helps make a holiday perfect too.

What's the best thing about being a writer?
There are so many things, but the two I appreciate the most are making up stories for a living and

chatting to my readers. I love hearing from readers and being part of the wonderful community on my Facebook page and in the Alex Brown Books Reader Club. I love seeing pictures of my readers' pets, their current crafting projects or simply knowing what they are up to as I settle down to write for the day.

What are you going to be doing this summer?
Apart from keeping my fingers firmly crossed that everyone enjoys *A Postcard from Italy*, I'll be writing a new book for next year and then going on holiday to Spain with my family. We go to the same villa every year and I love the anticipation of looking forward to having a wonderful time in the sunshine with my husband and daughter.